2011

A collection of prose and cons, cranks and pranks, etchings and petroglyphs, bon bons and bona-fides, tall tales and tattle-tails, goofs and gaffes, word plays and sword play, nouns and pronouns, verbs and proverbs, pratfalls and pitfalls, witty aphorisms, falsified documents, wine notes, laundry lists, and occasional moments of unexpected lucidity.

2011

A collection of prose and cons, cranks and pranks,
etchings and petroglyphs, bon bons and bona-fides,
tall tales and tattle-tails, goofs and gaffes, word plays
and sword play, nouns and pronouns, verbs and
proverbs, pratfalls and pitfalls, witty aphorisms, falsified
documents, wine notes, laundry lists, and occasional
moments of unexpected lucidity.

Bob Mayfield

Mienmymaw Pubs.

This is a work of fiction, and should not be construed otherwise.

To Lois Baker Janzer, teacher, poet, translator, mentor, and the one who always knew I had a book in me. I'm only sorry this is too late for you to see.

Table of Contents

Part I 1

The Death of the Short Story 3

I Killed Sarah Palin for Christmas 6

Katy Riley and the Dilemma of
Unspeakable Proportions 9

Writer Rampage 18

January 21

Journalists Gone Wild 24

Yakinsak 27

Tin Tinnitus 35

Koko 40

The Introduction 48

Joseph, Redacted 52

A House So Random 62

The Horrible 67

The Deification of Buster Posey 69

Ffimmicks 77

The Artist Addresses His Muse 80

Sparky Misses Out 83

Ona Maria 93

Half-Time 104

Part II 113

Ozzie in Oslo... 115

Workout... 122

Passport to Happiness 128

The Hawk, the Dove, and the Power of Imagery...................... 134

Buck 145

She's All That.. 153

The Baron von Easley: Or, I Should've Turned

Left at Albuquerque 162

Ozzie On a Plane... 170

Paris... 176

Katy Riley in Pakistan 185

App Pro Poe 196

A Joke (Edited for Clarity and Brevity)............................. 199

Molly Begolly 203

How I Became a Bestselling Novelist 208

The Ultimate Pen 213

Grampa Udresson Recollects... 225

That's All, Folks.. 227

Part I

The Death of the Short Story

Today the Short Story was officially declared dead.

It had been on life-support for a long time, and while many were hopeful and optimistic that the Short Story might recover, it was not to be. The only humane thing to do was pull the plug.

The announcement was made on the steps of Library of Congress by Doris Oates, CEO of the Federal Bureau of Fictional Narratives.

As cotton candy clouds drifted above the tree-line, and a chilly breeze sent leaves fluttering by, seemingly whispering discontent, Oates in a somber and sometimes wistful tone, read an e-mail sent out to all writers, editors, and publishers; "Today we sadly announce the passing of the Short Story. Once a staple in a strong line-up of fictional narratives, the Short Story simply could not recover from the hard times it had fallen upon. Overwhelmed by big fat novels, 15-minute celebrity memoirs, comic books, Internet, cell phones, tooth decay, arrogance, hubris, NPR, outsourcing to essays, the Short Story simply could not survive, and rather than allow a once proud and mighty fictional form fall prey to complete irrelevancy, we have decided to end its long, noble run. We mourn with all of those who have toiled so long in the planning, writing, editing, and publishing of the Short Story. A memorial service will be held on Skype tomorrow at noon."

Most readers were apparently unaware of the horrible, squalid existence the Short Story had fallen into since its heyday BK (Before Kindle). "I assumed everything was fine (jubilantly)," said

3

ex-Short Story writer, Tony Mungo, "but then I guess that's what happens (long pause, stares into the camera), you turn your back, next thing you know, something marvelous and inspirational disappears (heavy sigh). Well, we'll always have O. Henry (fade out)." Today Mungo writes for the popular television series, 'You're Gonna Put Your Eye Out.'

NPR, once champion of the Short Story, but which now jams the airwaves with cheesy memoir/essays, responded through spokesperson Alfred Notred, "We feel bad for the Short Story, but frankly it had its day. Today it's all about pithy, gently ironic essays, those cute and smug pieces by David Snordaris and Mitch Allium. Yes, Short Stories once dominated, and we'll remember them fondly, but in the end, they were like dinosaurs. In fact, just like all those loveable, rubber toys I had when I was a kid and my alcoholic mother would stagger into the room yelling at me to put away those stupid little dinosaurs and come to dinner, and when I got to the table, there was nothing but a near-empty bottle of vodka, and my brother and I would race outside into the ally to fight over food scraps out of the dumpster behind the old Arctic Circle..."

O, shut up.

Arthur Krohn, Short Story editor for the online New Jerseyist magazine, says the decision was long overdue. "Given the elements of the Short Story –one-dimensional, simplistic, the, sorry, I-don't-have-time-for-character-or-plot-development attitude, no wonder it hit the skids. I've seen the quality totally tank over the last decade. Most submissions make me want to puke. And when's the last time you've seen a collection of Short Stories on the best seller list? When's the last time you've even seen a collection of Short Stories that wasn't self-published by some gray-haired, pony-tailed, ex-hippie instructor of English at a community college? No, it was dead long ago, they didn't need no stinkin' announcement."

When asked why the New Jerseyist continues to run Short Stories, Krohn leaned forward, and in a hushed tone said, "Shh, don't tell anyone, but for the last 5 years, we've been using a computer program that randomly selects titles, plots, characters, and by-lines. It's great, you push a button, bingo, Short Story. No one's noticed the difference."

4

Though it wasn't until Edgar Allen Poe and his ilk popularized the modern Short Story in the mid-19th century, its roots go as far back as the Homeric Hymns of Greek antiquity. "Certainly many of Ovid's works fall in the category of the Short Story," said Sir Reginald Oreganold, Professor Emeritus of Literature at Hovid University, "Chaucer, Boccaccio, and my god, the Arabian Nights, all are really just Short Stories held together by a simple frame. Nay, you can't kill the Short Story, my friends, any more than you can kill history."

Shortly after the Oates announcement, a small band of renegade Short Story writers stormed the Library of Congress and barricaded themselves in the remaindered room, and are said to be pounding away angrily at typewriters, producing single page Short Stories out of spite. Spokesperson, Susan B. Shed, who has been writing Short Stories since she was an angst-ridden teen-ager, whipped out a defiant e-mail through her blog, and Facebook page: "Oates, who put the throne under your ass? You can't tell us the Short Story is dead, not when I have a stack of unpublished Short Stories the size of the Encyclopedia Britannica under my bed. Take that, FBFN."

"We wish them well," Oates responded from her ofice. Leaning back in her chair, hands clasped behind her head, she continued, "While the pen may very well be mightier than the sword, it's no match for the rejection slip."

Long time comic book writer/editor/publisher Stan Leaky laughs off the whole affair; "Listen, we in the comic bizz know how this works. We've been doing it forever. You take a popular, but maybe fading superhero, and kill him off. You drag it out for months, with fanfare, hoopla, pageantry...and you sell a gazillion comic books! Then a year or so later, you bring your superhero back to life! 'O hey, look, he was just frozen in an iceberg.' Hahaha. More fanfare, pageantry, huge sales. I'll tell you, that's what's going on here. A publicity stunt. In another year the great announcement will be made; 'The Short Story is back! We thawed it out!' New improved, stronger than ever." Leaky winked, "Mark my words."

The Short Story is survived by Facebook, Twitter, texting, and a lingering sense of foreboding.

I Killed Sarah Palin
for Christmas

God, I hate those Christmas stories where some kid dies, usually –but not always- freezing to death. Most times the kid dies on Christmas Eve, though sometimes right on Christmas day. One horrid story has a kid actually drowning on Christmas day. That was cheery. Or how about the one with a kid getting run over by a sleigh (slay?!). But my favorite is the Dostoyevsky story where some poor kid goes out begging for food Christmas Eve for his sick mother and ends up freezing to death at the foot of a statue of St. Jude. Yeah, Merry Christmas to you, too, Fyodor.

So, when my kid, Slugger, and I set out on Christmas Eve to bag a Sarah Palin, I made damn sure I didn't accidently shoot him. I pulled down my Double-barrel 47 Refudiator Rifle from the wall, handed Slugger an axe and boning knife and we headed out into the wild.

There'd been a sighting of wild Sarah Palins roaming around Rogueback Rim. My Crazy Cousin Jamie told me a friend of his had bagged one two days earlier, so I was feeling lucky. Lot of folks up here in the tundra were sick and tired of those Sarah Palins making off with livestock, pets, mail boxes, and yes, even small children. Besides, nothing makes a good Christmas dinner like a 4-point Sarah Palin.

Snow had fallen to about three feet deep, but I had my hip boots on. Slugger was up to his neck in snow, but y'know kids, they can handle it.

We trudged 5 –maybe 10- miles uphill, past Crosshair Ridge, down Blood Libel Creek, then up to Rogueback Rim, where the wild Sarah Palins run. I grabbed my collapsible shovel and dug us an ice cave, about 5 feet wide and 30 feet deep. Told Slugger to go inside and make himself comfortable way in the back, where he'd be safe. Then I gathered some twigs, branches, brush, and got a big roaring, fire going right at the mouth of the cave.

I chopped down several Serbian Spruce, sawed them to logs about 15 feet long, stacking them atop one another to form a good solid wall. Then hunkered down behind it, and waited.

I'd been there about two hours, when I called Slugger to come join me, and got a little nervous when at first he didn't answer, but finally he came limping out of the cave, his feet encased in ice. The fire had melted enough of the snow that once he got outside, it re-froze around his feet. That's okay, he's got some pretty good boots. Couple holes here and there. He was hacking and coughing from the smoke. I told him to quit whining. He crouched beside me, and we waited together.

At first you don't see them. You hear them. A whole pack of Sarah Palins, musta been upwards of two dozen, howling, a high-pitched, cackling call. Unmistakable. If I weren't already shaking from the cold, those cries would've sent shivers up and down my spine. I shook Slugger, "Hear that, boy?" Slugger was looking a little sluggish. I was starting to worry about him. But both of us perked up as the cackling and howling got louder. They were close. Real close.

Slugger, who was having a hard time keeping his eyes open, lifted a weary arm, "There's one, Paw."

Sure enough a Sarah Palin, a big one, sprinted from the tree line into a culvert, maybe a hundred yards away. I put her in the sites of my 47 Refudiator and squeezed the trigger, ka-pow! First shot, dropped her! She flopped on her back, Ugg-booted legs pin-wheeling in the air for a couple seconds, then falling still.

I grabbed Slugger by the scruff of his neck and we rushed out to finish the kill. Yup, that's a Sarah Palin, all right. Big strappin' thing. Slugger handed me the knife, and within a half-hour I had her gutted and cleaned. Must've had a good eighty pounds of meat, shoulder, rib,

7

thigh, breast. I thought briefly about taking the head, mount it on the wall, but I didn't want that thing staring at me while I'm trying to eat. I split the meat evenly, putting half in my backpack, and the rest in Slugger's. We returned to camp.

"Whaddaya say, son," I cried cheerfully, "we could get that fire roaring again, roast up some dinner, and spend the night in a nice, warm snow cave, or we could trudge back the 5 or 20 miles home through snow in the dark. Whaddaya say?"

Slugger's lips trembled. His eyes flickered. I knew it. That's my boy. "Okay, Slugger, let's head on home."

It was about a five-hour slog, and by time I pushed through the cabin door, there was my Crazy Cousin Jamie, drunk. He'd polished off the whisky, and was staggering around the cabin trying to find more hooch. "Sit down, Jamie, me boy," I said, "we got us some fresh Sarah Palin ribs to throw on the fire." First, I fetched a case of hard cider I had hidden in the wood pile, then Frenched the Sarah Palin rack, tossed it on the grill over the fire, and me and Jamie commenced to having a wonderful Christmas Eve celebration. I musta passed out somewhere around midnight, and when I woke up Christmas morning, my Crazy Cousin Jamie was gone, and so was the rest of my cider.

I went out to get the paper, and damn, I'd forgotten about Slugger. He'd been kinda lagging behind last night, and I was sort of in a hurry to get home, so I relieved him of the Palin meat, and hurried on, and once seeing Crazy Jamie at home, forgot all about the little bugger. But I figured, he's a good, tough kid, he'll be alright. Sad to say, though, there was Slugger, arms wound round the mail box, frozen stiff as a carp. Least he made it that far. That's my boy.

Well, there ya have it, another kid freezing to death on Christmas Eve story. God, I hate that.

Katy Riley and the Dilemma of Unspeakable Proportions

Ask Aunt Wilma

Dear Aunt Wilma,

Help! I got a dilemma (who doesn't, right?). Four guys, all crazy about me – or so they say (but I don't necessarily believe guys).

One of them's married (I know, I know). One is a widower, and he's kinda uptight. This one other guy is just plain outrageous (I actually dated him once). The last guy is Mr. Mysterio. All I know is he's Arab, (well) educated in England, and sounds like he travels the world a lot (but then who can believe a guy?).

So the real problem is they're all customers of mine. I bartend, pretty high-end joint, some even call it a wine bar.

But this leads to some awkwardness, as they all tend to show up at the same time (lunch crowd), and over the last couple months they've all started saying stuff (2 me) about each other. Y'know, little digs. Nothing too mean. But it's pretty clear, they see each other as rivals. So far, no fist-fights, as they're all civilized, with good jobs (except maybe Mr. Mysterio), and they treat me with respect.

So onto the dilemma. Like I say, I dated the outrageous guy a couple times, and while he's a bucket of fun, loud, and frankly kinda obnoxious. Fun, but crazy fun. In the long run, I think, no go.

The uptight widower is very attractive, neat, considerate. Two kids. Girls. We have lots in common. But there's a seriousness about him that bugs me.

Mr. Mysterio is like a tornado. He comes roaring in, patting everyone on the back, standing around the bar, never sits, roving around, talking to everyone, mostly about himself, tall-tales, hilarious, but suspiciously vague. Usually going on about some foreign intrigue or other. He's always telling me he's going to whisk me off to Dublin, Paris, Rome, Beijing, Rio, Qatar, etc. And then, like a tornado, he disappears. He can be gone weeks, then one day, like he never left, comes whirling back in, tall-tales and all…no clue what's up there.

And then, the married guy. Heavy sigh. Yes, he's the one. He comes in, I have to gulp for air. I cover it up by being rude to him, but he laps it up, him and his big, soulful blue-green eyes. He's funny, in a sarcastic way. Deeply interested in me, always asking how I am, and at even the tiniest hint of something wrong -health, wealth, or lacks thereof- he's all sympathetic, and there for me. He keeps hinting his marriage is an unhappy one. Never sure if his wife is going to pack up and go. I don't know, is he just trying to get in my pants?

Final piece of the puzzle. I'm a single mom (yeah, made some bad choices along the way), doin' OK, but sure could use some stability ($$$) in my life. Don't exactly need, but definitely do WANT a guy in my life.

Anyway, there it is. Advice? Don't want to make any more bad choices.

Dilemmaed in Haven, New Conn.

Dear Dilemma-ed,

Sounds like you've already made up yr mind. And the choice is: BAD. Don't even think in any way, shape or form about Married Guy. That's crazy talk, girl. Don't do it! As for obnoxious guy. No way. 'nuff said. Mr. Mysterio. Same deal. You need a real presence in your life, not the great disappearing act.

And so we come down to UW (Uptight Widower).

You state yourself you need and desire stability, but it sounds like you're retreating from the one fellow who might offer exactly that. So what if he's serious. And uptight? Maybe he's truly interested in you, but is uncomfortable sharing in a 'crowded market.' It also sounds to me like he's the one guy who might have a firm grip on life, if as you say, he's let on that he's crazy about you, and can still maintain his calm, seriousness in your presence, this indicates the seriousness may be about you. Not only that; a widower with two kids? A single dad knows what you're going through in life ('lots in common', right?), and while it may sound like the pilot for a sit-com (plug in a VHS of Brady Bunch, or With 6 You Get Egg-Roll), seriousness = security = stability.

And I hate to say this, toots, but as a bartender you are to your clientele both glamorous and dangerous. Bartenders (if yr like any and every one I've ever met) are outgoing, flirtatious (in a good way), and come off as attractive, if not seductive to the customer. And besides, what are guys doing when you're waiting on them? Drinking! Take this into account when all your suitors are lined up at the bar telling you how crazy they are for you. Then toss a grain of salt over your shoulder. It's very easy for these guys to convince themselves that you are the one and only, when ten minutes later they're off to the next bar or back home with the wife discussing vacations and laundry. And Puh-lease, do not fall for 'hints' from Married Guy that his marriage is on the rocks.

The point is, IF you feel it necessary to date guys you meet in a bar (sorry, honey, no other way to put it), you had better be very, very selective.

But if yr gonna make the leap, my money is on the Widower.

Dear Mortgage Doctor,

Help! I got a dilemma. I live in a rental (duplex), and I just got informed by my landlord that I have 6 months to move out, cuz he's selling the house.

So I guess I should buy a house or something. How do I go about qualifying for a loan? I have no debt cuz I pay everything in cash (I've had some problems with checking accounts and have decided they are evil), but I've been told to qualify for a loan I need to have some kinda credit score. I'm hoping it's more like a golf score than a bowling score, cuz I suspect it's kinda low.

Of course, I do have a fall-back situation. There're a couple guys crazy for me, and it might be simpler to marry or move in with one of them. But who knows how long that would last (guys!).

One guy for instance, seems like he's fairly well-to-do, he comes in (I'm a bartender) three/four times a week, very soft spoken, nice, polite, neatly trimmed hair, and he's let me know he's sweet on me. Problem, he's kinda, ummm, old. I think he's been divorced a couple times, and has grown and gone kids, and he lives in a condo by the river. But, I don't know, would I just drag down his credit score?

Then there's this guy who's a contractor. Always talking on his cell, wheeling dealing, and I know he's interested in me. But y'know, with the housing market being the way it is, I don't think he's doing so well right now. But that has to change, doesn't it?

Then there's this widower who has a good, steady job, and we get along great, lots in common, but I don't know. He may be seeing somebody else right now, cuz though he always lets me know he likes me, he never asks me out. Hints, but never spits the words out. I don't know if he just doesn't like the fact I'm a bartender, or maybe he's shy. In any case…

Then there's this married guy who's asked me out a couple times (easy, easy, just for coffee), but I ain't playing 'the other woman', though to be honest, I really got a crush on this guy. And if he's asking me out, the marriage must be on the rocks. Or am I the one on the rocks?

So, in any case, I got 6 months to clean up my act and find a new place. One way or the other. Though I should still work on my credit score. Can you help?

Dilemmaed in Haven

Dear Dilemmaed

From the sounds of it, you probably do not qualify for a home loan, or if you do, it would be in the Tuff Shed category. However, to be certain, there is a formula to calculate eligibility: take the total of the last two years declared gross income, divide 12 times by your monthly bills, including food, rent, utilities, and other monthly obligations, such as recurring installment payments, credit cards, auto payments, personal and education loans, to that add the dollar amount you have saved for a down payment (if any), take this figure and multiply by the ratio of the distance between work, home and the dentist, add undeclared tips, and multiply by the number of hours you spend watching reality TV; if this number is equal to or greater than zero, you may or may not qualify for a loan.

As for repairing a damaged credit score, there are several things you can do, but it may require more than a few months.

First, buy a pair of scissors and cut up any and all credit cards (along with pictures of any married guys).

Second, be sure that you pay all your debtors on time. For someone who can't balance a checkbook this might be difficult, but it must be done.

Third, don't be lured into any bad debtors, like payroll loans, dog-track, casinos, or scratch-and-sniff lottery tickets.

Finally, since you only have 6 months before eviction, the likelihood of marrying (particularly an already married guy) is pretty slim. However, if the widower is well off, go with him. You can check his and other credit scores at Yahoogle McDougall.

Good luck! (And steer clear of the married guy.)

Yours,
The Mortgage Doctor
(From a Radio transcript)

Roy: Hello, yr on BarTalk.
KR: Hi guys, this Katy Ri…
Tim: No last names, please.
KR: O, uh, Katy from Haven, New Connecticut.
Tim: New Connect-a-cut. Love it. Where's Haven?
KR: About 15 miles south of Heppner.
R: (Laughing) O, you're a big help, Katy.
T: Is that Katy with an 'i e' or Katy with a 'y'?
KR: 'Y,' of Course.
T: Of course, Katy with an 'i e,' is just showboating. What can we do for you, Katy with a 'y'?
KR: Well, I got a dilemma that involves a bar, a car, a guy, and some ethics thrown in to boot.

R: We might be able to help with the bar and the car, we might even be able to help with the guy, but ethics?

T: I don't think so.

R: Go ahead, Katy, what's up.

KR: Okay, I have this old clunker that I'm afraid to drive anywhere but back and forth to work, because everything in the world is wrong with it...

T: I thought this had to do with a bar?

KR: Well, see that's just it, I'm a bartender...

T: O good. Please, continue.

KR: And sitting at the bar, quite frequently, a little too frequently, is this guy, who just so happens to be a mechanic...

T: A-hah, the plot sickens.

KR: Right, and you see, I dated this guy a couple times, and yr gonna kill me when I tell you this, but, I really and truly only went out with him on the 2nd date, because on the first date he fixed my carburetor.

R: I bet he did (Laughter).

T: That's the only way I ever got a second date, too.

KR: Come on, guys, look, he's a nice guy, just, y'know...

R: You can say it, Katy, there can't be more than 4.5 million people listening right now.

T: He's a doofus, right? You can level with us, Katy.

KR: Well, that's a little strong.

R: Well, okay, he's a minor doofus.

T: A doofus in training.

R: A doofus wannabe

KR: (Laughing) Let's just leave it at that. See, the problem is, he keeps asking about the car. How's the carburetor? How's the muffler? How're the belts? My god, how many pieces does a car have?

T: (Laughing) Pieces? A car has pieces? It's not a jigsaw puzzle, Katy.

KR: Yes, it is. Now, here's the thing, clearly he's angling for another date, and just as clearly I need work done on my car, but the complicating factor is this other guy...

R: Ooooo, Katy. I knew it, yr trouble.

T: Yr a heartbreaker, aren't you, Katy.

KR: No! I'm a bartender, and guys come in to drink, chat, that's my job, I'm supposed to talk to people, and I don't know, it's not like I'm anything super duper...

T: O, I bet you are, Katy...

14

R: Are you...lemmee see, how can I put this delicately? Katy, are you...ummmm, zaftig?

KR: (Laughing) What is that? I don't think I want to answer that question.

T: She's zaftig.

R: She is.

T: Katy, go on.

KR: Okay, so this other guy, is just as often at the bar, and I'm like crazy for him...and I really want him to ask me out, but all the while I'm cringing while this other guy...

R: The doofus.

KR: Mechanic! Is there asking about my radiator and water hose, clearly trying to get a date with me, I can see this other guy is repulsed by the whole thing...

R: What does this other guy, your dreamboat, do?

KR: I think he's a writer, or something.

T: A writer?! Forget it, Katy, he can't help you.

R: Anyway, let's take a step back...just how many things are wrong with this car?

T: Yeah. Then we can figure out just how many dates you gotta go on with doofus before the lover boy takes over.

R: You guys!

T: Hey, did we call you? Did we? No, you called us, come on, Katy, 'fess up.

KR: Okay, this car, like, everything leaks, there's puddles of oil everywhere I go, no one wants me to park in their driveway....and there's all sorts of noises, whistling, clanking, clicking and clacking, it runs like it's stuck in mud, there's blue smoke pouring out the back...

R: Okay, Katy, that's enough. Look, I hate to tell you this, but yr gonna have to marry the mechanic.

KR: No!

R: It's the only way, Katy. Marry him, and by your 25th wedding anniversary, he may have this car running just fine.

T: Can yr dreamboat wait for you for 25 years?

KR: No!

R: Waddaya mean, no. We solved your problem. Katy, you called with a problem, we solved it.

KR: Come on guys, seriously...

15

R: Okay, Katy, look, by your description there're way too many things wrong with your car for anyone short of a Miracle Worker to fix…

T: And we're assuming you don't have the financial wherewithal to, say, buy a new car.

KR: Right.

R: Well. There is another possibility. How rich, or well-off, is the guy you really like?

KR: Not that much. Though there is another guy, who's pretty well-off and he's clearly got a thing for me…and he's a widower, so he's available.

R: Okay, let's say you ask out the rich widower.

T: Yeah, there's gotta be a Sadie Hawkins dance coming up…

KR: This isn't high school.

T: Sure sounds like it.

R: Ask him out. Tell him…ooo, ooo, I got it, here's what you do, Katy. Ask him out, and say, 'I'll drive. I'll pick you up tomorrow at 6.' So you pull up, splashing oil all over his driveway, and the neighbors are calling the fire department because of all the smoke, hubcaps are rolling into the bushes, dogs are barking all up and down the block, and he comes out and you open the door for him…

T: Ooo, that's a nice touch.

R: He starts to get in…looks around and says, 'forget it, here you can have my car! Take it, please, just get this piece of junk…'

T: Pieces of junk.

R: '…get these pieces of junk out of here!' And there it is, Katy. You get a new car, maybe one date, then go back to your loser writer.

KR: (Laughing) Actually that's not a bad idea.

R: Are there any other guys, Katy? I got a feeling we're only scratching the surface here.

KR: (Laughing) Not that many.

T: Five?

KR: Little more.

R: Eight?

KR: More.

R: Four hundred and seventeen?

KR: (Laughing) Ten. Tops.

R: Ten? Sheesh, Katy, you must have what it takes. You put the 'tender' in bartender.

KR: Hey, what can I say, guys like me.

16

T: Okay, so we got a mechanic, a useless writer, a widower, who else?

KR: Well, there's a contractor, and this older fellow, but...

R: Contractor? Great! Katy, do you need a new deck? How about a kitchen remodel?

T: Katy, Katy, you got to take advantage of this. Are any of yr suitors computer nerds? You could get your own website.

R: Certainly, there must be a dentist. You can get all new teeth.

T: What about a golf pro? There must be a golf pro in the group.

R: Is there an astronaut, Katy?

T: Katy, one date a week, just one date a week, and you can have a car that runs like new, a remodeled house, your own website, whiter teeth, you could lower your golf score, and fly to the moon. Katy! You got to start taking advantage of this situation. One date a week, that's all it would take.

KR: Will you guys stop, it's not like that at all. But, I do kinda like the idea of asking out...the widower.

T: Well your choices are clear. Marry the mechanic, or ask out the wealthy guy, and forget about the poor schlub you really cherish, tough luck for him. No one said life is fair. Leave him standing by the roadside...

R: Holding one of your hubcaps.

T: ...that's all there is to it, Katy. Marry the mechanic or hogtie the widower.

KR: I'm gonna do it.

R: Katy, it's been a pleasure talking to you.

KR: Bye, guys, thanks. (Hangs up)

T: Bye, bye...sheesh, she sounds like twenty miles of bad road, doesn't she?

R: More like a whole freeway system. Remind me next time I'm in Haven to steer clear of the bars.

T: Get a slurpie at the local Am/Pm...

R: You got that, brother. Hello, you're on BarTalk....

Writer Rampage

A writer recently went on a rampage in Littlefield, New Connecticut, leaving scores of citizens rendered in faithful prose, some to the point of Hi-Def lucidity.

While only three of the victims required treatment at the local Urgent Care for exposure, there may be countless others scarred for life,

"I've never seen anything like it," says Littlefield Prose Police Chief, Sandy Lott, "We may never know the full extent of the damage. Many victims will never come forth for fear of having a reader recognize them, and well, regard them as a person written about. Like my buddy, Leonard. Haha, I didn't know Alice was his second wife."

Writing under the corrosive pen name, Sue Denim, the author preyed upon innocent, heretofore unwritten about subjects, allowing readers an inside look at their foibles, visages, and questionable sartorial choices.

"I've never been written about before," says a tearful Ira Ravenforth, "I had no idea it could be so devastating, so…so… humiliating." He goes on, sobbing, "I thought tube socks were the *in* thing."

Some people never get over of the shock of seeing themselves in print, according to local psychiatrist/yoga instructor, Luigi Bord, "It's like hearing your voice on a recording for the first time. What? That doesn't sound like me. I don't have this high, pitched whiney, nasal voice, do I?" Bord says, in his high-pitched, whiney voice.

The writings began to appear more than a month ago, mostly short vignettes featuring local folks going about their daily routine; shopping, getting the oil changed, downing a hard one -or two- at lunch.

"It was obviously an inside-job from an outside person," says Butch Custody, owner of the mercantile shop on Main Street, a locale where many of the vignettes take place. "The writings purported to give a real-life feel to the town," he continues in his whiskey-soaked voice, rubbing the stubble on his chin incessantly, "but there was a note of mockery about them, a smug I-know-you better-than-you-do tone. That pissed off a lot of people."

It wasn't long before town folk began looking at each other suspiciously. Are you Sue Denim? How do you know so much about my Betty Boop underwear?

Particularly disturbing was the portrait of a local couple (who will remain unnamed for fear of retribution). After 25 years of a prosperous, loving, faithful marriage, the Edisons decided to remodel their kitchen. "I can't tell you how it tore me apart to see my choices of cabinets appear in print," says an embittered Lois Edison, in a bright gingham dress, red smock, and black flats, "it was like they knew our contractor…wait a minute, the contractor…he was always walking around with a clipboard in hand, taking notes…could he be this Denim?"

The Edisons have since reconciled, agreeing that the backsplash needed more color.

"I don't know what would lead a writer to do this," says art matron, Arlene Abbot, "there's plenty of fictional folk out there to write about, you don't need to violate real people. They've got jobs, relatives, some of them even have a purpose in life, why rip their soul out by making them available in print?"

"This happens all the time in Big Cities," says Mayor Mina Mayer, "writers write about each other with ferocity. But they're used to it. A barb here, a jab there. All part of the process. You develop a hide like a rhinoceros." Mayor Mayer pauses, glances about furtively, "But here in Littlefield? Never."

The rash of writings have disappeared -for the time being. While many fear the writer is simply lying low and may re-emerge with even more scabrous portraits, others think –or hope- she/he has moved onto another town, ready to cause more destruction.

Not everyone was disturbed by the outbreak of writings. Tony Booskeep, owner of Hooligan's Sports Bar, says business is booming, thanks in part to the fact that many of his loyal customers were profiled in the pieces.

"You can almost see him –or her", Booskeep says, wiping down the zinc bar with a soggy, filthy towel, "huddled in a corner, notebook in hand, scribbling away. Kinda spooky, really."

One of his loyal customers, Rockin' Chair Clem (not his real name), who was the subject of two profiles, sums it up best, "You can write about me all you want," he says laughing, "just be sure you spell my name right...hey, wait a minute there, young fellar, you writing about me? You get back here, you little..."

January

Its vastness can only be measured in nuisance.

It begins with a cry, a shutter, and the smell of pot and liquor, and sweeps across the darkness, until finding a breach, light enters, and is sucked into a misty blue sky, the roar, racing against wind, until sunshine wipes all but the immense lassitude of an inner quiet, broken, cacophony, and gaining on the ground, the crunch of metal, rubber, and resistance, and rotation of events tumble off into the arms of solitude, the grace of speed, gray depths and the warm dirty snow collapsing into darkness, and all is still, frozen earth, no match for the electric pulse, and all that is green is dying, and the face of forever dons a mortal mask mocking the moment, the present, a gift to the unprepared, staggering toward justice, yet mounted without diligence or care, neutered by the smell of awe, the sound of gargling water, un-furrowed brows of wind, a crash strangles the night, and the dam-sky bursts open and what gushes forth, hell-bound, cement shine, all the gray swill of touch and sense, is layered, geographic time, immortal mounds of stone, piled shoulder to shoulder, swelling like birth, but smelling of death, the struggle against dirt, sky, river, and light continues with fingers rubbed raw of flesh, knuckles blistered and bleeding, and finding no remorse, only a shift of gratitude, moored, idling, undulating with the click click click of the digital clock, no menace, only warning, sweeping belly to ground, face to pavement, a word unpronounced, but enormous in intent, drops like candy, and its sentiment is felt by all humanity, though none recognize it for what it is, the shame of silence, and a wing tracing an arc through the sky, belief, helium, balloon, so puffed up it pops and no one feels the exhalation, the passage from what once was to what shall be, stuck in the squalid moment, unmoving, unmovable, a roiling fog rises from the ancient river bed, once dry and crusted, now perpetuated by an oily sky, as morning shifts its weight, varnished wooden prairies unfold across the landscape, rush of sentience and incapacity, hooves screech, halt, proceed, a tumbleweed shouts, a lost moment rolling into the white placid fields, icy elbows, fingertips scorched frozen, the untimely grunt of metal, lunging through glassy cement, darkness peeled away by orange blades, strands of sinuous gray cut into ribbons, a figure in pale yellow stands against the horizon, shaped and molded by an inert sky, and then as if all were forgiven, the fist unclenches, the hand opens and welcomes the notion of humility and familiarity, embraces the rotation of sun moon sky earth, hot and moist to still and cold, empty vessels waiting to be refilled, seeds exploding, the grain whispers to the spruce needle, 'just wait my friend, the day is nearly upon us,' and then silence burns the stem to soil, within a heartbeat an eternity passes like a kiss, the figure disappears, gobbled up by the horizon, the aching sky reaches behind the curtain, but its loss is certain, the fulfillment of life with minor deviances, the twig bent, springs forward, and the tree does not recognize the motion, tension, all movement ceases as a limb in pain seizes a piece of the wind, slipping through its leafless fingers, lies down, slumbers without embrace, longing for the hug to suck up existence beyond love and yearning, to huddle against a boulder and wish it confirmed and stable, roll, roll away, to absorb its strength, durability, rubbing it as if a petroglyph, or stalagmite might reveal the very nature of soul/spirit, when all one really needs is to slip into water so hot the bone sizzles from the heat, and fresh air, down the wilderness track, left behind, or so far out in front the loneliness examines itself as a species not yet created or long extinct, to end is the only way to begin, to empty all the bullets, anger, self-pity, reliance on others, ignorance, calm, but the investment is too much, the intent too flimsy, and the resolve beyond scope, if only the eye meeting eye, flesh upon flesh, heartbeat against heartbeat, the fingers dwell on resistance and acquiescence, the tongue dips down to sip from the river and lurches forward spitting its gestation back upon the earth, a rage within the soil swells from a deep unsettling far below the surface, an eruptive force sends shock after shock aloft, uplifting boulders and splitting granite, until with a force unmatched by heart and passion, at the spot where energy enjoins matter, nature spews forth its animus, a release of all spirit held bound at the center of the earth, of the universe, of a single soul, split by time and memory, and the ripples on the river-sheen settle to a calm wave upon wave, and as light succumbs to dark revealing the eyes of the skies staring down from a vastness unimaginable, suddenly a fatigue wiggles free of energy, and it's hard to recall centuries ago on Union Square in San Francisco, the smell of pot, the cries of sardonic joy ringing in the New Year, and here on the brink of time, at the end of the arc carved out by a hawk's wing, silence is wasted on itself.

Finality, the course is run, release, the end. Turn the page. January is at long last over.

Journalists Gone Wild

When Katy Riley first noticed a rash of abandoned journalists slumped over nearly every table at her favorite coffee shop, she decided to do something about it.

Relying on her experience socializing feral cats, she would sit at Starbucks for hours on end, laptop open, just waiting, smiling, making occasional eye contact.

"At first they're hesitant," she says, "but once they realize I'm not gonna hurt them, they come over, ask what I'm reading, hoping it's the last article they got published."

The first abandoned journalist she befriended ended up getting a job as barista at Starbucks (not the one she frequents, but the one next door). Soon, she was herding abandoned journalists into other fields, like bartending, bicycle delivery, and Zumba meditation.

The wave of abandoned journalists began two years ago when the newspaper industry went down the toilet. Thousands upon thousands of journalists were suddenly released into the wild, which only goes to show just how bloated the industry was to begin with.

"Our newsroom had hundreds of people milling about," says ex-wine columnist, J.J. Jabberforth, "many of them literally doing nothing but walking around with pencils behind their ears talking onerously about pull-quotes and sub-heads. We found out later, most of them were 'editors', which is code word for dead wood."

Many abandoned journalists tried blogging at first, but "It's like rooting around in the dumpster behind McDonald's," Jabberforth continues, "if you're not the first one there, all the good stuff is taken. Trust me."

Jabberforth, who was widely admired in the industry for his outrageous 'ledes', recently found a position flopping a sign around at passing traffic at the corner of 4th and Main, advertising Papa Puck's Pizza.

There are no reliable statistics as to the true number of abandoned journalists. According to JETA (Journalists need Ethical Treatment just like Animals), tracking abandoned journalists is like census-taking among the homeless. JETA's statistician, Luigi Bord, explains, "You hang out at bus stops, happy hours, computer repair shops, and food co-ops, and ask around, 'How long have you been abandoned? How many abandoned journalists do you know?' Etcetera. You get a number, but who knows?"

While much of the data is anecdotal, it does appear that after two years of hemorrhaging, the number of first-time abandoned journalists is dwindling.

"Which makes sense," Bord says, "there aren't many real journalists left."

According to JETA official, Ova Yonda, the first thing they require of new admissions, is spay or neuter. "You don't want these things propagating," Yonda says. She also warns, if you find an abandoned journalist, do not take it home as a pet.

"What they most need is a livelihood, a *raison d'escribe,*" Yonda says, "we try to find them a position that synchs with their previous work. Lots of food writers have found entry-level jobs at chicken processing plants. While those with op-ed page background often make great garbage technicians. Sports writers tend to excel as car wash attendants."

Political cartoonists and advice columnists are the worst, she claims. "Not only are they useless in the real world, they're even more useless in their own made-up world."

She shakes her head, "Some of our admissions have tried their hand at writing fiction, you know, the Great American Novel. Well, I've seen a couple manuscripts, and they read like the Merck Manual."

Still, JETA is making progress, "We've placed many abandoned journalists in the world of politics. After all, journalists root around in the same squalid world as politicians, so they make effective interns, spokespersons, and even speech writers. They have a facility for reducing the most complex issues to simple cliches, because at the end of the day, it's about parsing, vetting and ratcheting up the gravitas."

Yonda sighs, "Although, politicians have about the same shelf-life as a jazz columnist."

Another area of the private sector which has proven to be fertile ground for abandoned journalists is the coffee shop. Katy Riley

25

says she has steered a number of her clients into the profession, one even opened her own independent shop. But, alas, she had no business experience, or even basic common sense, and the shop closed after two months. "She thought all her old friends in the business would come out to support her," Katy Riley says, "and they did…except they just wanted a free cup of coffee."

Her client (whom she declines to name) is now a cashier at Starbucks (not the one next to the one Katy Riley frequents, but the one across the street from it).

The worst cases, both JETA and Katy Riley agree, are the self-delusional abandoned journalists. They continue to go to land-use hearings, city council meetings, scribbling notes, and asking misleading or uninformed questions. They do random interviews. Many with 'pop culture' background hang out at happy hours, open mics, and Mongolian Grills, pretending they're reviewing the 'scene'.

"It's pathetic," says Katy Riley, "they refuse to admit they have no venue. I've tried over and over again to get them to see the world as it is, and all I get is this, 'and what was your middle name again?' Who knows, maybe they're blogging somewhere."

One thing is clear, abandoned journalists are a tough fit for much of society. "Personally I don't trust them," says owner of Lew's Bar and Grill, Lewis 'Campy' Tuffthud, "they come in here with their rumpled clothes, beat-up laptops, order one drink and sit here for hours, eatin' up all my nuts, staring around the room, making everyone nervous. I'm thinking of cancelling happy hour. Speaking of which, you want another one, bub?"

"They got no work ethic," says house painter, Lenny Robert Lennyhall, "I gave one a brush, a can of paint, and a ladder, and he looked at me like I just handed him a live grenade. 'I don't do ladders' he says, 'I'm afraid of heights.' And so he takes a job as a house painter? Whad he think, the house was gonna bend over for him?"

And of course wherever there are unfortunate, gullible people, there are unscrupulous individuals (who are not even politicians!) to prey on them. Katy Riley (who declines to give her middle name) says one of her clients recently told her she'd found a job as an instructor at a journalism school. Suspicious (because who would go into journalism right now?), Katy Riley investigated and found that Fred's Pilate Zumba Nail Salon and School of Journalism charges a 'users fee' to all their 'instructors'.

Needless to say, she counseled her client to keep looking.

Yakinsak

Just down from the Rattlesnake Hills, loaded with loot, and ready to rock and roll, I stumble into Yakinsak, an old mill town, now pretty much coastin' on the apple-packing business. I know just what I'm looking for, what Jumpin' Jimmy calls the best little brothel in all the Northwest. And lo and behold, a storefront window right here on Main Street, in gold letters, Lilly's Brothel. That's pretty bold, I'm thinkin'.

And I soon found out why. I walk in, tuck my hat under my arm, and am immediately greeted by Madame, a discreet, elderly Chinese lady. "Are you here for the special?" she asks.

"O yeah," I say. It's been more than a month up in the hills with nothing more than the Money Machine (our code words), and Jumpin' Jimmy and the gang. I sure am ready for 'the special.'

"Do you prefer exotic, or classic?" Madame says, unfazed by my enthusiasm.

"Exotic, of course."

"Young and wildly creative, or experienced and deliberate?" she continues, as if reading down the menu.

"Mmmm, them there's two mighty tempting choices, but y'know, I feel like I'm in the mood for young and wild."

She bows slightly, and says, "Follow me." She leads me upstairs, down a narrow hallway, opening the third door on the right, I follow her through a darkened room to a purple curtain with gold cords and gold lace trim. She pushes aside the curtain. "Please," she says waving me in with her right hand.

"Thank you, thank you very much." I'm a bit on the eager side, all but tripping over my boots as I enter, and see a most gorgeous Oriental young lady, sixteen-years-old, 17, tops, sitting behind a small table, her head bowed. She raises her eyes to me and smiles, almost imperceptibly. "Come, please, sit down," she says.

27

I do.

"Please, spread your hands out on the table...no, no, palms down." Ooo, sounds kinky. I do as she bids. She examines my hands then asks me to dip my fingers in a bowl of very warm water. Hmmm. They soak for a good long time. She lifts my hands out, and takes what appears to be a small scalpel and works very meticulously around the cuticles of each fingernail, gently clipping off hangnails and slivers of calloused skin. While I'm wonderin' what the bejeebers is going on, she pulls out an elaborately engraved wooden case, and removes an array of tiny brushes, molds, clippers, and a dozen or so variously colored bottles. And then...she starts painting my nails. Okay, pretty weird ritual, I'm thinking, but I'm the one who asked for exotic.

She begins with a base coat of black, then fills each nail with a different set of designs –diamonds, stripes, snail curves- each in a differing spectrum of colors –turquoise, gold, bright red and orange. After a while my fingernails look like a wild assortment of butterfly wings. It's awesome watching her go about her business –her art- head bowed, eyes narrowed in concentration, fine beads of sweat on her forehead.

Just as I'm thinking we're about done, and ready to get on to 'the special', she says, "Now, please, take off your boots, and we'll do your toes..."

Two hours later, and two hundred dollars lighter, I step out onto Main Street. Okay, that was weird. I glance back at the window, yup, still says Lilly's Brothel. A façade -for a nail salon? I'm thinking I might just race back up in the hills and kill Jumpin' Jimmy, or at least do him some serious harm. But then across the street I spy, Hooligan's Bar and Grill. Man, I could use a drink.

I push through the swinging doors, but, what's this? Yeah, there's a bar, alright, long, and curved at the end, barstools, and several flat-screen TVs overhead, some flickering with sports shows, and one with cartoons, but the bar itself is cluttered with a toaster, bread box, knife block, coffee maker, paper towel rack, spice rack, dish drying rack, microwave, and there're three kids sitting around watching cartoons, and what appears to be a husband and wife behind the bar, washing dishes. Seated at the bar are a couple old fellars, and a grandma. Okay, I can deal with this.

I step up to the bar, the husband guy comes over, "Nice nails there, buddy." And, oddly, he seems to mean it. "Can I get you something?"

28

"Sure could use something to drink."

"Billy," he says to the oldest of the kids, "could you get the young man a drink?"

"Sure, Pops."

Billy goes to a fridge in the corner and pulls out something and brings it over and sets it before me. It's a colorful pouch with a tiny straw attached to it. Strawberry, it says.

"Do you…er, have anything stronger?" I say.

Billy winks at me, "Know just what you mean," he says, takes my Strawberry juice and returns with a similarly colorful pouch, but this one says Lemonade, "my favorite," Billy says.

Hmm. I pull off the straw, stick it through the little hole, take a sip. Not bad. Little on the sweet side.

The guy behind the bar says, "Sorry, I didn't get your name, I'm Sam."

I tell him my name.

"Welcome." He introduces his wife, Mindy, "and this here's uncle Benny…"

One of the old fellars turns to shake my hand, "Nice to meet ya."

"And this is Mindy's dad and mom, George and Liddy."

Cheerful little family.

They go about chatting amongst themselves; homework, laundry, what movie they might watch tonight. They're careful to include me. Sam asks if I'll be staying for supper. "No, no, many thanks, but gotta…meet someone," I say.

I finish up my lemonade, ask what I owe, and Sam says, "On the house."

Dark had fallen on Main Street, and I don't just mean metaphorically. What in the name of juniper berries is going on? A nail salon fronted by a whore house. A bar, home to a nice suburban family? Down the road aways I come upon Trueblood Hardware and Mercantile.

Hmmm, okay. I peak inside, there's some activity going on. May as well check it out.

I push inside. I hear laughter, loud talking, coming from the back, and wander down the paint brush aisle, and come to the counter. Big register, some point-of-sale items. A mixed gender group of eight people are standing around with glasses of what appears to be beer and or cocktails. They glance my way, newcomer, stranger, a few smiles, then return to chatting. The man behind the counter greets me, "Can I help you?"

"Well, gotta admit, I was looking for something to drink. Something hard."

The man smiles, directs my attention to the wall behind him where row after row of bottles nestle cheek by jowl; every kind of vodka, scotch, brandy, rum, whiskey, port. "And of course, we have beer on tap."

Boy, do I brighten up, "Lemmee start with a beer. Do you have an IPA?"

"Comin' right up."

I get my foamy glass, nod to the folks, who all seem friendly enough, and wander up and down a couple aisles. Hardware, from every size nail, screw, to every thickness of wire, to hand tools, mops, ladders. Above is a mezzanine stuffed with work benches, cabinets, shelving. Pretty nice supply. By time I wind my way back to the 'bar' and the group of happy folks, some of whom nod my way, I can't help but blurt out, "Strange little town you got here."

One of the fellows laughs, "You like, or no?"

"Didn't mean to offend," I say.

Most of them chuckle, "Don't worry my friend, we get that a lot…can I buy you another beer?'

"Only if you'll let me stand you one."

"Fill 'er up, Johnny!"

After a couple more beers, and having engaged in conversation with the happy folks, more and more people file in, finally one of the fellows comes over to me, "You know, young man, I can see by your nails, that maybe you have an ulterior motive for visiting our happy little town…"

"Well, as a matter of fact…"

He leans over and whispers, "Two blocks down, around the corner on C Street, Dan's Barbershop. Tell 'em Joey sent you." He smiles, we clink glasses, and he returns to his friends.

Not wanting to seem too eager, I polish off another beer, pay a fairly hefty amount, leave a pretty good tip, and on my way out, give a tip of the hat to my new friends, who in return offer me plenty of hearty and jolly farewells

Dan's Barbershop is right where Joey said would be, on C Street, right next to the bank, though by now, I'm pretty sure it's not a bank. I take a deep breath, push my way into Dan's, expecting anything, when

30

Madame, a small, discreet Chinese lady greets me. I gulp. She's wearing pretty much the same thing as earlier, I think. But that's been a few hours and many beers ago. I point, "Weren't you at Lilly's this afternoon..." I say.

Her eyes dart back and forth. "No."

Hmm. I must've looked a bit puzzled. Sure looks like her.

"May I help you?" She says.

"Well, I'm here for...for...."

"The special?"

"Huh?...you sure you're not...o wait, uh, Joey sent me."

"Ah yes, then you'll want the special."

"Umm, okay...but I've already got my nails done."

She glanced at my hands. "Very nice...but we don't do nails here."

"Good."

"Do you prefer exotic, or classic."

Okay, joke's on me. I'll play along. "Let's try classic this time."

"Excellent choice. And do you prefer young and wildly creative, or experienced and deliberate? "

Oy. "Ummm, how's about experience?"

"Very well." She bows slightly, and says, 'Follow me." She leads me upstairs, down a hallway identical to the one at the nail salon, and we pass through the third door on the right, and through a darkened room approach a purple curtain with gold lace trim. She pushes a small opening of the curtain, "Please," waving me in with her right hand.

I'm nervous, and a bit edgy, if not angry, but when I step into the room, it is...glory be! A boudoir. Four-poster bed, lots of fluffy velvet red pillows, curtains, night stand with a bottle Champagne chilling in a bucket, two Champagne glasses, but most pleasantly, incredibly, standing aside the night stand, this tall drink of water, stunningly, long legs in fishnet stockings, tight fitting red with white trim teddy showing off every lovely curve. She's pretty, with high cheekbones, short dark hair, maybe late 20s early 30s. "Hello," she coos, deep, sultry voice.

"Well now, howdy."

"May I poor you a glass of Champagne?"

"Only if it's real Champagne," I say.

"But of course, Tattinger."

"I prefer Bollinger," I say with a smile, "but I suppose I can slum it."

She glances sidelong at me as she pours, "You seem to know a lot about wine," she says.

"That's my job, ma'am."

"Really?" She tips the glass up just right to keep the effervescence from spilling over the edge.

"Yup, up in Rattlesnake Hills, wine maker," bit of brag on my part.

"Come tell me about it." She stretches out her long legs on the bed and props herself up against the cushiony pillowed headboard, and pats the spot beside her.

"I'm a bit dusty," I say carefully, "don't mind if I take off some clothes, do you?"

"No, in fact, I insist."

I strip down my skivvies, stretch out next to her, accept the proffered glass of Champagne. "Well it all started some years ago when I stumbled upon this vineyard…"

And then I proceed to regale her with tall-tales on how I became a wine maker for a wealthy investor, "We like to say he has more dollars than sense," (my favorite joke)…how we planted the vineyard, started making wines from other vineyards while waiting for ours to mature, etc., all the usual stuff you can read in any interview with any wine maker. But this was me. All the while she's attentive, asking appropriate questions, laughing, nodding, agreeing. About midway into my story, she slips down into a prone position, props herself up on one elbow, and slowly undoes the straps of her teddy, tosses it aside, exposing a silky black bra, barely containing luscious, voluptuous breasts. I continue with my story of how certain clones impart different flavors…

At one point, without interrupting me, she turns her back, and says, "Do you mind," indicating the latch on her bra.

"Not at all." I pop it open for her. She wiggles a bit, and tosses the bra across the room, lays on her back, massaging the flesh beneath her breasts. "Of course, we knew Cabernet would work here, but what about Zinfandel?" She's slipping off the stockings and is now completely naked. She continues to listen intently. While I'm describing our fermentation regime, she reaches over beneath the night stand to a little fridge and pulls out 6 chocolate covered strawberries. She eats one very slowly, and puts another one on her navel.

"Hungry?" she says.

"Am a bit peckish," I say, and lean down and pluck the strawberry from her belly –gingerly- with my teeth and gobble it up. "Delicious," I say, "anyway, it turns out the clone 357 wasn't really suited to our soil, so we had to rip all those out and start all over again…"

"O no…"

Over the next couple minutes, she puts one after another strawberry on her navel, and I nibble away.

While I'm explaining the blending process, she reaches into the fridge again and pulls out a small dish of what appears to be whipped cream –real whipped cream- and a jar of black caviar. With a small spoon she spreads some whipped cream over each nipple. She shivers a bit, almost gasping. Then with another small spoon she tops each breast with the caviar.

"Help yourself," she insists.

I do.

"Very tasty," and the chill has made her nipples firm, like raisins, "…but harvest was delayed that year about two weeks…" She tops off her nipples again with cream and caviar, and I help myself.

She's been refilling my Champagne glass all this while, but I notice she's not having any. "Aren't you drinkin'?" I say.

"I'll have a sip of yours."

She takes my glass and licks the rim, then puts the glass to her lips, but instead of sipping, runs her tongue around the inside of the glass, then dips it into the wine, and hands the glass back to me. "Thanks," with a mischievous grin.

"My pleasure," I say, and after taking a sip, I have to admit it tastes much better now. "And of course," I say "once you got stuck fermentation it's the devil's own time getting it goin' again…"

She must've had a timer somewhere, maybe in her head, because just as I'm telling her about the bottling process, she says, "Sorry, cowboy, but we've got about 2 minutes left. Just to let you know."

"'ppreciate it. Well just to wrap it up, I guess the whole point is, once the wine gets in the bottle, then comes the hard part…sellin' it."

"Do tell," she says. I stand up, stretch. Pull on my shirt, slip into my britches. Pull my boots on. She's smiling wistfully at me.

"Thanks for listenin', Ma'am, y'know, it gets kinda lonely up there in the Hills, just me and the boys and the fermenting tanks. Sometimes I just need to get some stuff off my chest."

"I had a great time. Thanks, cowboy." She winks, "And next time you're looking for a good time, just ask for Molly."

"You bet I will, Ma'am."

Back on Main Street, another two hundred dollars lighter, it's close on midnight. No way am I goin' up in the hills tonight. I'll need a hotel, and I know just where to find one. Chuck's Butcher Shop is still open.

And sure enough, they have a room available.

Tin Tinnitus

Woosh, woosh. Like someone brushing a long, thick mane. Woosh, woosh.

I first noticed it when I awakened in the middle of the night. As I was trying to go back to sleep, my left ear pressed against the pillow, I kept hearing this 'woosh, woosh' sound, like a broom on shag carpet, or a cat licking a microphone. I thought maybe my wife had bought a new clock, and it was pressed against the wall or bed, so regular was the 'woosh, woosh.' I paid it little mind, and fell asleep.

The next night, I got up at 3:57 am, took a quick pee, and back in bed, head on pillow, 'woosh, woosh,' even more pronounced than the previous night, and this time each 'woosh' had a metallic ping to it, like an echo chamber, or reverb. I had a tough time going back to sleep, puzzling over what it could be.

When I awoke that morning, my wife was in the shower, and so I rooted around the night stand on her side of the bed trying to find some timepiece or whatever it might be, and while fiddling around managed to unplug an extension cord, which unfortunately, led to her computer. Ooops.

When she got out of the shower, I apologized, and as she snarled and re-booted the computer, I fetched her a cup of coffee. We sat in bed sipping coffee. I asked if she'd bought anything new that might be making that 'woosh, woosh' noise, since it was coming from her side of the bed. She looked a little befuddled, "What noise?"

"That 'woosh, woosh.'"

Her eyes narrowed with concern, if not scorn.

"Don't tell me you can't hear that," I said.

We were both quiet. She listened, then looked at me pathetically. "Woosh, woosh," I said, sheepishly. "You don't hear it?"

"Are you nuts?"

I got up on my knees in bed, and looked out the window above and behind the headboard, maybe it was a tree, in the breeze, brushing up against the house. But no, all was still outside.

I sat with my coffee, my wife beside me, glancing over occasionally with barely concealed alarm.

Once she got up to get dressed, and while she wasn't looking, I impulsively checked my pulse, and the 'woosh, woosh' was right in time with it. Trying not to panic, I checked it regularly over the next couple minutes, and every time the pulse was in perfect synch with the 'woosh, woosh.'

Very strange. The 'sound' was so clearly coming from outside my head.

By time the next night came along, and I got up to go pee, and back in bed, 'woosh, woosh,' right in synch with my pulse. It was irrefutable. The sound was inside my head.

I was clearly going nuts.

The tell-tale pulse continued. The 'woosh, woosh' took on different characteristics, sometimes there was a metallic ping to it, sometimes the squeak of a mouse, or a 'Wee Wee!' Every now and again I got this syncopated thing going, like, 'woosh, hey, woosh, hey, woosh, baby.'

I cleaned out my ears. I quit drinking coffee. I yawned incessantly. Nothing changed. While most obvious in the dead of night, during the day, in the absence of all ambient noise, occasionally I'd catch the 'woosh, woosh.' But it was extremely faint.

Then one morning while trying to go back to sleep, listening to 'woosh, woosh,' the cat climbed on the bed and began nudging my feet, thinking I was going to leap out of bed and feed him. Instead I gave him a kick that sent him sailing, and just as he hit the floor, he whistled. Not a plaintive or startled whistle, more of jolly 'yee-ha!' whistle.

Now, having never been inside anyone else's head, I cannot with any certainty say that I am the only one who can hear internal events as if they were external. Every now and again, I'll hear a clap of thunder, or the sound of an F-15 landing, but I know it's inside my head. These are momentary and occasional bursts, and I accept them as part of the dangers of being human -internal organs emitting bizarre and unpredictable noises.

But a cat whistling? If it only happened once, I'd have just assumed I was insane and let it go at that. But a couple nights later, as the cat leapt off the bed in anticipation of me feeding him, he hit the floor and whistled.

It wasn't long after that I heard music. Faint. Distant. Couldn't even tell what kind of music it was. Brass band? Emo? Ragtime? Marimba band? My daughter, Sallie Sue, often leaves her radio on when she sleeps, and I figured maybe she'd cranked up the volume a bit too high. So, dead of night, I trudged upstairs to turn it down or off, but as I got closer to her room, the music was still distant, very faint. My hands got clammy, my heart played tom-toms against my rib cage. As I approached the doorjamb of my daughter's room, I could tell it wasn't a radio.

Then a brilliant notion occurred to me; maybe I'd left the radio on in the garage. I often listen to humorous NPR shows while working in the garage. Maybe they play Marimba music in the middle of the night, y'know, for very learned insomniacs. I went back downstairs. The cat was in the laundry room. Staring at me. No, I'm not feeding you. I brushed him aside with my foot. As I opened the door to the garage, the cat whistled. I didn't need to go into the garage. I knew the radio was not on.

The music was inside my head.

Once you've gone crazy, anything's possible.

While I had (at first) mentioned the 'woosh, woosh' to my wife, I said nothing more about it, and certainly nothing regarding the whistling cat, the Marimba Band, or the buzz below my left nipple. That started a few days after the Marimba band. Like a very gentle electric buzz. I usually carry my cell phone in my shirt pocket, and I just figured I was getting a text message. But no. I'd left my phone in the car. Just a gentle buzz, an inch below my left nipple. Comes and goes.

You would think at this stage, it was high time to start contemplating the 'what', 'how', and 'why' of a bunch of renegade organs bursting into song at whim. I sure did. The 'what' was pretty obvious. My innards had totally rebelled.

As for the 'how', something -or some set of things inside me were expressing themselves as if external. I'm not an electrician, but my best guess is the brain is wired in one way or another to every other organ, artery, capillary of the body, and can pretty much make of them what it will. A pulse, a temblor in the brain, synapses bursting. Like a ventriloquist, my brain was 'throwing its voice,' making all these internal ephemerae speak as different characters.

Most intriguing, was 'why'?

In Poe's 'Tell-Tale Heart' the 'why' was guilt. Was that the case here? Did I do something wrong, so vile and heinous that guilt was making my innards do the cha-cha?

I always like to say I don't do anything wrong, because, frankly, I don't do anything. I'm as sedentary a soul as one could find. My sins are so few and minor as to evaporate upon inspection. I adore my wife and kid. They tolerate me. It's a good working relationship. What could I have done so wrong as to be consumed by guilt? Sometimes I'm sardonic. But I don't think there's closet space in hell for that. Occasionally I'm inattentive. Sometimes I forget what I'm doing, or supposed to be doing.

Surely, nothing so hideous as to set my internal organs into riot mode.

The other possibility was 'Gaslight.' Someone was trying very subtly to drive me nuts. Was my wife having an affair with Charles Boyer? Or a sound effects man? 'Make the cat whistle? I can do that!' I preferred to think I was crazy.

So when the sound of gravel rattling around in a tin cup started, I ignored it. Just another internal organ rebelling. Or reveling.

Once in the middle of the night I woke up and didn't hear the 'woosh woosh,' and I thought, OMG, I'm dead! But then it started up again. Woosh, woosh. Never thought I'd be so glad to hear it.

38

That morning I got on Yahoogle, and typed in; 'hearing pulse in ear.' After three pages of links to sites hawking ear implants, hearing aids, and ear wax sculptures, mid-way down page 4, I saw it –Pulsatile Tinnitus. Hearing the blood rush through an artery behind the ear. Fearful, I went to a medical website. Yup, that was it, alright. A 'woosh woosh' sound caused by a blockage in the mid or inner ear, forcing one to hear the blood pulsing through the largest artery in the neck –woosh woosh. As far as I could tell, this blockage might signal a more serious problem. Like I could be seconds away from a stroke. Or, it might be something as benign as a brain tumor. Though more than likely it was simply a blockage.

With a little more research I found an article that promised to cure Pulsatile Tinnitus in less than two months. But to find out how, I had to buy the article. I'm sure the cure was 'wait two months, and it'll disappear.' I decided to save my hard-earned cash and just turn up the radio.

At least now I had a name for my lunacy.

As the weeks dragged on the Pulsatile Tinnitus seemed to grow ever dimmer and fainter, all but unnoticeable except in the wee hours of night. Either that, or I'd just grown used to it. Other sounds and sensations emerged and disappeared. Gargling noises, the sound of wind though a crack in the door, the occasional F-15 landing between my ears.

When after two months, the Pulsatile Tinnitus hadn't disappeared, I considered buying that article, but then I thought, no, between the 'woosh, woosh,' the whistling cat, Marimba music, occasional buzz, and rattling of gravel in a tin cup, my body in revellion was keeping me fairly well entertained.

And I didn't even have to pay for it.

Koko

Koko knows where the bones are buried.

Koko has her ear to the ground and nose to the wind.

Koko's eyes follow you around the room like a black velvet painting of Jesus on a bare white wall. Her little face will appear in the vortex of a triangulated space created by the counter, bar stool, and bookcase. Her watchful eyes lock on the kitchen as she lies on her bed in the living room. Even from the bedroom, if she positions herself correctly on the bed, she can see all the way into the kitchen. Ever vigilant, she watches.

Koko is a five-year-old Humane Society mutt. She was rescued by Brad von Easley, after what must have been a harrowing July 4th celebration, for according to records, she was found miles from her listed home. No one claimed her.

Koko quickly adapted to her new home. Her first job upon arriving was to take over the beds of both of Brad's daughters. One at a time. While the child was sleeping, Koko would creep onto the bed, stretch out, leaving no room for the previous occupant, and nothing would convince Koko (at least nothing the child was prepared to do) that the bed did not in fact belong to her. Mornings would find the child either on the floor, or flopped half on, half off her own bed. And Koko's head on the pillow.

Not so easily thwarted was Brad von Easley, who was more than happy to drop-kick Koko out of bed immediately she tried encroaching upon his space.

But Koko also proved to be extremely loyal. She followed close to the left side of whoever she was walking with, leading Brad to believe someone had been training her to be a seeing-eye dog. Except that she hated leashes, and would strain so hard against the collar, that she nearly strangled herself. Maybe she simply liked walking on the left side of people.

Her name came from her mocha color, but the kids wanted to change it to Liquor, because she quickly licked any hand, leg, cheek, elbow, whatever was within lapping range. Much to Brad's disgust, the kids often let Koko lick them on the face.

Koko knows only two stages of life. Eating, and waiting to eat. This is where her vigilance comes in handy. If she spies the cat tiptoeing out of the laundry room, she slips in behind him, gobbling up the remaining cat food (which she generally barfs up). In the car, if Brad leaves his tall no-whip mocha in the cup-holder, for even a brief time, to, say, pump gas, Koko has the cup shredded and licked clean, and is sitting up in the back seat, smiling, as Brad climbs back into front seat, snarling. When Brad is cooking, Koko quietly wanders into the kitchen, careful to walk on the pads of her feet, so that the toenails don't click, and avoiding Brad's swift foot, licks up dropped bits of food, be it animal, vegetable, grain, or shards of onion skin.

But there is one tower, one edifice that for nearly 5 years has eluded Koko's yearning. She does not know it by name, only reputation. It sits in the corner of the kitchen, metallic, about the height of Koko's head, and whenever food is present, this tower's lid will open, and perfectly edible food disappears into it. This desecration of everything sacred is beyond (Koko's) comprehension.

Koko knew that within this edifice resided all the great meals that ever existed, cradling the entire culinary history of this household. And she wanted in.

Dog knows, she's tried. She sniffs around it constantly (and o my, the smells!) and whenever Brad is readying to slip food into it, she is there, her head poised, waiting for the lid to open, waiting for food to slide from the plate, not into the maw of the tower, but into her own maw. But, alas, Brad's foot is quick to her butt and she scoots off, turning in time to see another fine meal disappear into the tower.

Koko's strategic planning may lack keenness, but not her intuition. If left outside too long, particularly on cold or rainy days, she discovered that by whacking at the brass knob on the front door, the door will magically swing open. O sure, a lot of shouting, and chasing ensues, but she's inside and snug beneath a bed, nice and warm, by time anyone catches up with her. She's tried similar strategies to get inside the tower, but with no luck. So far. But she is vigilant. She is watchful.

Now, it's not as though Brad is trying to starve Koko to death. Far from it. But if any dog on earth is satisfied with what it has already eaten, then it is not truly worthy of the name Dog.

Brad is, if anything, generous to a fault. If snacking, he'll often toss a piece of whatever he's gnawing on to Koko. Upon completing a batch of beef stock, Brad will hand her a big bone, which she accepts gingerly in her teeth, goes to the back door, awaits its opening, and takes it outside to tenderly strip it of tiny scraps of meat, and chew on the flavorful bone, sucking its succulent juices, until it's –well- bone-dry, and there's nothing left to do, but bury it.

Koko and Brad have had some rough patches over the years. Koko loves to ride in the car, and is a little too easily duped, with the result that sometimes she ends up at the veterinarian. There a spate of horrible, undogly things are done to her, including fingers up the rectum, the clipping of toenails, and worst of all, the cooing, reassurance of the aids who clutch her throat while all these monstrosities are enacted upon her –then they give her a tiny treat. The audacity! Koko refuses to talk to Brad for several days afterwards. Unless of course, he's fixing duck for dinner and tosses her some duck cracklings. O my, she loves duck cracklings.

Even more than duck cracklings, Koko loves goose. Koko does not know this. Koko only knows that when once in a rare while Brad roasts a goose, the singular enticing aromas fill the house, sending her into a swoon. So captivating is the smell of goose it once very nearly drove Koko to acts of violence.

It was some years ago (though Koko's grasp on time is a bit wobbly), and Brad was throwing a party. Lots of people milling about the house, most of them hanging out in kitchen. For Koko, that meant a lot of feet to avoid, but she criss-crossed, traversed, circled the kitchen, waltzing between barstools and feet, and enough food was dropped to make her efforts worth the hazard. A crumb here, a crumb there –it adds up.

And somewhere in the interstices of the various incongruous aromas that were swirling around the kitchen, a tantalizing new smell emerged. She couldn't pinpoint it, but it grabbed her attention. When the oven popped open those aromas whooshed out and very nearly bowled over Koko. She didn't get to see the goose (hey, down in front!), but she formed in her mind a picture of it; this is what Heaven looks like.

For the remainder of the evening she made the kitchen her stronghold. But for some reason, no piece of the goose, big or small hit the floor. Making her all the more brave and resolute.

It was only after everyone had gone home, the kids in bed, and Brad was cleaning the kitchen, that the goose finally entered Koko's realm of consciousness. As Brad stripped the carcass of meat, he tossed a piece Koko's way. O my Dog! Koko's eyelids flickered. Her brain went numb. Bright blinding light flooded over her eyes. A sensation of floating seemingly lifted her off the ground, and in her ecstatic state, she hovered over this rare piece of heaven on earth. But in reality, she was inching closer and closer, her head tilted upward, drool splashing in her large drops on the floor, and as Brad tossed little bits her way, she moved in for the kill.

And then it was over. Brad carried the carcass over to the metallic tower. Next thing she knew it was slipping away, forever, into the tower. What insanity! Working purely on adrenaline and instinct, Koko lunged at it. And for one brief crazy moment, actually had the goose carcass in her teeth. She could taste it, feel the crunch of bone, and my Dog, the aroma o goose, goose, I love thee!

But…Brad yanked back with equal force, and after a brief tug-a-war, Brad kicked, Koko squealed, and despite herself, let go the carcass and scampered round the counter.

Brad yelled at her, "Whaddaya trying to do, kill yourself?!" Which was all gibberish to Koko, but as she always paid more attention to intonation than content, she knew Brad was not happy.

That night, when everyone was asleep, Koko circled the repugnant tower for hours. She could smell the goose lying in there. Hiding, like Rapunzel, just begging for Koko to rescue her. To no avail. Next morning Brad suspected one of the kids had spilled soda pop on the floor, so much dried stickiness surrounded the tower.

Brad could also be cruel. Koko, when preparing to be fed (she saw the bowl, she saw the can), often would get, okay, a little eager. Brad would look at her, "Quit chomping your mandibles," he'd snap in that uncertain voice. Is this good, or bad? But then, just as he was about to set the dish in front of her, he'd pause, and say, "Do the

'Koko Dance.'" While the meaning was unclear, the implication was obvious. She knew the only way to get her food was to keep prancing back and forth, her forelegs to the left, her butt to the right, then the reverse, toenails clacking on the hardwood floor, her head bobbing and weaving...very humiliating. If the kids were around, they'd laugh, clap their hands and shout for Koko to keep dancing. All very embarrassing, but again, if it hastened the onset of food, she'd shamelessly do the Koko Dance. Usually by time the meal was set down, there was a splatter of drool a foot in diameter.

And so it was that one day, a new and unsettling atmosphere fell upon the household. The kids were off to their grandparents for the evening, and Brad von Easley spent all afternoon in the kitchen cooking, sipping wine, whistling, changing the music randomly, talking to Koko, occasionally tossing her a tidbit of something or other. She rarely knew what, as it barely hit tongue before going down the gullet. But Brad seemed happy, and that made Koko happy, if not a little leery.

The smells were enticing, not quite in the goose realm, but, then what is, other than goose?

And then the doorbell rang. So engrossed in this new mood was Koko that she hadn't heard a car pull up, and so, in way of overcompensation, she raced to the door, barking her fool head off, the hair on her back up, and ready to rip to shred anybody who might disrupt the kingdom. Brad, ever calm, kicked Koko aside, opened the door, and this new person came in. Female, though that was no concern of Koko's. This new person tried to pat Koko on the head, but o no you don't. Not just like that. Especially seeing as she smelled of...ick. Cat. Even worse, she didn't bring any food for Koko. As this person was of no use to Koko, she moseyed into the bedroom, climbed on the bed, and watched through the door, all the way into the kitchen. Just in case.

This new person seemed pleasant enough. Her name, though Koko, never quite caught it was Katy Riley. Her and Brad spent a good deal of time in the kitchen, talking, sipping wine. Some quiet laughter. Nothing raucous. Koko sensed something slightly awkward about Brad. She couldn't put a paw on it, but he was gentler, tamer, more given to listening than talking. Koko considered checking his nose to see if it were warm.

Then suddenly there seemed to be some food-related activity in the kitchen. Koko noiselessly slid off the bed, wandered across the living room to the kitchen. Yes, things were happening. Something was coming out of the oven. That's a good sign. Plates, silverware rattling. Ooo, this could be good. And then the food came out. Stuffed pork shops, garlic mashed potatoes, and bacon wrapped asparagus. Koko caught just a glimpse of this smorgasbord as Brad was plating it up, and she worked up a fairly healthy drool.

Thinking this Kay Riley might be an easy touch, despite the cat smell, Koko positioned herself beneath her barstool, when Brad said sternly, "Koko, get out of here." Huh? What? She gets to eat, and not me? Pfff. Koko ducked her head and slunk out of the kitchen, and somewhat miffed, lay down on her bed by the TV.

She watched. She listened. They ate. Forks clanging on plates. Joyous sounds of deliciousness. Koko brooded.

Finally it was over. Brad and Katy Riley strolled into the living room, turned on the TV. They sat together on the couch. Trying not to be too obvious, Koko wandered into the kitchen. The plates were still up on the counter. One leap, and she could easily get to them. But, Brad was right there. She could see the top of his head. Rather too close to this Katy Riley person. Maybe they were just sniffing each other.

Koko paced around the kitchen. Licked here and there, nothing much. She surreptitiously sauntered back into the living room, where Katy Riley was practically lying in Brad's lap. Wondering if she was missing out on something, Koko crept under the table and poked her head up between them. Maybe there was some food situation going on here. Brad said, "Will you get out of here."

Koko hung her head and returned to her bed, which, as it was just to the right and beneath the TV, put her at the center of attention. Though their attention didn't seem to be much on Koko, or the TV.

After a while, Brad stood up and headed into the kitchen.

"Lemmee put some things away, then I'll freshen your wine," he said, apparently, not to Koko, but to this Katy Riley. Koko watched from her bed as Brad scurried around the kitchen. Plates clanged. Faucet ran. Silverware clanged. Refrigerator door opened. Then Brad came into the living room bearing a bottle of wine. He refreshed Katy Riley's glass. They sat very close to each other on the couch. Then to Koko's amazement, they hugged and began licking each other's lips. How come Brad never licked Koko's lips? All the times she'd tried. This was troubling.

The hugging and kissing proceeded furiously, until Brad whispered something, Katy Riley whispered something back. They both stood, still clinging to each other. And then very slowly, all the while hands petting, lips smacking, they walked into the bedroom.

Koko, showing amazing patience, waited. After a moment, she got up and strolled into the kitchen, looked around, and then her eyes froze…she spotted it. The tower. Its lid wide open. Koko began to twitch. Her eyelids fluttered. She very nearly did the Koko Dance, so excited was she. She waited a moment. Was this a trap? Would Brad von Easley come racing out of the bedroom and give her a swift kick if she approached the tower? She paused. Listened. Sounds of laughter, then sighing from the bedroom. Then the door closed. Only muffled sounds.

Koko snuck up on the tower. She was careful. She'd never seen the lid wide open. Didn't want the click of toenails to force it closed. One false move and the chance of a lifetime was over. But this was no time to be careful. With one fearless leap she plunged her nose into the tower, and o, good Dog! The meat, potatoes, bones, bacon, asparagus, she gobbled it all, slurping it up, barely chewing, just gobbling the tastiest of tasty morsels, chomping, gnashing, gulping, then suddenly she snorted, something lodged in her throat, she gagged, she tried to spit, to cough, to hack it up, but no use, she choked, then thrashed about knocking over the tower, banging into the stools, her head reeling, the horrible sting in her throat, she staggered, tried to run, but blindly banged into the bookcase, she couldn't breathe, the pain, the pain, and as she thrashed, she began losing her grip on reality, blackness descended, her mind spun out of control, and the last thing she heard before departing this dog forsaken world was the sound of Brad yelling, he grabbed her, and then…Koko was gone.

"Yeah, we just got her back…"

Koko re-entered the universe. She was on her bed in the front room. She knew she'd been gone a long time. Everything was different. Her head was fuzzy, she couldn't smell anything. Her tongue was lashed to the roof of her mouth. She had no sensation, nothing but a dull ache everywhere. She heard Brad von Easley's voice. That calmed her. Somewhat. Her eyes barely open, she tried to lift her head to see where he was, but the pain was so intense, she simply sighed, and laid her head back down to rest. She listened.

"Doc says she'll be okay, but it was a close call…well, when she got into the garbage can she ate everything…pork chops, bones and all. Yeah, the vet had to give her a tracheotomy, then he realized she'd

46

swallowed bones, and immediately operated, more than two hours digging out bits of bones and other stuff...he said he can't believe she's still alive. He thought he lost her several times. I just sat in the waiting room crying, every now and again one of the aids would come out, looking hopeless, I thought for sure she was a goner...but the little turd survived. Just barely. Thank god the emergency vet is practically around the corner. Much further, she never would've made it. But even after, doc said it was such invasive surgery he gave her only a 50-50 chance of survival...but here she is...yeah, she's been at the vet this whole week....Cost? Bundles. Over five thousand dollars, so far. I guess me and the girls won't be going to Hawaii this year. But, whaddaya gonna do? Pain in the butt she is, she's still our Koko...no, the kids aren't taking it well at all....Lindy can't stop crying, and Marilyn walks around like she's been kicked in the gut....can't wait for them to get home though...I'm sure they'll go nuts seeing Koko...but she's pretty drugged out, and can't really be moved...yeah, pain pills, big time... hope she doesn't get addicted...no, Katy...it's not your fault...I'm just sorry it interrupted our, ummm...did you get home okay?...O well, maybe you'll let me make it up to you some time...or maybe it wasn't meant to be..."

Koko lay listening, panting, but lightly, for it hurt just to breath. Brad von Easley hung up the phone and walked over and kneeled beside Koko. He put a hand to her head. "Hey, ole gal, you're awake." She glanced up at him. "You dumb, stupid animal," he said, fortunately she didn't comprehend the words, she just knew that Brad loved her. "You know you scared the crap out of me," he said. Koko pried the tongue from the roof of her mouth.

"Thirsty, pup?" Brad stood up, "I'll get you some water..." he walked toward the kitchen.

Normally Koko would assume it was to get her food, at which point she'd leap up and follow by his left side into the kitchen. Then prance around, sniffing, licking the floor, ever hopeful, ever vigilant.

But not today. Because for some reason, she wasn't in the least bit hungry.

The Introduction

Hieronymus Uedtstre, the eponymous hero of this 19th century novel, lies on his deathbed, and to his grieving daughter makes the horrific confession that he is not her father, but in fact her mother. The daughter, enraged, and mortified beyond belief, brings a candle-holder down on her father/mother's head striking him/her dead.

This shocking conclusion, certainly one of the strangest surprise endings in all of literature, forces the reader to reevaluate everything that has led up to this brutal act. Not an easy task, considering the preceding 700 pages of elusive, thorny, abstruse, sometimes tortuous prose. But it is only when the last piece falls into place, in this case, when the daughter drinks the vial of cyanide, killing herself, that it all makes sense.

From the outset 'Hieronymus Uedtstre' confuses the reader. Norm Whomsky (whose 'Rendered Illiterate' first introduced Teapuddlian literature to American readers) suggests that this is the intent -the bewildering prose belies the simplicity of purpose –truth, persistence, and product placement.

The bravura language, often considered to prefigure Joyce ('I think that I shall never see/a poem lovely as a tree'), the characters with amalgam-like names (Ahsley Dushom, Pholone Thud, Niskrit Mthis), inconceivable plot twists, improbable coincidences, innumerable characters wandering in and out, having nothing to do with plot development or motivation, all conspire to make this a novel both perplexing and remote.

And yet 'Hieronymus Uedtstre', often called the Great Teapuddlian Novel, remains one of those oddities; most literary scholars know of it, but few have read it. Largely because, of the editions published in the U.S., most have either been poorly translated, irreverently bowdlerized, or severely cut (in some cases by half). But now, finally with this new translation by Salsbury Stu, complete and unabridged, and hermetically faithful to the original, we are now able to ask; What is 'Hieronymus Uedtstre', and how then shall the modern reader deal with it?

The author, Lyschschvavitz Dille, was a gardener. This we know from her only other published work, a collection of descriptors and meanderings from the back of seed packages from the upstart mail order company, Belcho. The work '*Mertle, Buuddle onk Snoflip,*' was published posthumously and never translated into English. Nor any other language. The title roughly translates as 'Shit, Earth, and Love (or 'Sex', as the Tepuddlian word *Snoflip* is ambiguous).'

And so 'Hieronymus Uedstrre' remains the singular work of Dille's that, confounding though it is, we must take on its own.

Let us first then tackle her prose style, which some have likened to that of a chemistry textbook interspersed with annotations by vandals. Less kind reviewers have likened it to a hornet's nest repeatedly wacked.

However one defines it, there is an excitement, a joie de vivre, a sense that the writer is insanely inspired by inanities, or, in the vernacular, just doesn't give a rip. Don't look for hidden meanings, are arcane symbolism, this is just straight-forward writing, like a drunk headed to a hanging.

There is agreement amongst scholars on one point: if this novel were told in any other style —poetic, elliptical, expository- it never would have been published. Or if it had been, it certainly wouldn't be read and disgust a hundred years down the road. So we must take at face value the fractured language, the awkward metaphors, puerile puns, and the inappropriately planted adverbs.

With this in mind, let us now dismiss the narrative arc of the novel, for to call this chain of occasions a 'plot' would abuse the notion. There is no sustained action, no concatenation of events leading up to a denouement, in fact, there is precious little to remind the reader that this is a novel. Plot, any notion of a plot, has been tossed out the window.

In one instance, we have one hundred pages of conversation between an ant and a clematis, followed by a 40-page explanation of the pollination of stevia (which as Whomsky noted, is horribly inaccurate).

Events are thrown at the reader without explanation or context; the year-long crossing of the Teapudllian Fjord, the discovery of Rudy's Ark, the troubled upbringing of the von Easley boy, the twenty-year construction of the Teapot Windmill, the Bees Wax Shortage of 1874, the anonymous tip that leads to the secret recipe for Coca-Cola -none of these events have continuity, either within themselves or as they relate to each other. There is certainly no 'development'. But, as Whomsky insists, 'Is that not the author's intent?'

All of these sequences then are background texture, like gray primer, to bring to the fore the real colorless focus of this work –the main character, Hieronymus Uedtstre. He is likely patterned after the author's husband, Ott Dille (whose obituary, written by Lyschschvavitz Dille, recites date of birth, longevity, and death –that's it). Like her own husband, our hero, anti-hero, is a cipher, a man (woman?) who merely occupies space. We have no visual, or psychological portrait of the title character. He could be a dwarf, or Gargantua. He could be 100-years-old (there are hints of this possibility), or a newborn (at least symbolically); we don't know.

And for Whomsky, that's as it should be. It is in the surrounding cast of characters that many have found delight. Inescapably, it is Maundy Teusday, the ostensible villain of the novel, who draws our attention, as he comes and goes, sometimes spraying Belcho seeds upon the ground, often throwing stones at starlings, occasionally annoying the Town Mayor, all the while taunting our supposed hero, and perhaps –perhaps!- fathering the daughter.

Sidekicks (or are they merely imaginary beings?), Benj Dorwad, and Glys Orin seem always to be on the fringe of whatever is (or is not) going on. The Baron von Easley puts in an appearance. The synonymous twins, Quaff and Swig, are always yelling at our hero from a nearby skiff.

And finally, the daughter, Hierowyn. Much has been made of the fact that it is only two pages before the end of the novel that we find out Hieronymus even has a daughter (there is no previous mention of wife/husband or lover).

For the most crucial character (excepting the title character) to appear out of nowhere, and so suddenly bring everything to a crashing conclusion seems at first glance exceedingly bizarre.

Whomsky points out, however, that this is in keeping with nearly every aspect of the novel. If nothing else fits the mold of conventional narrative, why then should we expect a responsible ending. Perhaps Lyschschvavitz Dille, after 700 pages of chicken fodder, finally said, 'to hell with it,' and in the tradition of the great Russian novels of the era, just kills off everyone.

Perhaps even more perplexing, because it is the entire *raisin d'etre* of the novel, is Hieronymus's ultimate confession. Are we to infer that he has had a sex change somewhere in the course of the text, and it just got lost in the thorny prose? Or is Hieronymus really Heronymus? Is it a sadistic joke the main character plays on Hierowyn? Was he/she taunting his daughter, inciting her to murder? And finally, is Hierowyn really his/her daughter?

Dille gives us no clue, perhaps, because, one suspects, she has no clue. In the final analysis, we can only take the written word for what it is. Unalterable. After the thunder of garbled prose, meandering plot threads, and unsustainable characters, a wayward daughter suddenly enters, kills her father/mother, and commits suicide.

And bang! It's over.

Enjoy.

David Utterford, MD PUD, Clark College
March, 2011

Joseph, Redacted

The problem with knowing a writer is, you might get written about. Just ask Joseph.

Joseph Inverness, a shy, introverted young fellow, met his future wife, an aspiring writer, in college. Joan Gaspereau worked on the college paper, writing humorous sketches, mostly about mundane matters on campus. Joseph was a phys-ed major, and standout basketball player, but not standout enough to get drafted. After college he found a job teaching weight training and toning at a local community college. After another year, he was made coach of the girls basketball team.

Joseph and Joan married. Joan upon graduating, looked for work as a newspaper editor, but could only find freelance work here and there. She soon became pregnant.

Joan was highly neurotic. Her fears included; gaining weight, close spaces, highly aggressive people, bright colors, large bulbous noses, excited conversation, tidy bathrooms, laundry, loud laughter, steak knives, crowded shelves, too many rainy days in a row, and anyone more neurotic than her.

To almost all of these inconveniences, Joseph complemented her perfectly. He was fastidious, methodical, well-organized, frugal, self-motivated, quiet, and almost pathologically dull.

During her pregnancy Joan began keeping a journal. In part, to keep her neuroses in check, and in part to amuse herself. She illustrated her pithy observations with crude, elementary drawings. She wasn't much of an artist, had never studied to be one, but had a nice eye and hand for contours, and dramatic, comical exaggeration.

Amongst her many friends, mostly hangers-on from college days, was a young lady who had gotten on at a small weekly. One day while visiting, she noticed some of Joan's drawings, then, with proper authorization, read the accompanying texts. She laughed out loud. She asked if she could show them to her editor. Joan thought it all a bit silly, but agreed.

Soon her drawings and writings became the 'With Child Diary' in the paper, following the wacky exploits of a young, pregnant mother, and leading up to the birth of Ronald Arthur, a robust, squalling baby boy, who seemed to contain more life than should be allowed in one so (newly) and totally unformed. Joan had figured the 'With Child Diary' to end at that, but quite the opposite happened. With this new, endless wealth of bubbly, bawling material, she could scarcely contain herself, and the Diary continued. Her drawings became a little more hand-steady, without compromising the raw comic nature.

Joseph seldom appeared in the early Diaries, sometimes as a foil to the half-crazed Joanne (Joan's *nom de cartoon*), but more often as an off-stage presence whose spirit entered but seldom interfered.

But then came the second pregnancy. Feeling that her comic world was far too claustrophobic, and that her readers were getting a little antsy with only two characters, Joan began featuring Joseph (named Peter in the Diary) more often as the solid, stalwart father/husband/breadwinner, making the bouncing boy, and the neurotic mother even more exaggerated. Peter was the solid core around which all the family flimflam flew.

Once the second child was born, Millie (Nellie in the Diary), the comic world exploded. Nellie's birth was not mere addition by one, but an entanglement involving exponential multiplication, as Joan drew on friends, neighbors, extended family, creating a whole world circling about her main characters.

Soon after Millie was born (and the account duly recorded in the 'With Child Diary'), Joan published a book, a sort of 'greatest hits' of the first three years of her Diaries. It was a thin paperback, locally published, and was an instant hit. Joan appeared on local talk shows, for which her neurotic, self-denigrating wit was perfectly suited. She was plain enough looking that she appealed to the 'Everywoman', and funny enough that the same Everywoman recognized her own foibles in Joan.

The book sold well, so much so it was picked up by a major publisher. With a few additions, a new snazzier cover, the book was published nationally, and was warmly reviewed in family magazines and newspapers across the country. Joan traveled to New York and Los Angeles to appear on a few low-level talk shows, and again her nervous, anxious, self-deprecating wit won over enough people that the book made a brief appearance on the trade paperback bestseller list.

Joan was approached by a national syndication, and asked if she would be able to produce a daily comic strip featuring her characters. She didn't think so. Her 'art' was too rudimentary, and it took her forever to draw one piece. She couldn't imagine cranking out 365 a year. Besides, how many funny ideas can one person have? Certainly not enough to fill a calendar year.

The national syndicate, speaking through a newly found agent, laughed off her reservations, saying of course Joan would have an assistant, or even assistants, if needed, to help with the art and to conceive and develop ideas.

Joan consented. Then fretted, and chewed her nails to the cuticle, until she came up with two months worth of strips all on her own just to get the strip off to a running start. And almost exactly on Millie's second birthday, Joan's syndicated strip began appearing in 56 newspapers across the country.

Throughout all of this Joseph was mildly stoic. He read the Diary, books, the strip, with slight amusement, feeling only a twinge at the invasion of privacy, and at some of 'Peter's' antics, the almost insanely sane center of the strip.

But life was good. The family of four moved into a house on the coast, still within driving distance of the community college where Joseph continued to teach and coach. They traveled, which gave Joan even more fodder for her strip, broadening its scope, and giving it a more national feel.

Yes, life was good.

As the kids grew, Joan relaxed into the cozy routine of producing a daily strip. She had a studio, one full time assistant, an older woman who was very nearly as neurotic as Joan, but in a completely different way. And was a far better and quicker artist. They worked well together. She also had a team of 'bit' writers who contributed ideas, and occasional storylines.

One notion Joan contrived to ease the tension of constantly coming up with new material, was to present the strip in real time, especially as regards the children growing up. When Ronnie started kindergarten, so did Ross. When Millie threw up on her first day at Montessori, so did Nellie. Although the kids matured in the strip along with the real-life kids, there was still a kind of distance, they were mere caricatures, whose real flesh and blood nature were hidden behind one-dimensional newsprint.

Though the gap was closing.

Joan gave Peter a dull job. He started as an insurance agent, but then she moved him into corporate headquarters. This gave Joan numerous comic 'office politic' opportunities, which she took full advantage of.

Over the years, Peter became a little more quirky, and Joseph wondered if he too were becoming more quirky. Joan presented extended storylines regarding some of Peter's odd hobbies. These were cast in a strange way, as if Peter were trying to rebel, or break away from the madness of the rest of the family and his work.

One storyline had Peter buying a brand new riding lawn mower, despite the fact they lived on a postage-stamp sized lot. Peter would ride around on his mower, hoisting a beer (that he never drank) from the cup holder, waving at neighbors, mowing the lawn over and over again. Joseph supposed this was funny... to someone.

In another, an excited Peter ruined a neighbor's going-away party by discussing model boat-building ad nauseum. In yet another, Peter attempted to coach Ross's soccer team, with predictably awful and hilarious (?) results.

As Joseph read these, he pondered his own life. Was Joan commenting on him and his work? Was he not thrilling enough, so that she had to make up quirks?

One day, Joseph was called into the office of the Athletic Director. A complaint had been lodged against Joseph that he had inappropriately touched one of the girls on his basketball team. The director thought the allegation an outrage, saying he fully supported Joseph, but...the college took these things seriously, and regrettably, he was forced to put Joseph on paid leave while an investigation into the matter was pursued.

Joseph was horrified. His mind raced. What girl? He ran through his calculated memory. Inappropriate touch? During on-court huddles, he might put his arms around the girls while giving them a pep talk. He may grab one by the shoulders when instructing or reprimanding. But inappropriate touching? The card catalog in his mind could find no trace of such an encounter.

He limped home to Joan and told her immediately. They went over the implications. Joseph worried that if the story got out, his wife's reputation might be tarnished. It may even put her strip in danger. Joan pooh-poohed it. She was supportive, almost furious that the college was punishing Joseph. No, it wasn't her reputation at stake, it was Joseph's.

Fortunately, the 'investigation into the allegations' was conducted with surprising delicacy. Non-uniformed police, and college counselors, interviewed everyone surrounding the incident, from assistant coaches, to fellow instructors, and all the girls on the team. Most had no idea why the interviews were being conducted.

In the end it came out that a misguided, but perhaps well-meaning associate instructor while passing by the gym one day during basketball practice observed Joseph patting a girl on the butt, and, she, this assistant instructor, thought, he had left his hand there a bit too long. She admitted that it may have been closer to 'lower back' than butt, and that 'leaving too long' was a subjective matter.

The poor girl around whom these allegations circled, realized she was at the center of whatever it was that was going on, and was so ashamed at having jeopardized her coach and team that she insisted on quitting. But she was a much-needed forward, although, mostly coming off the bench, and Joseph and his assistant coaches persuaded her to stay, if for no other reason than to assure everyone that nothing untoward had happened.

The complete exoneration, along with the subtlety of the investigation, left Joseph thrilled, a sense of triumph over adversity, almost like winning a championship game. He and Joan celebrated with a rare bottle of Champagne.

With that ordeal over, their lives drifted back into dormancy. For a while.

Two months after this incident, Joseph, who only occasionally read the comic strip, one morning opened the paper, glanced at Joan's strip, recognized himself as Peter, and then much to his horror, read a four-panel introduction to a new storyline. In it, a forlorn Peter returned from work to tell his wife that he had been accused of making unwanted advances on a co-worker. Peter was put on paid leave while an investigation into the matter was underway. The conversation between Peter and Joanne was almost word for word the one between their real-life counterparts. Joseph nearly chocked on his English Muffin.

He sat for long moments, numb, listening to his breathing, the pulsing of his blood.

Joan had already left for the studio. Should he call her? Demand an explanation? She had never said anything to him about this new storyline. Joseph was so angry he slammed the paper down, sending a teacup crashing to the floor. As he picked up the pieces, the words, so amazing to him, pounded in his brain: 'How could she?!'

He would definitely have a talk with her that evening.

All morning, he got more and more worked up. Several times he had a hand on the phone to call her. But then he'd stop. Was he being childish? Too sensitive? He didn't think so. The words returned; 'How could she?'

As the day wore on, his anger, confusion and befuddlement subsided. At late afternoon practice, somehow the sight of his back-up forward out on the floor, hustling, sweating, working her tail off, put everything back into perspective. He laid a hand on her shoulder and complimented her for doing such a good job.

On his ride home, he decided not to force the issue. He'd say nothing. If Joan wanted to bring it up, let her. He'd take the high road. But of course, Joan said nothing about her new storyline. Joseph bought a new teacup, bit his tongue until it bled, and never confronted Joan.

The storyline played out over several weeks. Peter worked for a national powerhouse insurance company, and an (evil) investigator from human resources was called in to look into the matter. It was found that woman in question had filed harassment charges in two of her previous jobs. All of Peter's co-workers defended him. Then much like the real story, Peter was exonerated when the woman confessed that perhaps she had made too much of an idle comment. Everyone was relieved. Peter returned to work. The final panel showed Joanne, alone at a table, feeling isolated and uncertain, with the thought balloon: 'I wonder.'

So that's how Joan felt? Did she think that maybe, just maybe, Joseph had 'inappropriately touched' this girl?

Joseph paid closer attention to the strip now. He noted how his children were portrayed, especially the older son. Not exactly an all-A student, klutzy at sports (much to his father's chagrin), Ronnie was a good kid, but he excelled at nothing. Ross, however, was the brightest kid in class, won science awards, and was the leading scorer on the soccer team.

Nellie was pretty much a straight-up match for Millie, as she came off as spoiled and self-involved in the strip.

While it was bad enough to plunder your own family, Joseph felt some people should be off-limit. When Millie's best friend, a girl who spent the night often, was an incessant talker, fidgety, flighty, and really quite annoying, got drawn into the strip, Joan portrayed her just as she was. Except that in the strip, the girl was diagnosed with ADHD. There was an ongoing storyline involving this, including counseling, and eventually medication.

Joseph felt Joan had gone too far.

But he never confronted her about any of this. Was it because 'Peter' in the strip would never do so? Acceptance and toleration being the norm?

Joan's blurring of the line between reality and caricature -Joseph would be the first to admit- certainly lent the strip authenticity, but it also gave it a kind of catty soap opera feel. Because the 'reality' was so exaggerated. Peter, for instance, couldn't just be a workaday Joe, no, he had to be in the running for Vice President of the company. It wasn't good enough for Ross to be on the high school newspaper, no, he had to be the muck-raking investigative reporting editor/writer standing up to all the authorities to break a story that would make national headlines (this idea based on a profile Ronnie wrote about a gay teacher).

Whenever anything significant happened in their lives, Joseph could almost gauge when it would appear in the strip, as there was always a lag time of about two months. Although sometimes, depending on the severity of the situation, it may be more than a year. As when Joseph's father died.

It was an awful time for Joseph. He wasn't a very emotive person, but when his father suffered a stroke, fell into a coma, and after many weeks, he and his mother had to make the gut-wrenching decision to take him off life-support, it crushed Joseph. For the first time in his life he considered going into therapy. He had no grip on his

58

emotions, couldn't function at work, and was forced to take a leave of absence. He had never felt so lost and lonely in his life.

It was more than a year later, when Joseph was finally beginning to feel his old self again, Joanne's mother in the strip suffered a heart attack. She lay in a coma for weeks (in the strip it took months). Once again, Joseph read this with disbelief. It was as if he had to suffer through the pain all over again. But worse, because in a way, Joan was robbing him of his grief.

And then when Joanne and her father made the gut-wrenching decision to take her mother off life-support, Joseph almost crumbled. He could barely stand the sight of his wife. When the mother died in the strip, something in Joseph also died.

As the years marched on, life continued inside and outside the mirror of the strip. When Ronnie went off to college, so too did Ross. When Millie kissed her first boyfriend, so too did Nellie. When one of Ronnie's friends got addicted to prescription drugs, so too did one of Ross's friends. When Joseph took his team to the regional championships, Peter finally made Vice President. When Ronnie brought a young lady home on spring break, introducing her as his fiancé, so too did Ross.

It was about this time that Peter's quirkiness developed into what can only be characterized as midlife crisis.

Which forced Joseph to look at his own life. He seemed fine. He was approaching 50, but there was such an ease and stability to his situation, why would he want to ruin that? If he was having a midlife crisis, he was the last to know about it.

But along with Peter's definite midlife crisis (expensive toys, unexplained absences, going out with 'the boys'), a strange undercurrent flowed through the strip. Peter seemed to have no love for his wife. Joanne fretted about Peter's feelings, confiding in friends that she feared he was having an affair, or that he found her unattractive, or that he no longer cared for her. Of course, in the strip, these fears were always proven to be unfounded, and 'the humor' was in Joanne's lack of self-esteem.

There were plenty of other storylines that began to nag at Joseph. In one extended sequence, Peter dreamed of taking a solo vacation, an adventure all alone. He was forever pulling out maps, reading travel books, talking up exotic places. He bought camping gear (along with a ridiculous pith helmet), and almost bought a motorcycle. And, of course, Joanne turned this into a huge melodrama, fretting, and driving herself and everyone around her nuts. The resolution, after weeks and weeks, was that Peter and Joanne's brother (a frequent visitor to the strip) decided to rent a van and drive across the U.S. to Las Vegas. Joanne was mollified, Peter got his 'big adventure', and a chaperone.

The 'tone' of all these stories involving Peter, seemed to be leading, even to the undiscerning eye, inevitably to…divorce. Peter's estrangement, Joanne's constant consternation over everything about their relationship. It seemed she was willing the marriage to come to an end.

Would she do that in a comic strip?

Even Joseph would be hard put to say exactly when it all began to takes its toll on his psyche, his work, and the marriage. He would never say to his wife; 'It's me or the strip. One of us has got to go.' He was proud of her work. She had crafted a wonderful if moderate, national success. She was not a bestselling author, but a pretty darned good selling author. He could never deny her that.

But it was becoming more evident that the pressure of having your every move, mood, tick, and mannerism scrutinized, analyzed for its comic effect, and then if deemed worthy, thrown up in front of a worldwide audience was too much to bear. If he were to graph it out, the arc went slowly up for a long time, then at first moderately down, then swiftly dropped, and finally a complete dive off the chart. Joseph knew the end was in sight.

He waited until Millie left home for college (yes, in the strip, Nellie followed). Joseph tried to be assertive, tried to warn Joan what was coming, tried with all his might to convey that he needed out of the marriage. And maybe it worked. Because one day at practice, he was approached by a young, very nervous legal intern who handed him some papers. Divorce papers.

Relieved. Stunned. Saddened. But as ever, civil and well-mannered, he bought some toiletries, and rented a hotel room.

He could not talk to Joan. Not directly. So he talked to her through his kids. Neither sibling seemed stunned by this development, nor did they express much in the way of sorrow or sympathy, towards either parent. Had they been aware long before he (and maybe even she) that divorce was imminent?

And Joseph waited. He opened the paper to the comics every morning with a strange anticipation. Two months went by. Nothing. Five months. Nothing. The divorce was final. Nothing.

When (and how?) was Joanne going to tell Peter she was divorcing him? Joseph was curious to know Joan's take on the situation, and she would no doubt reveal it in the strip. In some decipherable form, masked, for sure, but she would tell him.

More than a year went by, and Joanne and Peter remained married in the strip. Peter continued on as the sane, devoted husband, even taking Joanne to Europe for their 25th wedding anniversary. Joanne of course suffered jet-lag, hated French food, argued with Italians, cursed English cab drivers, thought Stonehenge boring, while Peter had the time of his life.

Even after Joseph re-married (a school teacher with no writerly aspirations), he waited.

And then, as in real life, Peter and Joanne became grandparents, starting the comic 'baby' cycle all over again. If changing diapers was funny twenty-five years ago, why shouldn't it be funny now? Especially when grandpa was doing it. Millie (and Nellie) remained stubbornly single, a well-educated, career woman who had no time for husbands and babies. She was the only interesting one in the strip.

Though, one odd thing developed in Joseph, he actually began to like Peter. He sort of admired his life, and his mild and reasonable reactions to Joanne, family and work. He seemed a perfectly rational, likeable fellow.

Still, every day he opened the paper, certain that Joanne would finally make the big decision –after months of hand-wringing and suffering, no doubt- to divorce Peter. Or perhaps she would reverse reality, and make Peter the onerous one to file for divorce. That would probably be more suitable to the self-deprecating Joanne/Joan. Or perhaps she'd be cruel, and simply kill Peter off.

He waited. But no, that day never came.

Ever dull, ever dutiful, Peter lived on forever.

A House So Random

Naida, the daughter of a powerful doge, suffered from brachydactylia, was blennioid in shape, collected harquebuses, lived in a Rundbogenstil house with vasa murrhina windows, tended to melodramatize any situation, dabbled in Babism, could be at times lightsome, though if provoked, might cause a ruction. She also cultivated turpeth, wore her hennin with a saucy tilt to the right, and often would nectarise her tea with stevia.

One day, while eating a cuneal slice of savarin, she…

"Papa?!"

"Yes, honey?"

"Will you please put away the dictionary, you're gettin' way too obscure, if not totally obnoxious."

"But, honey, I finally stumbled on an awesome gimmick for telling a story, I'm flipping randomly…haha, get it, random? –through 'The Random House Dictionary of the English Language, the Unabridged Edition,' and using header words to make up a story."

"Story. What story? Yr just stringing together mismatched phrases."

"Haha, I know. You should see some of these words, they're not just obscure, they're totally bizarre. And they drive my spellchecker crazy…their mixeableness is awesome."

"No, it's obnoxious. You're supposed to be telling a story."

"Okay, honey, I'll try…"

…leapt over an acequia, and bumped into a minister without portfolio…

"Papa. You need a plot!"

"Hey, don't derogate my plot…it's like dead-anneal, which you can test with a deformeter, it takes time, and the occasional decasyllabic word to get through the dreck…"

"At least get out of the 'Ds'."

"O, man, I could wallow in the Ds the rest of my life. Check this out; dichogamous. Ever hear of that?"

"No, and I don't even want to know what it means."

"Or disarticulator? I've seen articulated buses, but what happens when a disarticulator gets a hold of one? Haha."

"Okay, Papa, have your fun."

"Hey, Sallie Sue, did you know that H is the most boring letter in the alphabet? But ho, look what I just noticed, 'header' is a header word. But…and this is a big but…it's not defined as what we call header. Five definitions and not one is our notion of header. Wow…when was this thing published? Hmm, 1967. Way back in the Pre-Computic Age. I wonder if header is more of a computer term. Headers, footers. Maybe they weren't headers back then. But what else would they be called?"

"Stupid?"

"Wait, let me Yahoogle it. Hey, here we go, they're actually called 'guide words', or 'guidewords'. Lemme look up 'guide words' in the Random House Dictionary… 'guide words. See catchword, 2nd definition.' Ah-hah! Here it is. Yup, they are called guide words. Catchword, guideword –Borrrrr-ring. Forget it, I'm stickin' with headers. Stet. This is the 21st century, after all."

"Papa, will you please just get on with the story. Give us a plot, something?"

"Hey, hon, look; 'plot' is a header word! Haha, okay. You want a plot, I got it, see what you think of this…"

Naida lived in an involuted dwelling, and one day while hanging from a rundle, Ozzie entered bearing a jar of yill. Ozzie, a first year softa, was dressed in his usual viridescent tobe, looking excessively of nuptial plumage. Ozzie and Naida were best of friends, despite the fact their differences were many and supermundane. On the one hand, Naida had a connate sense of loyalty, was doughty, and circumspect. While Ozzie was a voluptuary, as well as obsequent, and many thought him irresolute, otiose, sweer, and something of a simp. But Naida knew that when properly motivated, Ozzie's energy level could only be measured by the megajoule, and due to his strict stratigraphy of thought, he could cut-and-cover with the best of them. While Naida might be accused of preciosity, Ozzie had a more synoetic relationship with the great unwashed.

After the intussusception of belly-wash, Ozzie cut a mean kazachok, that's when Naida suggested they go for a walk. They set out on the road from Pharsalus to Dneprodzerzhinsk. Naida wore samite culottes, and Ozzie carried his jereed of alerce. The goldfinny were singing, and the two friends stopped to pick cuckooflower, astilbe, and to gaze at the rafia. Out on the lake, in a boat with a mutton-spanker, a few Gwari were fishing for sea cucumber.

Suddenly they heard a screechy shofar, and with voices shouting skimble-scramble they were set upon by brigands each bearing a gonfanon.

"What sortie is this?" cried Naida, but she was struck thuddingly on the head, rattling her encephalon.

When she regained consciousness, she found herself and Ozzie, feet in gyve, before Periander, tyrant of Corinth.

One of the tyrant's entourage cried, "Ordure in the court."

"I thought I smelled rotten damson," muttered Naida.

Then Periander, pounding his dorje, spoke darkly;

"So Ozzie, we meet again," he said derogately. "Last time we met was during your perpetration of an insurrection against me, determined to overthrow my realm, and set up a dinarchy."

"What a screed," Ozzie replied exiguously, "you wound my izzat. I was just trying to get the masses to understand that fainéant is the opiate of the people. Besides, it was a mere flapdoodle. I did nothing maleficient."

"Your loquacity convinces me only of your lassitude," Periander said.

64

"Yea, verily, but tell me, where in your pandect does it say this is a judicable offense?"

"I AM the law here, you are obligable to me alone. Lemme apprise you of your punishment. Death. Off to the hangman with you. Ha! What is your rejoinder, pouter? You have nothing to say, either you are presbycusis, or you suffer ankyloglossia."

"Neither, actually, it's just that, if I am about to die, I need to set my affairs in order. I have so many debitors and so many tangled financial obligations, so much commerce to tend to."

"I don't give a tinker's dam about your sorry affairs."

Naida, fearing Ozzie was playing the footle, spoke up, "Periander, I will stay in Ozzie's stead while he deals with his affairs. Keep me until he returns."

Noting the pulchritudeness of Naida, Periander quickly gave his assentation.

As a departing Ozzie past under the arcature, Naida grabbed him by the nuque, and hissed in his ear, "You better return, you little gilse, or I'll have you excrementitiously stuffed."

"Hey, no prob," Ozzie replied. "It's a lead-pipe-cinch. I'll return as quickly as my dilligentness allows."

Not to be too colloquialist, but then…he went that-away!

For months Naida wore a shroud over her shorn head, all the while keeping an eye on her horologe. Though kept under watch and ward, Periander treated her well, teaching her the caseation of Gorgonzola. She dined well on succotash and salmagundi.

After a year had passed, and no Ozzie, Periander called Naida before him, "My patience is at an end," he said. "I'm not waiting a vigintillion days for Ozzie to return, so I'm afraid, my dear, the day of reckoning is at hand. You must die in his stead. But I'll tell you what, your irisation sets me astir, and I will spare your life if you agree to sleep with me."

Hiding her flusteration, she said, "I don't mean to rankle, but you're married, and just a little creepy as well."

Angered, Periander thundered, "Your passionlessness is your erring. So be it…off with your recidivist head!"

"Wait," a voice from the parlor cried, "I have returned!" Astonished, everyone gaped. They thought at first it was a whangdoodle emerging from the rickshaw, but in fact it was none other than Ozzie, lade with hyssop and cowherb.

"Though some would call me intestable," he said with jocundity, "I have settled all of my worldly affairs, from Ross and Cromarty to Mayfield, Ohio, right down to the last lira and dinar. So Periander, release Naida and allow her safe-conduct out of your rotten borough, and do with me as you will."

Periander rubbed his jaw, and seeing that the agglutinative relationship between the two friends was incomparable, he decreed them free to go.

As they went pitter-patter through the dalan, Naida grabbed Ozzie by the lith and gave him a shog, "Your cuncatorship very nearly cost me my life, if not my virginity."

Ozzie put a hand on her pectoral girdle, "You're a bewitcher, for sure, but you know I would never allow for that...at least not from that weasel. If anyone is going to denudate you..."

Naida gave Ozzie a playful dope-skelp, and they continued their perambulation.

As the sun set over the Cottian Alps, they returned to Naida's dwelling, and followed the declive into her bower, and exhausted, fell onto a bean-bag chair, and appressed together, the two friends fell into a stertorousness "Zzz."

"Great story, Pops."

"Really, you like it?"

"Little on the clumsy-side, but at least it was a story. Where'd you steal it from? Or dare I ask?"

"Haha, yr right, it's from the D's again, Damon and Pythias. Some Greek myth. I gussied it up a bit, natch. Pretty nifty, eh.

"I suppose. It's certainly better than your little 'Finnegan's Wake' riff of earlier."

"Thanks, hon. So there it is folks, the first short story ever written based on header words –or guidewords, if you prefer- from the Random House Unabridged Dictionary (1967 edition), I hope you enjoyed this special production, and we look forward to welcoming you back..."

"Mama, Papa's breaking the fourth wall!"

"Well, tell him he'd better fix the other three first..."

Ah, phooey.

The Horrible

In what corporate managers can only refer to as a regrettable mix-up, a Haven, New Connecticut Humble Bee's Restaurant and Grille, recently served baby formula to an adult male.

Regular customer, Fynn Fnüdl, ordered his customary glass of Riesling, and was served what he described as a milky, cloudy, but very high in protein drink.

His daughter, Sallie Sue, who was sitting across from him at the time, said her father began "talking silly", and "acting really foolish. Not like there's anything unusual about that," she added.

As a safety precaution Mr. Fnüdl was rushed to a nearby baby clinic and treated for what was diagnosed as a lactose loogie. He was released under his own cognizance only after nurses confirmed he 'did his doody'.

Fynn Fnüdl, a revered, respected and widely unread wine writer, commented later, "I was expecting my normal rush of 13.2 percent alcohol," he said through an interpreter, "but due to the dark circumstances of the bar area, where a jello-wrestling contest was under way, my mind was distracted."

His server, Katy Riley, said she was shocked. "How could a veteran wine writer not notice he's drinking baby formula? I'm gonna start reading his blog just to see how bad a writer he is."

Riley said after serving Fnüdl, she slipped into a tight-fitting t-shirt and got into the ring of jello for a match against the bartender, Jennifer Rigg, so she didn't specifically witness the debacle at table 65.

Fnüdl claims to have not noticed the drink switcheroo until he had nearly finished his glass. "Seeing Katy down there, splashing around in lime green jello…well, let's just say I wasn't exactly concentrating on what was in my glass. All I remember is she was throwing a forearm over her opponent, and I was screaming 'pin her, pin her!', when I suddenly felt this overwhelming urge to burp. Sallie Sue came over and rapped me twice on the back, and I let loose this enormous belch, and that helped. But still and all…"

General Manager and referee of the jello-wrestling-match, Erin Gobra, said he was sad and dismayed that a loyal customer had been served an inappropriate beverage. "He comes in here quite a lot, and for him not to get the alcohol content he's looking for is just plain wrong."

Gobra said he didn't notice anything amiss until after the match was over. "He was sitting with his daughter at the edge of the bar area, and there was a lot whooping and hollering, and then when Katy pinned Jenn, I heard this loud 'goo-goo gah-gah,' and looked over to see Fynn drooling. It was pretty scary."

Blame for the mix-up was placed on the similar packaging of the Riesling and baby formula, which sit right next to each other in the cooler. The Riesling, a Gallo-by-Golly Product, comes in a brightly colored pouch, as does the instant baby formula, which is produced by subsidiary, Baby-By-Golly. "The only difference," Gobra said, "is there's a picture of this baby on the Riesling pouch, and a big fat gnarly snake on the baby formula."

"Next time he comes in," Katy Riley commented, "I'm gonna pour him the baby formula again. I can't wait to see him hold his glass up to the light, swirl, sniff…'Mmm, love the bouquet!' Wine connoisseur? Ha!"

Fnüdl, who is home resting, and teething, said he is ready to forgive and forget. "After all, they gave me a $10 gift certificate, and a free jello-shot."

"Thank god it wasn't the other way around," he said, "and some toddler wasn't served a glass of Riesling."

The Deification of

Buster Posey

Brad von Easley was dozing off. It was his fourth night on the road, and he was mentally and physically fatigued. The Super 8 room smelled of stale coffee, Lysol, and cat urine. He was propped up in bed watching TV, a pre-season baseball game, Giants vs. the Mariners.

Even though he was drowsy, and frankly, had a couple glasses of Syrah in him, he couldn't believe what he was hearing. He thought maybe the Spartan nature of the room, combined with enticing aromas of any Super 8, was making him hallucinate.

The voices of the play-by-play and color announcers sounded familiar, but he couldn't quite place them. All he gleaned were their names; Ernie and Howard. But the words they spoke caught his soporific attention:

"Buster Posey steps up to the plate. As all of baseball, and most of the rest of the universe knows, Buster had a phenomenal rookie season, and if he can even come close to repeating that amazing season, the Giants stand a good chance of making it back to the World Series... Posey takes ball one.

"Many people don't know, Ernie, but when Buster was in Triple-A, he went to New York, and had lunch with Derek Jeter, Willie Mays and the late Mickey Mantle. He asked each of them, 'What it's gonna take for me to get to the majors?' Well, Derek Jeter, knowing he might meet Posey one day on the other side of the field, maybe even in the World Series, was the first to speak; 'First, you have to eat 18 raw rotten eggs every morning, then for lunch down 14 tequilas, and every night before bed, set fire to your hotel room curtains…'

"Willie Mays said, laughing, 'Buster, don't you believe a word of it, you just work hard. Hard work, determination, that's what it takes. You got the stuff behind the plate, you got the arm, but it's all gonna be about your bat…hitting for average, power, and knocking in runs, that's what it's gonna take, and that means hard work, and a good bat…'

"Well, just at the moment the late Mickey Mantle interrupted Mays and said, 'Buster…what a great name, Buster! You're gonna make it on account of your name alone. Buster Posey, now that's a major league name. As for the bat, son, come with me…'

"Buster takes ball two. Low and inside."

"So as the story goes, the late Mickey Mantle led Buster Posey to the Gates of baseball's Val-Hall of Fame. There the guardian, Branch Rickey, sat chewing on a cigar and wanted to know what Mantle was doing here with this kid who was so clearly still alive. 'Just want to show 'im the ropes,' the Mick said. 'see if he's got what it takes to make it to the bigs. And maybe get him a new bat.' Branch Rickey chomped hard on his cigar, and said, 'Ok, but make it quick.'

"Buster stepped onto a glowing green baseball diamond so huge in dimension the outfield disappeared over the horizon, but more amazing, he saw Ty Cobb playing catch with Lou Gehrig. The Babe was leaning on a bat, chatting with Stormin' Norman Cash. Satchel Paige was throwing batting practice to Hank Greenburg.

"He was also amazed to see an enormous tree right in the middle of centerfield.

"'See dat, kid,' Mantle said, 'that's the tree of Yaz, and it's where your next bat is coming from.'

"They strolled beneath the tree which rose a hundred feet into the sky, its branches short and stiff. 'Take your pick, Buster,' Mantle said.

"'Of what?'

"'Bats,' Mantle, laughed, 'one of them branches is your future bat.'

"Buster circled the trunk of the tree sizing up each branch. The Mick scoffed, 'You don't want low-hanging fruit, do you?'

"So Buster climbed up into the gnarly branches, first encountering a squawking cardinal on a lower branch, 'This one, take this one,' he squeaked, but Buster climbed higher, where he found an oriole perched, 'Here's a great one, you'll love this one,' the bird chirped. But Buster continued his ascension, as high as he could go, on ever skinnier, wavering limbs, until he selected what seemed to be the perfect branch. He put his hands around the base and it felt good. He plucked the branch and was surprised that it came off in his hand as easy as an apple.

"'Good choice,' shouted the Mick from far below.

"He scampered down, where the late Mickey Mantle said, 'Now just dip it in Batters Creek.'

"Buster hadn't noticed the creek running alongside the tree, but as he did, he saw it was quite shallow, barely enough to cover the bat.

"'Might want to go out a bit deeper,' the Mick said.

"Buster did…"

"Olivo is going out to the mound, and here comes Wedge out of the dugout. They're gonna talk over how they want to pitch to Buster."

"…so Buster waded out further into the creek until the water was up to his thighs, and dipped the branch into the water. And when he pulled it out again, it was a perfectly formed 34-ounce bat.

"'Let's see what you can do with that,' the Mick said.

"So Buster got in the batter's box, squared up, and Satchel Paige threw him a bender, and Buster spanked it over the walls of Val-Hall of Fame, out onto Shoeless Joe Avenue.

"The Babe, who'd been watching all of this with a snarky grin, came over to Buster, 'Yr gonna be a great one kid.' And with that Val-Hall of Fame disappeared and Buster and Mantle were back in the New York diner, sitting with Willie Mays and Derek Jeter, who was still going on, 'You gotta crawl over busted glass to every game…'

"Buster got up, paid the bill, and left. The next week, Benji Molina went down with an injury and Buster Posey was called up for his first stint with the Giants…"

"Buster takes a called strike on the outside corner. They're staying away from him, Howard."

"That seems to be the game plan, and who can blame them? Hey, Ernie have you seen this?"

"What is it? Looks like, I don't know, an egg cozy in Buster's number 28 uniform."

"Well, sort of, Ernie, it's the Buster Egg Posey. It's a giveaway on Easter. The first twenty thousand fans get a free Buster Egg Posey. How 'bout that?"

"Well, as my gramma used to say, I take mine soft, but I don't mind hard boiled…low and an outside. Ball three. It's three and one."

"To continue on with my thought, Ernie, Buster only stayed up in the bigs for a couple weeks in 2009, but before going back down to Triple-A, he was called into the Giants's front office. 'Buster,' he was told, 'we know yr gonna be a part of this organization for a long time, at least, until the Yankees sink their teeth into you and offer you an eight-billion-dollar contract, but prior to that, if you want to make it up here to stay, yr gonna have to sharpen the mental aspect of yr game.'

"'How do I do that?'

"'You must visit the Buddha.'

"So in the off season, Buster traveled to Japan, where he took some batting practice with the Hanshin Tigers, then set off on his journey to visit the Buddha. He found him resting beside a fig tree, dressed in brilliant blue and white. Buster started to tell the Buddha why he had come, but the Buddha raised his hand, 'My son, if you are to improve the mental aspect of your game, you must do three things. For you see, a high batting average is not a material thing. Yes, there is the bat, and there is the ball, but these are but states of mind. To have discipline at the plate, you must have discipline of mind, and discipline of spirit. To achieve this state, you must focus on three things.'

"'What are these three things, Buddha?'

"'Water, air, and beauty.'

"'Huh?'

"'My son, to what part of a healthy life to you attribute the use of water?'

"'Umm, I drink it a lot…I, umm, shower in it…'

"'Indeed, without water, there would not be life.' Buster immediately thought of Batters Creek. 'Water is awareness, consciousness, it allows you to see, to feel. Water also is humility. Your mind is an ocean, Buster, it fosters, contains and feeds life. You must therefore always dwell in the moment, just as water never leaves the ocean.'

"'And what of air, Buddha?'

"'Air and wind, so ephemeral, it cannot be held in your hand, and yet its power is undeniable. While the wind can lift trees, and raze mountains, it also soothes, and calms. Air gives you power over fear.'

"'And beauty?'

"'Need I say anything of beauty? If you must ask after beauty, then I cannot teach you anything.'

"Buster realized he must be humble before the Buddha. He asked what he could do to enhance and develop these qualities within himself.

"'First you must be self-less. You must submit to water, to air and to beauty. You will stay with me for three weeks, and in each of these three weeks we will focus on one of the three qualities, and at the end of this period, if you are worthy, we will put you to the Test of Nine Pitches. Are you up to this, Buster?'

"'I am, Buddha.'

"'Then let us begin.'

"And true to his word, Buster lived with the Buddha for three weeks, subsisting on nothing but figs, nuts and berries, lemon grass soda, and sunflower seeds. The Buddha rarely spoke, but would often point to plants, animals, earth, and Buster would name these things, and address their qualities. The Buddha would have Buster lift his nose in the breeze, and Buster would relate the smells and sensations. In the morning, Buster would tell the Buddha of his dreams, and the Buddha would explain how each dream represented some characteristic of Buster's.

"At the end of three weeks, the Buddha asked Buster, 'Do you recall your last at bat when you were in the majors?' Buster thought a moment, 'Yes, like yesterday.' 'What then was the last pitch thrown to you?' 'Umm, high and inside, but the ump called it a strike, and I was…' 'Forget that! Cast it from your mind. And when you return to the bigs, let us say that same pitch is thrown to you, what will you do?' 'Swing, if they're going to call it for a strike…' 'No, you said it was a ball. Do not swing. You cannot control the will of others, only your own mind. If it is ball, then let it be a ball. Now let us say, you have two strikes on you. The pitcher has thrown you a steady of diet of sliders on the outside of the plate. What do you do?'

"'I try to anticipate…'

"'No! Have you not learned anything? You must not anticipate. Dwell in the moment. If you swing and miss at a high and outside pitch, dismiss this from your mind. That is in the past, it has no relevance to the Now. To anticipate is to recall every pitch you have ever seen in your life, from T-ball to Right Now, and will only confuse your Being.

Anticipation is failure. You must stay in the Now. Concentrate on the Now. When the ball leaves the pitcher's hand, focus only on the ball, see every thread, every speck of dirt, every turn of the ball. You must erase the thousands of screaming fans in the stands, the cameras, the lights, the crying of "popcorn, gitchyr popcorn!" and eliminate the past, deny the future. You must, in short –see ball, hit ball.'

"'I will try…no, I will do as you say, Buddha.'

"'Good. Now, can you tell me how water and air will aid you? And in what manner beauty will give you power over material things?'

"'These things are in my mind, Buddha. With water, I will not anticipate, I will stay in the moment. Through air I will find the ball, and if it is good, I will hit it, if not, I'll let it go. As for beauty…it is knowable, but unspeakable.'

"'Are you sure?' The Buddha smiled, 'you seem hesitant.'

"'I am certain, Buddha.'

"'Good. You are ready. Perhaps.'

The Buddha then took Buster to a wide-open field of blazing green, with a mound and batters box. He summoned Randy Johnson, Sandy Kofax, and Bugs Bunny. Then he said to Buster, 'Each will throw three pitches to you, you must either hit each pitch, or take it for a ball. If you fail, then we must start our training all over again. Buster grabbed his mighty Yaz, and stepped up to the plate…"

"Buster fouls off that high, inside pitch. They're not gonna give him anything to hit, Howard."

"Can't blame them, Ernie. So to continue, Buster steps into the batters box, and Johnson lets fly a 95 mph fastball right behind Buster's right ear. Buster ends up flat on his back, eatin' dust. But he took the pitch for a ball.

"Then Randy threw a wicked a slider, 89 mph, but Buster picked it up. He saw the spin of the ball, and thought to himself 'Slow the game down, live in the Now.' And while the ball started in the middle of the plate, it ended up low and inside. Buster took it for a ball.

"Buster thought he knew what was coming next, the splitter… but then he stopped himself. The Buddha said, never anticipate. And sure enough, when the ball came out of Randy's hand he saw the rotation, and knew it to be a fastball, on the high end of the zone, and he swung mighty Yaz, and smacked the ball 542 feet from home plate.

"The Buddha nodded in approval.

"Then Sandy Kofax toed the rubber. His first pitch was a fast ball, with a lot of movement, and it ended up a quarter of an inch off the plate. Buster took it. The next pitch was a belt-high heater, and Buster drove it into left field. Then came Kofax's famous big sweeping curve. It started out in right field, and about mid-way to the plate it was over first base, and by time it got within three inches of the front of the plate it was right down the middle, but another inch and it was way inside. Buster took the pitch for a ball, much to the delight of the Buddha.

"Then Bugs Bunny took the mound…with, of course, his usual hijinks and shenanigans. His first pitch, he tossed up in the air, and blew it over home plate, and Buster spanked it into left field. Bugs's next pitch, he simply rolled through the dirt, but just as it was about to cross the plate, the ball leapt up, and Buster took it, high, for a ball. Then Bugs decided to throw his famous change-up. He wound up, his arm pin-wheeling, but when he released the ball it suddenly stopped, then whirled, curled, slowed nearly to a crawl, then started diving, jumping, and just as it was about to cross the plate it sped up like a bullet, but Buster –being Buster- with his incredible reflexes, got his bat on the ball and dropped it down for a perfect bunt.

"And with that, the Buddha smiled and disappeared. His work was done."

"Buster fouls that one off. Boy, he had a good pitch to hit, too. I bet he wishes he had that one back. A young man from Scottsdale, Arizona, caught that ball. I bet he'll treasure that one forever."

"Just to complete our thought, Ernie, last July when Benji Molina was traded to Texas, Buster was called up to the Giants. But his first week, he went hitless. Y'know how that can snowball, anxiety sets in, you start doubting yourself, and pretty soon you can't hit the ball to save your life. Then one day, Buster got benched. And that's when he realized what he had to do. He had to face the challenge of the Nine Innings of Composure."

"Do you remember all nine, Howard?"

"Well, the first three have to do with reigning in negative feelings. Inning One, you must pass through the Forest of Anxiety. Inning Two, one has to scale the Mountain of Fear. Inning Three, one must cross the Sea of Self-Doubt. Buster did these with little or no trouble at all. Then Innings Four through Six are about shoring-up positive thoughts. First, one must plough the Field of Confidence, then Sow the Field of Trust, and finally, Harvest the Fruit of Self-Awareness. These too, Buster completed without difficulty. But the last three Innings are the hardest, because you're put through a series of tests: Inning number Seven, one must defeat the Giant-Wolf of Ambition. Buster, with the help of Yaz, did this. Inning Eight, you must free yourself from the Ice of Desire. Again, with the help of Yaz, Buster accomplished this task. But it's the Ninth Inning that's the killer…"

"That's the Inning of Fire, isn't it, Howard?"

"It is. And it's real fire, Ernie, no movie-special-effects here. Buster entered the Dugout of Fire, holding aloft his mighty bat, Yaz, and the first thing he felt was Fire on his right elbow, 'Omigod, am I gonna have elbow problems?' he thought. But he put it out of his mind. Then his knee got engulfed in flames, 'O no, a blown-ACL.' But, he managed to put that out of his mind. Next was Fire to his wrist, then ankle, then lower back, hammie, and each time the doubts came, the anxiety started to set in; 'Am I gonna end my career with an injury, or worse yet some kind of incurable disease, like Crohn's, or Lou Gehrig's disease.' He was in the darkest part of the Dugout when he noticed ahead of him, a dammed-up creek, Batters Creek. And above his head, he saw dangling from a stalagmite, a blue and white stone shaped perfectly likely a baseball, and without thought, Buster got in his stance, and through all the pain flaming from shoulder to hip to ankle and foot, he swung mighty Yaz, and smacked the stone ball into the heart of the dam, busting it to smithereens, and the waters of Batters Creek came flooding out, dousing all the flames. Buster emerged from the Dugout…unscathed.

"The very next day he returned to the line-up, and Buster went 3 for 5, knocked in 3 runs…and the rest, as they say, is history. Buster was in the big leagues to stay."

"It's three and two. Vargas winds, kicks, delivers…ball four! Unbelievable. Buster did again. What an at bat! I tell ya Howard this kid is phenomenal, he's got it all."

"You said it, Ernie. Determination. Discipline. Composure…"

Brad von Easley got up and turned the TV off.

Ffimmicks

'Former farmer, Fynn Fnüdl, found funiculars fascinating…' that's about as far as I got with the first chapter of my novel -'Phhhh'- composed solely of words beginning with the letter 'f'. I'd considered starting the second chapter with; 'Fabled FBI fox, Felicity Foxhaven, fiddled feverishly for five farthings…' but I realized I was trapped. How you gonna develop a plot, let alone characters, without articles, pronouns, conjunctions, and very few prepositions (for!)? And dialogue? Impossible.

A quick flip through the 'fs' in the Dictionary, reveals some odd nouns, precious few verbs, and really not much in the way of fabulousness. I considered cheating, like; 'Fifteen finutes beFore finishing fer fingernails, Felicity Foxhaven fainted.' But that's just dumb.

Why even consider such a nutty proposition? Well, gimmicks sell. As a severely underpublished novelist, slash short story writer, I'm constantly trying to come up with gimmicks to attract attention, like my dancing dog dangling dangerously dabove downtown Dubuque.

Somewhere in the back of my puny brain I remember a novel written (and published!), in which the author never used the letter 'e'. You realize what that means? No 'he' 'she' 'the', and no 'e-mail.' Imagine. As I recall, this novel was originally written in French (no 'le' no 'asseyez-vous' no 'envoy') and translated into English. Two books, two different languages (each language with an evident 'e'!), and neither containing an 'e'. It was written by e e cummings…haha, no, it wasn't. At least, not to my recollection.

Maybe I should try something a little more subtle, like an entire novel without the letter 'z'. But wait, then I wouldn't be able to use my favorite character, Ozzie. Ozzie's been with me since the beginning, when I wrote and published two short stories for my high school literary journal, 'Drizzle' (I was an editor, so I couldn't legally send myself a rejection slip).

Ozzie appeared in a story I wrote for my college rag, 'Stagnant,' and was also the star of my (self-published) novel, 'Slim Chance on a Fat Dime'. Readers went zzzzz.

Ozzie also made cameo appearances in many of my mainstream works. But every time I try to go 'commercial', I flop like a flounder. As with my erotic historical romance novel, 'Come in the Wind.' That's when my agent quit returning e-mails. I thought I'd hit it big with an updated translation of the New Testament; 'Bad News for Modern Man.' (Hint; surprise ending!) That drove my agent into retirement. Although my unauthorized sequel, 'Harry Potter and the Fiery Car-Wreck,' drew some attention, mostly from lawyers. My agent went in to the witless protection program after that.

Of course, nothing flops farther faster than when I stick with my usual 'experimental' fiction. Word plays based on algorithms, characters patterned after subterranean geological formations, and plots following global weather patterns, etc. It's no wonder I'm underpublished.

I suppose I could try a novel without using the letter 'q' -but no, wait, I still wouldn't be able to use Ozzie. For you see, Ozzie's real name is Osmondi Hasan Hussain, and in the Bush I Iraq War, he was a translator for US troops. He came under suspicion as a double-agent, however, and after the war was over, and realizing his life was in jeopardy, Osmondi sought asylum in England (where he was educated), and there led a double-life for almost a decade, teaching abstract Arabian art at his alma mater, Oxford, and shuttling back and forth between Great Britain and Pakistan. Then came the Bush II Iraq War, and he once again resurfaced as a translator for NATO troops. When an entire Italian squad, except for their translator, was wiped out by an IED, Ozzie once again came under suspicion, but before any investigation could be conducted, he was secretively whisked away to America, where he took up residency in Haven, New Connecticut, curating Persian rugs for a local textile company (Ozzie's family made its fortune in the transportation business, running mostly guns, oil and rugs). He took the name Oswalt H. Houseman, and for all appearances, was a good US citizen.

But local FBI agent, Felicity Foxhaven, was not so sure. She'd been tracking his shadowy past, and keeping tabs on his various travels to Afghanistan and Pakistan where he maintained questionable, if not, outright illegal ties to Taliban sympathizers. Trying to knot together his many aliases, along with his numerous passports from as many countries, Felicity Foxhaven thought she had enough evidence to prove Ozzie was in fact a 'Gentleman Jihadist,' that is, one who sympathizes with and finances potential terrorists, without ever sullying his own hands.

But, you see, to tell this whole story, I need a 'q', because Ozzie was born in Qatar.

So maybe I'll take another shot at 'Phhhh'; 'Four fancy Flemish females, fling fish far, far from Flanders…'

The Artist Addresses His Muse

Goll-dang, man. I have this groovy idea for a hot, new, riveting short story, full of action, suspense, murder, mayhem, quinoa recipes, and the answer to last week's crossword puzzle, but it is just not coming together…here I am, and I got nothing. Nothing. Come on, Muse, I have a deadline, like yesterday, and…Nothing.

And you know how editors are about deadlines, 'I don't want it good, I want it now!'

So, come on Muse, infuse me with some creative hair-pin turns, some fiery pits, and lethargic frogs. I need inspiration!

…nothing at all.

This is ridunculous.

O Muse, why do you frustrate me so? Do not deny me. Give me sustenance, or at least a phrase, something to get the juices flowing. A word play, an ironic observation, a sardonic comment, a corrosive jab, a soothing lament, a jarring metaphor, an untimely remark, a nasty thought, a contradictory image, an expressive rhyme, an alliterative aphorism, a crunchy colloquialism, a stunningly inappropriate remark, a memory of collapse and defeat. Something! A beginning, a portal into the creative tornado, a middle, fat, a concussive conclusion that cancels out everything preceding it, wiping out all trace of history, rejecting everything that shall or could be. Or maybe just a jingle for a Pepsi commercial. Something! O Muse, why must Thou frustrate me?

I mean, in the olde days, no sooner had the cursor started blinking than I was off and running, I could barely keep my feet beneath me. Witticisms, and gems aplenty flew off my heels like sparks. I Could bedazzle in an instant, seduce with a sigh, or expound for hours at length. Today I sit staring at a glowing blank sheet of screen, not a word oozing out. Come on Muse, it's not like I'm on deadline or anything.

Satisfy me, O Muse, you've always been there for me, and in this, and I will commend you to all nature and humanity, I will burn offerings of post-it notes, bar napkins, ratty old notebooks, at your marble altar. Please, condescend to inspire me with your mercy, and inspiration.

And if your ethereal magnificence isn't enough to inspire me, then perhaps, O Muse, you could at least do me the favor of helping me borow generously, that is, rip-off some other author -we won't call it plagiarism, just re-gifting. Maybe something from Shakespeare, Homer, Joyce, nobody reads them anyway. But -for Zeussake- do not get me involved in any sci-fi crap. I do have my scruples. Or maybe You could dig up a tale by Cervantes, or Borges (with whom, BTW, I share a birthday), we could change a word or two here and there to sort of disguise the 're-gifting'. But if we're going that route, I'd prefer ripping-off, err, borrowing, from someone with gravitas, Gaddis, Rabelais, Kafka, Camelieu…Haha, did I ever tell you the story, O Muse, you'll get a kick out of this, in my previous life as a bookseller, a customer, this gorgeous little blonde, with almond eyes, and ruby red lips, approached me, the fearsome, ruggedly handsome, and somewhat scruffy bookseller, and dropped this bon-bon from her luscious, sweet lips, "Do you have 'The Stranger' by Camelieu?"

Camelieu? No, I did not, O Muse, burst out laughing, as I am wont to do, for that would've been rude, and besides, would have shot to pieces any chance of me getting a date with this tasty little morsel, doubtful as that was. So, I fetched a trade paperback copy of Camus's 'The Stranger', and put it in her dainty, cream-soft fingers, and she looked at it with her dewy eyes, and said, "No, the author is Camelieu." Well, at that point I knew there was no point fooling myself, asking her out on a date, to what? Chuckie Cheeses? No, out of the question. What would we talk about? Dostoyevsky? Pynchon? Camelieu? No, it was pretty clear we were not cut from the same cloth, and so I gently persuaded her that there is only one 'The Stranger' and its only author *is* Camus, and when she had received her assignment (I assumed), she either mis-heard, misunderstood, or was misled. And so, O Muse, another opportunity out the window because I'm such a literary snob, elitist. I admit it!

So, where was I? O yes, supplication, a story, something to set my writerly chops chomping. Come on, O Muse, lay one on me.

Though I'm here to tell You, if You're not willing to help me in this matter, O Muse, I'm afraid I must question Your authenticity, Your intent, if not Your authority, because it seems to me Your job-description is fairly specific -inspire lowly writers, hacks, cranking out a story whenever the Editor snaps his/her fingers. I mean you've got no problem with the Louis Th'Amours and Danielle Steales of the world, but comes to me, the second most underpublished writer in the world, I can't even get a little love. What's up with that? Who do I got to sleep with to get a story out of this? Not like I'm asking for the world, just a little creative inspiration, Ole Muse.

Look, I don't want to have to go over Your head (can you say Zeus?), but I fear I'm gonna have to talk to a supervisor. Is there a manager on duty I can talk to? I know people in Olympian Places, O Muse, people with influence and authority who can put You out on the streets of terra firma indefinitely...A Muse today, amuse yourself tomorrow.

OK. Okay, you're wise to me, O Muse, you know I got no pull among the gods, I just thought maybe if I goaded You, You might in turn goose me, push me to creative heights never before achieved by a lowly subordinate writer like myself...I just thought maybe together, we could give birth to a Great American Novel, or at least crank out a so-so Short Story. But, looks like it ain't gonna happen.

O Muse, You once inspired me to greatness, remember what we could do together? Remember O Muse, the hi-hilarity, the depths of darkness, the uncanny wisdom, and otherworldly introspection? With You on my shoulder, I could conquer the world of Literature. Remember?

Maybe I'm trying too hard, performance anxiety. Maybe I'm asking too much of You. Then again, maybe You're a little too wrapped up in Yourself, maybe You got some hoity-toity God of literature You're trying to impress with Your patented advanced course on motivational writing. I think You're just a prose tease, maybe You don't like the cut of my jib, the gait of my walk. So, looks like Splitsville for us, O Muse, we're through, I'll just go slumming elsewhere for inspiration. Don't be surprised if You see me in a brothel, or more likely a bar, scribbling on a napkin, unable to afford a pint of artisanal creative juice.

Nope. Still, Nothing.

Alright Muse, I give up. If I can't even get one measly piece out of You, forget it, we're through, it's all over, adios. Too bad, all this hassle for what? A thousand words or so? That's all I'm asking, 1,000 words...we used to do that in the blink of an eye. You'd think....wait, wait a doggone minute...Hey, thanks, Muse!

Sparky Misses Out

"You got strawberries?"

Fynn Fnüdl was strolling through the rain-bespattered Littlefield Farmers Market, counting canopies, when he was accosted by Sparky. He was standing and grousing with Mimi at her Begged 'n' Borrowed booth. Sparky was somewhere north of 70, a small, white-haired ornery fellow, missing two front lower teeth, which along with a conspicuously jutting jaw, gave him a look somewhere between a wild boar and, well, a wild boor.

"I don't know," Fynn replied, "my wife thought she might bring some down today…but with this rain."

"I need about four/five pounds," Sparky said defiantly.

"Umm, I could call her and see if she's picking any…"

"Need 'em for tonight," Sparky continued, undeterred by the directional flow of conversation.

"I thought Don was gonna bring some down today," Mimi said. She and Sparky were of the same demographic, and had been friends since childhood. But while Mimi was stubbornly pleasant, Sparky was unpleasantly stubborn.

"I talked to him couple days ago," Fynn said, "he sounded pretty iffy."

"He came over yesterday and said he'd get Jessie to bring some," Mimi continued.

"Well…" is about all Fynn could offer. "I'll call my wife…" Through the steady hard drizzle he walked to his own booth, Fnüdl's Funny Farms Herbs 'n' More, grabbed his phone and called Ona Maria, knowing full well she'd never answer. She hates talking on the phone. Whenever she does answer, in a rare moment of magnanimity, it sounds like she's holed up in a cave, whispering intimations of despair.

He walked back to Mimi's tent. "Couldn't get a hold of her," he said drearily.

"You think she's gonna bring some down?" Sparky said.

"I don't know, she wanted to. But, this rain…"

"Wish I had Don's number," Mimi said sourly, staring at her cell, "I'd tell him to get his butt out there and pick some strawberries and get 'em down here."

"I need 'em for tonight," Sparky said.

"Well, my wife's picking up my daughter in an hour or so, if she has any, she'll bring them down…"

"I need four or five pounds."

"Papa." It was the aforementioned daughter, Sallie Sue, calling him. He ducked his head against the smacks of rain and returned to his own booth. "She wants to know if you can take seeds from heirloom tomatoes to grow new plants," Sallie Sue said, exasperated, and pointing at a lady standing in front of his canopy, flipping her umbrella open and close. Fynn wasn't sure, though he thought he remembered reading somewhere that heirloom seeds won't propagate.

"I thought that was just hybrids," the lady said. She was a regular customer at the farmers market, and a strange one at that. He often saw her standing in the middle of the market, mouth agape, eyes popped in astonishment, and her short graying hair, even on a windless day, fluttering with Medusal menace. Today she seemed particularly rankled to be out in the rain, only to be argued with.

Fynn Fnüdl splashed over, flipped through his seed catalogue, assured he wasn't going to find anything to confirm one way or the other his suspicions about heirloom seeds. "Nope. I don't know…"

Suddenly a voice barked behind him, "Your wife bringin' them strawberries down?" It was Sparky.

"I don't know.…"

"I thought it was only hybrids you can't start from seeds…"

"Could be, I don't have Internet access on my phone, or I'd Yahoogle it…"

"What time does the market close?" said Sparky, paddling furiously against the current conversation.

"Two.…"

84

"I'll be back at a quarter to," he snapped, "if you think your wife is bringing strawberries…"

"I hope so…"

"I need four/five pounds for tonight…."

"Would anyone else here know if you can start plants from heirloom seeds…"

"I'll be back…" Sparky wandered off between the two rows of canopies, and escaped view around the Littlefield Parks and Recreation Building.

Fynn waited till he was out of sight. "You might want to ask Chandra, she starts a lot of stuff from seed…" He pointed across to the Little Haven's Flower canopy. The lady tentatively backed away.

Fynn Fnüdl's phone buzzed, and did a little dance on the table. He opened it to see a message from Katy Riley. She was at her daughter's soccer game, and was miserable. 'dont know y they dont jus cancel stpd game,' she wrote.

He texted back, 'Soccers never canceled. During Katrina kids were still playing soccer.'

Came right back: 'lol. this suks and were getting r butts kicked.'

As he tried to think up a witty reply, he heard a cry, "Mr. Fynn."

"Yo, Mr. J, what's up?" Jared Sandoval, he of the Little R and R Farms, was standing shivering in the rain.

"I'm soaking wet, starving, gotta pee, and in desperate need of a drink. And I don't care who knows it. Wanna go get a burger at the Hunt 'n' Trap?"

"Ummm, yeah, I could use a glass of wine…Sallie Sue, can you watch the booth?"

"I don't know, pops, all these customers…" Fynn Fnüdl walked away safe in the knowledge that his daughter had at least inherited his mundane sense of humor.

The Hunt 'n' Trap Sports Bar was a wet, windy two blocks away. Fynn and Jared pushed in, and the first thing they saw was Fynn's neighbor Don standing at the bar, guffawing mightily, holding aloft a large mug of beer. While Jared went to take a pee, Fynn approached Don, "Hey, I thought you were going to bring some strawberries down to the market today."

"Can't get anybody to pick," Don said, taking a swig off his beer.

The phrase, 'And you can't pick?' popped into Fynn's head, but he managed to keep it bottled inside. "Got you a sale of four or five pounds, if you brought them down."

"If I could get someone to pick…"

Fynn took a table by the window, just so he could keep an eye on the steady rain.

"What a shitty day," Jared said, stripping from his sweat shirt, and sitting down.

Fynn ordered a glass of Riesling, Jared got the Grizzly Beer and He-Man Burger. They sat quietly staring out the window until the drinks came. Jared grabbed his large mug of beer, "This oughta take the chill off," he said, taking a huge gulp.

From his spot at the table, Fynn could see Don shooting pool in the back room with friends. One enormously gutted fellow was wearing a tee-shirt, swelling to accommodate the words in large font; 'Bullets. Booze. Broads.'

"Nice sentiment," Fynn muttered, but Jared was ripping into his burger and didn't hear.

"So other than soaking your sorry ass out in the rain while not making a dime, what's new with you?"

Jared waited till he had swallowed most of what was in his mouth, "Well…I got fired."

"What?!"

"Or quit, depending on how you look at it."

Jared went on to relate a story of how his boss, a Mussolini impersonator, had been sending him monthly to Indonesia to train staffers to open a new office. After a year of training, the office was set to open, and so the boss takes Jared out to lunch, 'You did a great job training our Indonesia team, now, guess what?'

"'What?'

"'We're closing your department and sending all the work to Indonesia. How's that for a kick in the balls?' I thought, I have two choices, I can punch his lights out, or stalk off. Not wanting go to jail over that asshole, I left. And I haven't been back since. So I don't know…basically I'm job hunting right now."

"Not the best of times to be pounding the streets."

"I got some promising leads. Best one, start my own business. I spent the last 14 years in this business and I've got so many contacts, clients, suppliers, some just begging me to go out on my own. I got a client list five pages long. But, I spend all night tossing and turning, just thinking of all the problems owning your own business. But really…it's the best way to go, I just need to pull the trigger."

Fynn was never quite certain what Jared's 'business' was and was always afraid to ask, as Jared might reasonably assume he hadn't been paying attention all these years. He thought it had something to do with engineering, pipes, or micro-chips.

They further discussed the pluses and minuses of starting your own business, until beer, wine and burger were gone. So was Don. Maybe he'd gone to pick strawberries, but Fynn seriously doubted it.

On the joyless walk back, far from abating, the rain had actually picked up some gusto. "Hey, honey, sell anything?"

Sallie Sue didn't even look up from her texting, just shook her head.

"O well, insult to injury." Fynn Fnüdl took his place in the center of his Sur-Shade Canopy where, like a cow, he was beginning to wear a brown spot in the grass from standing in one place so long. He listened to the rain pelt the canopy.

As a diversion, he re-arranged his display of plant starts, tomatoes, peppers, and dried herbs, oregano, basil, chives, lovage, lemon balm, and the 6 bags of fresh arugula.

Suddenly Sallie Sue jumped up, and waved, "Mother!" Fynn saw the small dark figure that was his wife approach, bearing a large box of strawberries.

She set them on the table. They were packaged in quart containers. "Wow, those look great," he said.

She was wearing a dark hoodie, and against the rain had all but disappeared into the recesses of the hood. Or herself. "Thanks for bringing them down, I've already got most of these sold."

"What're you going to sell them for?" she asked plaintively.

Fynn weighed one of them, came to just over 2 pounds. "Whaddaya think, five bucks?"

Just then Mimi came up, "Ah, strawberries…those look great."

His wife took a step back, burrowing deeper back into her hood. She wasn't terribly fond of talking to people.

But Mimi was. "You just pick these?" Getting into her personal space. "Wow, look at those, you know what variety they are?"

Ona Maria shook her head, "I planted four varieties."

The strawberry patch was the only portion of the gardens that Ona Maria showed any interest in. And it wasn't just interest, it was if she had a genetic connection with the fruit. Savoring a strawberry for her wasn't merely chewing and swallowing, it was a form of worship. Submission. So Fynn allowed her to take over the strawberries. And they responded to her as most of her followers do, with a cultish devotion and trust.

Mimi helped herself to one. "O," she swooned, "so good. How much you selling them for?"

"Whaddaya think, five bucks?"

Mimi scowled, "What's that, a quart? At least five bucks, but I'd go six if I were you. You can't buy strawberries like this in a store."

"We'll go five, give 'em a deal this week."

"You gonna set some aside for Sparky?"

"Yeah, I better." Fynn pulled two with the berries piled high and put them at the back of his table. That left him with six to sell.

"Think that'll be enough?" his wife asked.

"Yeah, we'll have more next week, won't we?"

"Tons."

"Okay, yeah."

"Set one aside for me," Mimi said. Okay, only five to sell. Mimi strolled off just as the wild lady with the fixation on heirloom seeds returned, and immediately her eyes locked onto the strawberries, "O my, look at those." She reached down to pick up and examine one of the quarts. "How much?"

"Five dollars," Fynn said cheerfully. "First of the season."

"Five dollars?!" she looked like she just swallowed a rat. "O, forget it." But she stood there looking at the berries.

"You think that's too much?" Fynn said.

"Five dollars?" she asked incredulously.

His wife, needing to escape this unpleasant scene, said to Sallie Sue, "Ready for Zumba?"

Sallie Sue picked up her purse, "Think you can handle it, pops?"

"I don't know, the crowds might come swarming down any minute."

"Let's go," his wife said, and to Fynn, "okay, we're off."

And with that the two of them strode away, leaving Fynn and the lady staring at the strawberries.

"Five dollars," she muttered. "I think I'll call my daughter, maybe she wants some."

Fynn decided he wasn't about to dicker.

"Five dollars?" she repeated.

"I think it's a fair price."

"Hmmm." She finally set the strawberries down. "I'll call my daughter," and with that she hesitantly walked off, as if Fynn might suddenly cave.

Within minutes, first Amanda from the booth beside his bought a quart, then a couple wrapped in plastic macs, out for a jog, stopped and bought a quart. Then a lady whose daughter was on Sallie Sue's soccer team, bought one. And finally, Chandra came over to see what all the hubbub was about and bought the last one.

No one complained about the price.

He hoped the lady with the seeds returned for strawberries, "Sorry, sold out." Not gloating, just, well...gloating.

He recognized immediately the extremely attractive young lady standing in front of him. He hadn't seen her since last fall, when she came to his table, commended him on his witty and informative newsletters. The manner in which she had talked to him, lo, these many months ago, as if they were old friends, or old lovers, seemed a bit incongruous to him at the time. He kept staring at her, in part because she was very pretty, but also because he kept thinking, 'Do I know you?' He figgered, no way. He wouldn't forget a lovely face like that. She had dark hair, fair luminescent skin, cocoa brown eyes, almost perfect teeth, and extremely delicious looking lips. Slender but not frail. And she was so earnest. A naive earnestness. They chatted for a good long time, she asking intriguing and leading questions, and he replying vaguely if not misleadingly. She offered nothing about herself. It seemed like a game of tag. Or keep-away. When she asked in a rather off-handed way if there were a good place to get coffee nearby, he directed her to the Old Mission Theater a block away. He considered offering to join her, as that seemed to be her intent, but in the end decided against it. She bought some cabbage and left. He hadn't seen her since then, some 7 months ago, but he thought about her, and their strange encounter, just often enough to remember her name.

"Well, hello, Felicity."

She looked surprised, stunned even. "You remember my name…"

"No, I call everyone Felicity. Gotta be right eventually," he smiled.

She smirked, "O, right." In on the joke. "Just wanted to say thanks for keeping me on your newsletter, I really enjoy getting them."

"Thanks," she was every bit as pretty as he remembered, even though she was bundled up against the chill and rain, and wore a cap over her dark hair. But it all conspired to make her face even prettier. "Care to sample some arugula pesto?" he said.

"Arugula pesto? I didn't know you could make pesto out of arugula."

"You can make a pesto out of anything…well, maybe not anything. Oatmeal."

She laughed, "Okay, I'll try it." He spooned some on a cracker for her.

"Arugula's a bit on the spicy, some might even say, bitter side…"

He watched the pesto disappear behind her lovely lips, her eyes lit up, "O, that's interesting." Puzzled look, "So how would you serve that?"

"I like it on an English Muffin, with a little goat cheese. Or on bruschetta, with a slice of chicken or duck. Nice spread for a tomato sandwich."

"Hmm." Felicity thought about it. "How much?"

"I'm selling them for three bucks," he held up the little tub of pesto.

Felicity chuckled, "Three dollars? You should sell it for more than that."

"Well, just trying to hook you."

"Okay, I'm hooked. I'll take one. You should really charge more."

She put the pesto in her bag, and looked around the market, "No food booths here?"

90

"No, sad thing, I can't get food here. We're just not big enough."

She spied the strawberries he'd set aside for Sparky. "O, those look great, are they...?" but she could tell by the grimace on his face they were not for sale.

"Sorry, I set 'em aside for a guy...but if he's not back by 2, I'll sell them. If you're around then...I'll save one for you."

Felicity shook her pretty head. "Can't. Busy."

"Pity. I'd hate for you to miss out."

They stood smiling at each.

Suddenly Felicity looked down, and cried out, "O stevia, I've heard of this."

"Yeah, sweet as sugar, but zero calories. Excellent substitute."

She bent down to read the strip excerpted from the seed catalogue he'd taped to the table. As he explained how difficult it was to grow, he thought maybe he had a sale, but she put it back down. Then looked him square in the eye. "Is there a good place for lunch around here?"

"The Hunt 'n' Trap Sports Bar, just a couple blocks away, umm, is okay for burgers and fries. Kinda seedy. A little farther down, on Frontier St. is the Sam and Ella Café, they have good food. Sandwiches, salads, pasta, pretty good stuff. And good wines by the glass."

"Really? Sounds good." Felicity, paused, glanced at her watch. It was 12:30. She started to walk away, then turned, "Care to join me... for lunch...glass of wine?"

Fynn Fnüdl looked around. Dang. "Yes, I'd love to, but, alas, I got no back-up," he said. "My daughter's off to Zumba, and..." Lame excuse. But...

"Pity," she said, coquettishly, "I hate to see you miss out."

Fynn pursed his lips, "Story of my life."

And with a smile, and a quick turn, Felicity walked out of his life.

The last hour and a half of the market dragged by like a long bad movie shot with popsicle sticks and rubber-duckies, no sound, washed out colors, and a vague clicking of reels turning.

To while away the Chinese water-torture moments, Fynn tried to snap a clear picture of the rain cascading off his canopy. But he couldn't capture the essence on a cell phone, at least from what he could see. It's hard to take a picture of misery.

At twenty minutes before two o'clock, Mimi came down to look at the strawberries. "Sparky never came back, did he?"

"Nope, and if he ain't here in 6 minutes, I'm selling them."

"You know, he just lives over there," she pointed through a brace of trees at the edge of the park, "that brick house on the corner, the one with the big garden."

"Big garden? So why isn't he growing strawberries?"

Mimi shrugged, "Good question."

"I had to hide yours and Sparky's, people kept wanting to buy them."

"Better not sell mine," she laughed, and returned to her post.

Fynn kept glancing through the droplets dribbling from his canopy, hoping to see Felicity come waltzing back into his life. Changing her mind, or itinerary, for his strawberries. Short of that, at least to see Sparky coming to claim his four/five pounds of strawberries. For tonight.

But neither did.

At ten minutes to 2 he sold the last of the strawberries to Coach Bob, who just happened to be driving by, saw the twelve colorful, sagging, soggy canopies impaled against a gloomy sky, and out of pity, decided to stop. He asked after Sallie Sue whom he had coached from grades 3 to 6 in basketball.

At 2 o'clock, Fynn rang the closing bell, and started packing up the herbs 'n' more from his table.

Mimi came over, "Sparky never did show up."

"I know."

Mimi handed him six one-dollar bills, "No, it's only five," Fynn said.

"What? Could easily sell them for six." She grabbed her quart of strawberries, and taking a bite of one, said, "I'm gonna tell Sparky I bought his strawberries, and then I'm gonna tell him just how good they are."

They both laughed.

Ona Maria

Ona Maria was born of a broken home. Her father was shattered glass, and her mother a busted twig.

When she reached her majority, Ona Maria slipped through the cracks and floated into the world. She looked back only once to see her house crumble into the slumber of silt. She changed her name and drifted to foreign shores, and after many landings and departures, finally settled in America. If settle is the right word.

For Ona Maria was constantly in flux. She began as a faerie, spun into an earthworm, jumped the banks to become a river, and emerged as a meandering spirit. She realized early on that her true nature was mutative. Either formless and timeless, or solid and determined. She existed twice as herself, one as a variation on the other, both refusing to engage in one another.

By age 21, Ona Maria was Queen of the Faeries, a sorceress, a goddess, and a marooned, submerged soul. That's when she met Fynn Fnüdl. He was of similar heritage, third generation removed. Linked by heritage, but little else, certainly not inclination, looks or lifestyle —for, while she was many, he was one. While she was formless, he was burdensome as a rock.

She was teaching a Nordic Yoga class for underperforming entrepreneurs. Fynn's girlfriend at the time, Naida, was a manager at the local Burger Hop, and was forced to take the class if she wanted to advance any further in the meat-grinding fast food corporate world. To sooth her jangled nerves, and to further ensnare Fynn, she insisted he join her. It was one of those 'If you really loved me' moments, and he manned-up, bowed his head, and sheepishly followed.

And without falling out of love with Naida, Fynn fell in love with Ona Maria.

How could he not find her fascinating? She was small, dark, exotic in dress, manner, and perhaps in looks, though he couldn't be sure of the latter, as she allowed neither windows nor mirrors to contain her visage. She was constantly in motion, always managing somehow to hide behind or within herself. Fynn attended four classes before he thought he might be able to pick her out in a police line-up.

Intrigued, he sought to introduce himself to this whirligig of possibilities, approached her from behind, but, alerted by a faerie, she suddenly turned around, and like an explosion became fully visible, her piercing eyes, the left one cocked, her pursed lips, her thick neck. She thrust out a hand, and snapped, "Ona Maria."

In reply he muttered his own name, and started to offer something in way of an apology, but she as quickly spun away in a cloak of divisibility.

Whether maintaining his love for Naida was a noble or stupid thing mattered little, for one day Naida discovered Ona Maria teaching Fynn a new improvised Yoga position that involved body parts engaged in ways that defied space and gravity. She screamed, ran at Fynn with a plastic fork, only to miss and eject herself out the second-story window, landing precipitously on the soft cushion of an awning below. She shimmied down the escalloped pole with the help of a kindly, handsome, vaguely Arab-looking fellow, to the sidewalk, and the two set off hand in hand, as if old lovers. Which they would soon become.

Thus did Ona Maria and Fynn Fnüdl become the 'curious couple' exemplar.

Despite their immeasurable differences –he loved conversation, she did not. He laughed a lot. She, not at all. He was disorganized. She had no material possessions to organize. He loved to travel, but she despised everything that took her away from herself.

Whatever kept them together? It may have been the sex, as Ona Maria was part contortionist, part mystic. Her small, but heavily contoured body gave her both flexibility and strength. Making love to her, Fynn often felt himself trapped underwater, entangled in seaweed, twisting, gasping for breath, hanging on for dear life, while Ona Maria skimmed across his vision like the shadow of a night owl. So badly did he ache afterwards, he always came crawling back for more.

*   *   *

Ona Maria moved with equal agility and strength laterally through the real (or, perceived) world. She taught, at various times, everything from Yoga to Tai Chi, Pilates, massage, aura management, meditation, aroma therapy, hypnosis, palm reading, Tantric Bowling, Zumba, Actuarial Sex, martial arts, mid-wifery, juggling, trapeze, kick-boxing, and cage fighting, while also performing bar mitzvahs, weddings, séances, and cattle auctions. So vast and various were her skills, that she accumulated over the years a devoted, if manically eclectic, following, including everyone from cowboy to existentialist, from truck driver to New Age musician. In fact, the numbers and persistence of her followers was almost cult-like. If asked to drink Kool-Aid, they would.

She did not need business sense, as her intuition always put her ahead of any business model one could anticipate. She knew what people wanted, even before they did. From the proceeds of a particularly successful seminar on Time-Travel Sharing, she opened the first Karma's Tai Chi Chai Tea Café. A theme exercise/tea room, she would first lead a program of Tai Chi, Yoga, Pilates, or Zumba on the back lawn beneath the sprawling maple tree, then gather everyone inside on bean-bag chairs for spiced tea (all of the spices, including the sweetener, stevia, homegrown, of course), served with arugula pesto soup and rice crackers.

When she tired of that venture (as she did with most things that subjected her to a place and time), she sold it to a franchise -ironically the same one that operated the chain of Burger Hops- for tens of thousands of dollars.

*   *   *

If sex held the curious couple together while circling in different orbits through the galaxy, it was the birth of Sallie Sue that bound them together on earth.

As a writer, Fynn Fnüdl, worked mostly from home, and so became the 21st Century template for Mr. Mom.

He had earned his stripes in the environmental world, writing first as journalist, reporting on the growing Global Warming movement, and then as essayist/critic. He constantly received new 'green' products for his approval, mostly because he took an activist approach –you'd see him testing a Bulgarian vegan-fueled scooter (didn't work), a solar powered cell-phone (unlimited daytime only minutes), a power-generating windmill with attachable water mill (did everything from grind grains to powering his irrigation system), and the ill-fated Indoor Carpet Garden (attracted too may bugs).

His notoriety hit the fan, when he wrote a cover story for 'Sustain This' magazine (with a smiling Fynn himself demonstrating), championing the first 'Green Toilet', which he designed, and was basically an inside outhouse. No flushing, no pipes, no odors, the iToit was a totally re-imagined toilet. Its swivel, height-adjustable seat was ergonomically designed, and through a vaporized opening, waste shot down through a slurry of diatomaceous earth, seaweed, beneficial nematodes, and naturally occurring sulfur, and was immediately converted into composting material, and rolled into an outside bin where it could be blended with other vegetable and compostable leftovers. This blend became a fertilizer so potent, that Fynn Fnüdl's garden was a wonder of the Quad-County area. Every fall, he led popular skateboard and bicycle tours through his extensive gardens.

And so with the birth of Sallie Sue, Fynn was happy to continue plying and prodding the Earth while Ona Maria returned to pin-wheeling through the cosmos. While she was off to a weekend Levitation Convention, Fynn and Sallie Sue would rent a yurt on Rattlesnake Lake. While Ona Maria led a showdown between competing Pilates and Zumba forces, father and daughter would be at the movies, watching the latest Disney/Nickelodeon concoction. While Ona Maria was walking a high wire between 100-year-old Spruce trees to call attention to the scourge of childhood obesity, Fynn and Sallie Sue were off to a softball tournament.

If she were jealous of the relationship between her daughter and common-law husband, Ona Maria never showed it. She knew Sallie Sue loved her, and regretted it. Because she also knew eventually, somehow, she would disappoint, if not completely dishearten and alienate her daughter. In fact, it was part of the plan.

As the years passed, and father and daughter grew closer and more *sympathique*, Ona Maria sidelined herself, loved, but not loving, sanctioned, but invisible. She also made certain there would be no second child.

*   *   *

As Ona Maria's empire grew, and Fynn Fnüdl's renown increased, they became the most visible, eccentric, and to some, the most annoying couple of their small community. Fynn attended most of Littlefield's city council hearings, and whenever he stood, council members cringed, and secretly muttered, 'Dear god, will you please shut up.' He hastened curbside composting, he harangued until a communal garden was available on every block, he started a Farmers Market, he turned the school lunch program into the healthiest program in the county. He badgered and browbeat until no house or building was built in their community unless appropriate user fees paid for sidewalks, parks, and schools. Littlefield, a small suburb of Haven became a rolling greenery of bio-swales, riprap, playgrounds, bike and hiking trails, dog and skate parks –all due, in no small part- to Fynn's influence.

His reputation and influence weren't confined to the suburbs of Haven. He had some while back received a proposal from the CEO of a California start-up, a clean water company, H2Wow! They needed someone to help promote their upcoming, revolutionary, life-altering product that would extract hydrogen and oxygen from the very air we breathe and transform it into water. Wow! They were still in the testing phase, but the plan was to first roll-out a bottled-water product, eponymously named H2Wow! then gradually scale up to larger integral processes, waste water, tap water, drainage and revitalizing of ponds, streams, and tributaries, eventually to refilling the world's dwindling aquifers. The beauty of the process was that once fully functional, a portion of the water they produced would be shot through a series of pipe-dams, paddles, pulleys, and turbines, thus powering the equipment that produced that same water. Sustainable, baby! The CEO, a one Fusol Rimny, had read Fynn's pieces on waste, conservation, and way-out-of-the-box concepts, and thought his senses of mission and humor were the perfect fit to produce brochures, and advertising copy for their product. 'Whaddaya think?' For Fynn there was just a little too much wa-hoo about the request, puffery, and outlandish think-big-or-go-home attitude, for a product that seemed in theory simple, but in reality, was more than likely impossible. He left Rimny on the hook, though, replying that as they got closer to actually going live with H2Wow! he'd be happy to consider their offer. Obviously, he never heard back from them. And he's still breathing, not drinking the air around him.

And so it was, when the producers of a new reality show, tentatively titled, 'The Curious Couple Next Door', came to Haven, New Connecticut, looking for contestants, their lightning-rod instincts immediately directed them to Ona Maria and Fynn Fnüdl.

It was more likely Fynn's notoriety as the 'bad boy of green' that drew the attention of the show's producers, though it was Ona Maria that intrigued and beguiled them.

In the first interview for the show, the producers sat with Fynn and an extremely uncomfortable and uncooperative Ona Maria, and asked very basic questions, all the while a hidden camera taping them. Her expressions ranged from serious boredom to murderous outrage, when the camera could manage to focus on her at all. She squirmed, stood, paced, spun into a Reach for the Sun Yoga stance, stretched against the wall, all the while refusing to answer questions or talk about herself in any way.

Fynn, who was effusive, engaging, full of anecdotes, and humorous asides during the interview, assumed, because of Ona Maria's behavior (totally acceptable and predictable), there so was no way they'd be selected for the show.

He was wrong.

During the next interview, which was also filmed, but this time with their knowledge, Ona Maria and Fynn Fnüdl got light touches of make-up, just enough to cut down on the 'glare.' Though Ona Maria had plenty glares of her own that no make-up in the world would conceal.

Even on camera, Ona Maria was hard to see. Ducking her head, twirling in an Embrace the Heavens Tai Chi pose, or bending into a Yoga Warrior stance. The producers were mesmerized by someone who could dodge, evade, and virtually disappear on film.

Ona Maria for her part did everything in her power to thwart, subvert, and otherwise shrink herself out of sight, which, of course, made her all the more intriguing.

Before the interview was even over, they were offered a spot as contestants on the show. Ona Maria, despite all her goddess and faerie misgivings, agreed to take part.

*   *   *

The producers were very coy about the exact nature of the competition. They promised there would be no intrusion on their lives, but that all interactions would be strictly scheduled and planned in advance. No ambushes, no invasion of privacy. All they asked was that, once filming started, this curious couple act as naturally as possible.

To get them comfortable in front of cameras, Ona Maria and Fynn Fnüdl were put through a series of tests, preparations for the upcoming 'competition.' A camera crew followed them as, first they dined at a new, and what turned out to be terrible, restaurant (they found out later it was a fake). The second was a trip to Monsieur Toussade's Ear-Wax Museum. After the third test, a hike around Rattlesnake Lake, they realized that certain couples kept popping up, contingently, marginally. Were these their competition? And in what way were they competing?

As the 4th test, they met the host of the show, a bland-as-porcelain, washed-up actor named Warren Wayward, and the panel of judges -a pop-psychologist, a comedian, and a hip-hop artist. They also discovered the true nature of the show. Ona Maria and Fynn were to compete with seven other couples, and as with the 'tests', each week the couples would be put into a planned event (a doubles tennis match, an evening at the dog track, viewing -from box seats- a soccer game, a barbecue at Rattlesnake Lake Park, etc.), and each week one couple would be voted off the show. As apparently not being bizarre enough.

Finally, after all the tests and acclimations to this new reality, it was time to film the opening episode. All eight competing curious couples were to congregate for what was called a cocktail party. The host, and judges would be present, interviewing each of the contestants, in a 'casual, informal' setting, while the couples got to meet and mingle with each other.

Ona Maria saw this as an opportunity to reverse time and reposition her place in the universe.

*   *   *

The 'party' was held in the studio of a local TV station. One could only guess at what mood they were going for –was it supposed to be a scene ripped from 'Gone With the Wind'? Or a Vienna ballroom? The Roman Coliseum? The set was festooned with all the trappings of what appeared to be a political convention -balloons, tables set up at various stations, a bar, with a plastic looking bartender (Fynn had suggested Katy Riley to play the part, but the producers had ideas of their own). A jazz trio played (quietly) off to the side. For all the careful attention to detail, the setting couldn't be more false.

99

Ona Maria imagined this was how the producers of reality shows evoke reality -with unscrupulous contrivances.

The action was to take place in the center, as five cameras were set at the ends of imaginary spokes of a wheel, with the hub being a large circular buffet table. This layout allowed Ona Maria to skirt around the fringe, observing, dodging, part of, but not participating in the melee.

She wore a lacey, black cotton dress, very comfortable but revealing of her contours, both convex and concave. Her short dark hair erupted into the distracting spike here and there.

Because she did not drink alcohol, she had requested carrot/mango juice, and for this, she was more coherent than most. And more critical of the ensuing debacle.

Fynn had requested for himself a nice German Riesling, and was surprised to find a bottling from Dr. Vosken, one of the Pfaltz's most respected producers. At least someone knew their wine. Most of the other contestants drank punch or high-balls.

It wasn't long into the farce that Ona Maria had the revelation: It is only in a contrived setting that people reveal their inner horrible self. She also decided at that point, that henceforth throughout whatever should come of this show, she would remove herself from play -for that's all this was –child's play.

Unbeknownst to her at the time, the camera kept catching her concealing herself, usually positioned behind someone, or moving through a group, or turning her head, her glances darting in critical disavowal from couple to couple. Even to her own Fynn Fnüdl. Especially when he got into an 'argument' with the rogue fluvial geomorphologist over a proposed biomass plant on the edge of the Yrvl River. They lobbed sarcastic barbs at one another, which no one other than the combating duo seemed to comprehend.

While the exchange of sarcasm seemed intense, the key 'dramatic' moment of the evening came when the obese woman married to a dwarf (a character actor on TV), started snipping at a local restaurateur for her 'sluttish' dress. Her husband, a sex instructor at the community college, leapt in, and then the dwarf stood up to defend his wife, but was stepped on by the insurance salesman, whose wife was an attorney. Shouting and shoving ensued. The Lesbian couple rushed over to either join in the fracas or break it up, but were stopped when the gray-haired, pony-tailed denturist tripped over his

Birkenstocks into the buffet table, sending punch splashing all over the sushi and tortellini salad. His wife, a substitute teacher and goat farmer, screamed, thinking he'd had a heart-attack, and suddenly the focus shifted from battle to panic. The amiable denturist, dragged to his feet by the Lesbian couple, assured everyone he was okay. In the end, no punches were thrown, and after 30 seconds the scrum broke up, the denturist smiled and chided his over-reacting wife, and pretty soon everyone was laughing, apologizing, or over-explaining their actions.

The producers rubbed their hands together, this would make great TV.

* * *

It was in the can.

Episode One. The grand beginning. The producers thought they had a winner on their hands.

The first episode wasn't scheduled to air until October, a disturbing 6 months away. At that point, new episodes would be filmed every week, leading to the big blockbuster finale.

The first episode was the important one. Its purpose was to entertain, of course, but also to introduce the concept of the show, and the Couples Curious themselves, giving viewers someone to either root for or rail against. The tension between couples -intra and inter- would supposedly draw viewers back TIVO-ing week after to week to see who'd get tossed off the show. The judging criteria was simple, if very subjective. The panel of judges were to watch the trials along with a studio and TV audience, and comment (ridicule, dissect, joke). Afterwards, the judges would discuss who they thought was the most fascinating (curious!) couple, then expound on which was the most deserving of the ole heave-ho. Then the viewing audience would weigh in, voting by text, tweet, or Fratbook message, and at the beginning the following episode it would be revealed which couple was off the show. All of this was set to ear-shattering music, and heart-pounding dramatic pauses.

But first, there was one very important hurdle to clear: convince the network this was a sure-fire ratings hit. Or, put another way, prove that it was going to make the network a boatload of money.

To that end, the pilot was to be screened before the big-wigs at MussCTV, along with a cadre of potential advertisers, and a heavily vetted test audience. The producers were confident, but nervous. The vice president of programming was even more anxious. The potential advertisers appeared to be in a foul mood. The crowd, impatient and mean-spirited. Then the lights went down, and on the movie-sized screen, Wayward came practically running at the camera, "Curious Couples!" he cried, and went on to unconvincingly describe the scenario. The panel of judges was introduced to thunderous (amplified) applause from the studio audience. Then one by one the couples were introduced. Video clips of only the most embarrassing nature were shown. There were bits from the original interviews, and from the 'tests', but most of the footage came from the cocktail party, and almost everyone looked drunk. The Lesbian couple bickered. The fluvial geomorphologist and his wife came across as cold and aloof. The first scene of Ona Maria was her standing on her head. Fynn glared and made a snide comment –one that in real life was directed at the buffet table, but on tape looked as if he were snipping at his wife. One by curious one, the couples paraded across the screen. It ended with the denturist prattling on at length about how the only way to tell a person's true nature by their teeth. Then the attention swung to the judges, who were stiff, and their comments unremarkable. The comedian was not funny. But the pop-psychologist was. Not intentionally, of course. The hip-hop artist seemed to have wandered in from a completely different show.

The car-wax magnate walked out after 20 minutes. The vice president in charge of programming muttered incessantly to his secretary, not looking a bit happy. The CEO of Briddle Soap looked at his watch, mumbled something about an appointment and quickly scuttled out of the room. What little laughter came from the audience seemed derisive. Even before the credits began to role, every single potential advertiser had left, along with half the audience. There was supposed to be a Q & A with Wayward and the judges afterward, but the vice-president of programming dismissed them, and huddled briefly with the producers. The last member of the audience hadn't even straggled out the door, before the decision was made. The show was axed. The producers shrugged, packed up their pride and pitches, and moved on to the Next Big Thing: 'Top Chefs of Gilligan's Island'.

*   *   *

The curious couples had not been invited to the screening. All eight received news of the cancelation via text or email. Fynn

102

was crushed. He was working on a novel (or treatise, or manifesto -he wasn't sure which), entitled 'The Power of Earth', and being on a TV show (even a bad one) would have given the book project a great boost. Ona Maria was delighted. The faeries had done their work well.

As consolation, they received a DVD of the pilot show.

Ona Maria and Fynn, with much trepidation, sat down to watch it on their hand-crank TV. Sallie Sue, ready for a giddy and ridiculous ride, joined in.

Disbelief was the first reaction. Who were these people? It was so far removed from 'reality', they felt like they were watching strangers waltz through someone else's uncontested dream. Here were specks and flecks of their life, and yet none of it gibed with what they actually experienced. They kept going back re-watching certain scenes, trying to piece together the shards of reality that flickered by, attempting to match them with their memory. But nothing did match. Yes, there they were at the ear-wax museum, with the dwarf and his wife in the background. They recognized themselves at the phony restaurant, with the insurance salesman getting drunk and yelling at the waitress. And yet, while it was certainly Ona Maria and Fynn, it was not them at all. It was as if they existed in a fictive narrative so far removed from normal imagination that it reeked of genius.

Ona Maria, surprisingly, found herself enraptured. She couldn't take her eyes off it. As if a troupe of faeries had just performed an improvisational, extemporaneous dance on a blade of grass, in which everything and everybody metamorphosed into everything else. Reality had become so unreal that it could only be called –reality.

Long after the initial viewing, it continued to tantalize her. Often, when Sallie Sue and Fynn Fnüdl were at the movies, out for lunch, or at a bassoon recital, Ona Maria would take out the DVD, and watch it over and over. She saw herself dipping out of sight in a forest of people, only to re-materialize, and then disintegrate again. She became a duplicate of herself made into an imaginary object, visual but false, whole, but incomplete. It was as if a stranger had burst into her world to explain what she was doing on planet Earth, who these people surrounding and defining her were, and why she did not belong.

And she also understood that stranger to be herself.

Half-Time

F.F.: Wow. Okay, folks, that was some hectic kinetic first half. Action packed. Rapid-fire, non-stop, in-your-face, jaw-dropping, first-rate, hyper-hyphenating action. And talk about a cast of fully realized characters, stunning plot twists, outrageous word snags, and, of course, occasional bursts of lucidity. What a show. But now, it's half-time, and while everyone runs to the concession stand for popcorn, Tattinger, and corn frogs, we've got a dazzling extravaganza lined-up for you; interviews, a look back at some fascinating highlights, commentary, outtakes, and of course, a peak at what might be coming up in the second half. All of this...and a special appearance by none other than Fyodor Dostoyevsky! The great Russian novelist is on his comeback tour, 'No Crime, No Punishment.' That sounds like fun. So hang in there with us, folks. We have Howard and Ernie standing by up in the booth, but right now let's send it down to Katy Riley, who will take us on a quick look back at some first-half shenanigans, plus a few alarming and felicitous outtakes. Katy?

Katy Riley: Thanks, Fynn, and I think you said it best, if there's one word to sum up this first-half, it is -Wow! Let's re-visit a few highlights; one of my favorites was the story of a young Vor Thorgesson, who wins over the hearts and minds of everyone with his stoic enthusiasm, stalwart pride, and stolid common sense. But, then in one of the biggest 'whoopsies!' in history, Vor makes the mistake of sneaking aboard the massive Vasa man-of-war as it sets sail on its maiden voyage in 1628, only to sink 15 minutes later. And in that tragic accident we lost our beloved Vor Thorgesson –or did we?

F.F.: There seems to be a hint that Vor did survive. Don't you think?

Katy Riley: That's right, Fynn. Personally, I think we'll see more of Vor, but, hey, whadoo I know? Then, of course, in 'The Introduction,' we were treated to a first-rate mystery story, a big tasty who-dunnit, with intrigue...

F.F.: Katy? I thought it more a classic romance, a powerful statement on how love may emerge from the most bizarre and dangerous circumstances...

KR: But, Fynn, a guy gets murdered. Who Dunnit. Very clearly a murder mystery.

F.F.: Okay, okay, I guess we can disagree on the genre, but no disagreement on the masterful story telling...er, right?

KR: If you say so. Any-who...speaking of genres, you gotta admit, there was something for everyone in the first half. From kids to grandpas, lethargists to activists, libidinists to forbiddenists, PETAs to JETAs...even a couple nuggets for foodies. For instance, in the delightful 'Children at Whisk', not only are the playful imagination of kids brought to dazzling Technicolor life, we get a crazy recipe for Corn Frogs –frog-legs deep fried in corn dog batter. Not that I'd ever try it. And, in 'The Perils of Praline', our savvy chef takes us on an international culinary journey, including every foodie's dream come true, an eight-course *degustation* menu at Paris's three-star, Arpege. Man of my dreams, take me away to Arpege! Though, I gotta admit I was a bit grossed out by the carpaccio of whale in Bergen. Not to mention the garden snails of *Le Jardin des follies*. Eating garden snails? Really?!

And then there were the love stories. Heavy sigh. Who can forget the touching tale of corporate romance, with, Larry, the data entry computer geek wooing the CEO's daughter in 'A Lass and a Lackey.' Ah, love lost. Or, in 'Enter Texting', where iGeneration meets Old School, as Nadia bumps into crusty ole curmudgeon Viet Nam vet, Buck, while breaking up with her boyfriend via text message. Hilarity ensues.

But my particular favorite was the Jane Austin tale, although, I must say, Fynn, I thought some of the scenes a bit too explicit, if not, umm, er, never mind...

F.F.: ...You were going to say, Katy?

105

Katy Riley: Nothing. Forget it. And of course, there were some heart-wrenching, poignant stories, so sad, nearly broke my heart. I don't even want to think about poor little Slugger. How could you?!

But in the long run, I think it's fair to say, it was the humorous stories that carried the day. Nonsensical comedies, slap-stick, farce, flapdoodle, satyr satire you name it, it was comedic kitchen sink time...

But, y'know, Fynn, for every word that makes it into print, there's probably a dozen that end up on the cutting room floor. Let's take a gander at some outtakes. For example, in 'Fjord Fun', Udr Udresson confronts the wolf/dragon, Ole Firry. In a truly chilling scene on the frozen fjord, Ole attempts to blaze a hole beneath a homeward bound Udr, and send him to his icy doom. But, Udr cries out, "Ole, you killed my family, you ate my dog, you burned down my house, now villain, you will feel the wrath of Yaz!" and he slings his mighty sword lopping off Ole's head, and then bounces off the fallen dragon's body like a trampoline to safety just as the ice is giving way. Yowser, what a dramatic, heart-pounding ending. But, y'know what if it had ended like this: 'Phht. And the sword pierced Ole's heart, and he perished.' That, my friends, was the original ending. Don't know about you, Fynn, but that's pretty lame. It ended up on the cutting-room floor, the proper place for such crap.

F.F.: I think, Katy, not sure, but the aim was to emulate the brevity, and straight-forward narrative approach of the old Icelandic Sagas...

KR: Yeah, well, anyway, next up, and very intense, is the famous scene in 'Teapot' where the Baron von Easley returns to his homeland disguised as an old woman, and goes unrecognized by the townspeople. The proud Baron becomes so incensed, he storms into the village council meeting, throws off his wig, shoots the mayor, runs out and sets fire to the wind mill, then races to his ship where his crew is waiting, and they set sail for America. A truly incredible climax. But, what if we'd been treated to the original instead? Here it is, and I quote: 'So the Baron went to America, never to return.' Umm, how thrilling is that?

F.F.: Okay, Katy, point well taken, but maybe the idea was...

KR: I'm not done. In 'Mr. Goronsky's Comb-Over,' a dream-like tale of the young immigrant, Ona, who is kidnapped, and sold into slavery, and finally rescued by the vain Mr. Goronsky, only to be brutalized, tortured, and disgraced so fiercely she commits suicide. In the original her ghost –or is it a ghost?- seeks and reeks vengeance on Mr. Goronsky. In this case, I think the original was far superior. Because in the final version, Mr. Goronsky realizes his mistake, shaves his head, marries Ona, has a dozen children, and opens a cantina in Santa Fe. A cantina? Really? Really?!

Anyway, there you have it. Back to you, Fynn.

F.F.: Thanks, Katy, but you know, I'm not sure we're on the same page here. Well, never mind, I'll just mention, because you neglected to, you had plenty of super, steamy, memorable moments yourself…some between the lines.

KR: Let's not discuss it here, Fynn.

F.F.: Well, okey doke. Thanks, Katy, a brilliant job as always. And looking lovely in the pink chemise, if you don't mind me saying…

KR: It's actually a body tee.

F.F.: Okay. In any case, let's go up to the booth, where Ernie and Howard are looking every bit as beautiful. Guys?

Ernie (laughing): Beautiful? Fynn, you need contacts.

Howard: Hey, speak for yourself, I feel lovely today.

Ernie: Haha, and so you are, Howard.

F.F.: Fellas, what is your take on the first half, and how do you think it sets us up for what's to come in the second half? More of the same? Or total departure?

Ernie: I think while everyone is in agreement that this was a jam-packed first half, for me, Fynn, the big question is; can we keep up this kind of pace? I mean the whirlwind action, how you gonna maintain that? What do you think, Howard?

Howard: Can't be done, Ernie, and truthfully, shouldn't be. I think the rush we got in the first half has to give way to some contemplative, ponderous subject matter. I mean, how much footle and fluff can a person take?

KR: Ho, wait a minute, Howard. Footle? Fluff? Really?!

Howard: Sorry, Katy, but, yes, really. It's time to stretch it out a bit, open up narrative, give some breathing room to plot and character development...

Ernie: But you gotta admit, what works, works. Right, Howard?

Howard: Only so much, Ernie. The rapid shifts in tone, person, and time, all gets kind of vertiginous, if not downright aggravating for the reader. Personally, and I hate to say this, but I think what we truly need is more 'gravitas'.

Ernie: Gravitas?

Howard: Exactly. Some weight. Import.

Ernie: You mean, like some deeper meaning, some spiritual or conscious-raising experience?

Howard: Not necessarily. Profundity can take many shapes. I just think we need to see more depth. More...I'm sorry, the only word for it is gravitas.

Ernie: Well, maybe we can get a glimpse into the future, because right now we have in the booth with us a m a n w h o m a y b e t h e s u p e r s t a r o f t h e second half. Folks, say hello to Ozzie!

Ozzie: Thanks, guys, great to be here. In fact, it's great to be anywhere.

Ernie: Ozzie, for all the fanfare and fawning over you as a lead character, we've seen precious little of you so far. Is that gonna change?

Ozzie: I sure hope so, Ernie. I can't give anything away, but I'm guessing you'll see a lot more of Katy Riley and I...

KR: In your dreams…

Ozzie: She's such a kidder. Along with torrid romance, I think you'll see some intrigue, perhaps on a global scale, but, frankly, I'm not at liberty to discuss any of the particulars.

Ernie: Global, huh? Like wars, famine, tornadoes, and tsunamis…?

Ozzie: Wish I could tell you, Ernie, but frankly I think you're going to flip over what's coming up…

Howard: Question, Ozzie, in the second half are we going to see a little more…gravitas?

Ozzie: Howard, Howard, Howard, as you know, my friend, gravitas is in the eye of the beholder.

Howard: Ha, of course it is, Ozzie.

Ernie: You mentioned intrigue, Ozzie, and it seems to me your character is built around intrigue, at once sympathetic, but somehow shady and chameleon-like. Is that your choice, or the hand you are dealt?

Ozzie: Both, actually. I'm given a path, a direction, but I also have plenty of breathing room to allow my character to develop, and blend in with whatever the situation, whether it be an assassination attempt, or out on a hot date with Katy Riley.

KR: Keep me out of this.

Ozzie: O but my darling, you are involved. But to complete that thought, the direction is laid out before me. I do my best to adapt and accommodate.

Ernie: So it looks like we can look forward to some romance and intrigue in the second half. Anything else?

Ozzie: A little song and dance, at one point I'll be doing the plot in interpretative dance.

Ernie: Haha, well, we'll certainly look forward to that, Ozzie. One last question. You mention that you are given direction, a path, as it were, does that mean there is a plan for the second half?

Ozzie: Wo, Ernie, a plan? You know, my friend, you are delving into the thorny scrapes of theology, here. I mean, it's as if you're asking, does God have a plan? Or is it that humankind really does have Free Will? Once God, the clockmaker, sets the mechanism in motion, does he go take a nap, leaving us to live our lives, come what may? Maybe he hit the snooze button, I don't know. Or, perhaps the clock winds down. Ernie, these are questions that the greatest minds have pondered down through the ages, from Socrates to Calvin and Hobbes…

Howard: Haha! There it is -gravitas!

(*Laughter all around*)

Ernie: Okay, Howard, you win. You got your gravitas. Are you happy? And now I'd like to thank our guest, Ozzie, for joining us, it's been a real joy.

Ozzie: My pleasure, guys. And gals.

Ernie: Let's send it back to you, Fynn.

F.F.: Don't you just love it when guests are so intelligent, entertaining, and squeamishly elusive? I can see why he's a character to keep your eye on. But now…wait, is this it? Is this the moment?

KR: It is, Fynn! That helicopter over-head, keep your eye on it, there it is, the rope ladder is unfurling, dropping, and wo, look at all the balloons, thousands of colorful balloons rising and being scattered by the blades of the chopper, and you can just see him now, descending on the ladder, waving one hand, wo that's kinda risky, climbing down a twisting rope ladder one-handed, but that's him, Fynn, Fyodor Dostoyevsky…I don't know if you can see, but he's dressed in classic 19th century Russian bourgeois clothing, a tattered dark long-coat, boots, thick, pleated trousers, his heavy beard swaying in the breeze. And he's almost...yup, there he is, he's on the ground, and stepping up to the podium. Let's listen in...

Fyodor Dostoyevsky: Hello, Haven, New Connecticut! This is Fyodor from...Siberia. Haha, so you're asking yourself, what's a nice Russian fellow like myself doing here? (applause). Well, the Tsar sent me here with his felicitations...what?! You mean there is no more Tsar?! Oy, what's a Bolshevik to do? I'll tell ya, a lot can happen in a century. There used to be a big whopping peasant class in Russia, but thanks to Communism, not anymore...now in Russia, everyone's a peasant. Haha. No, just kidding, of course, the Russian Mafia's got things well in hand...including Putin. Hahaha. Here my friend, a bottle of vodka for your piece of land. No, but seriously, thanks to Communism, a no-talent like Solshenitzyn is lauded as a literary titan, which can only mean the titans have been chopped down to elves. Wo, boom, a jab to the kidney. Sorry, about that Solzshy, but really...Gulag? Never could stand the stuff. Speaking of football...we were speaking of football, weren't we? Haha, you know we had football in Russia long before you did. Of course, the football weighed 80 pounds, and came at the end of an iron chain. Hey, Vladimir, fake right, and go long, and then, run like crazy! Haha, Russian football, you gotta love it. And how about that Volga? She's so tough to navigate. And her sister wasn't too bad either! Haha. Y'know, just to get serious for a moment -yeah, right!- for those of you who have been following me on Titters, you know I have a new book coming out this fall, it's called 'The Idiot Goes to Texas'.... hahaha, no, wait, he's already there! Seriously, the title is 'Harry Potterovich and the Vampires Meet the Brothers Karamazov'. It's smack-down time! Haha. No actually, I've lightened up a bit, updated my FB status, as it were, cuz, y'know, you've got to keep up with the times, so my new work is in the mold of reality TV. Have you seen this stuff? Boy, you couldn't make up reality TV. I'll tell ya, last night I was watching two housewives going at it, and finally I just said, hey get out here, I'm trying to watch TV. Y'know in Russia we don't have reality TV. That's because the squirrel keeps falling off the treadmill...haha, that one never gets old. No, folks, I'll tell ya, it's a lot of fun here, I can tell the level of seriousness is just above that of Tolstoy (mock boos). No?! Don't tell me you fell for Leo and his melodrama? Anna Karenina under a train? Hey, 700 pages of pathos, bathos, and the Santa Maria, and wham, she throws herself beneath a train. Wo, hope I didn't spoil

111

the ending for you. If so, I just gave you back about 2 years of your life. If I'd written Anna K., I'd have thrown her under the train on page two. Down you go, baby! What novel? Barely worthy of a short, short story! No really, I loved Anna, much better than that Prince fellow from 'War and Peace'. Holy crud, reading that brick was like doing the backstroke through tree sap, while carrying a copy of Anna Karenina. Wait a minute, it is tree sap! Haha, no offense, Leo, really, you're the best at what you do. It's just that what you do, really, really sucks. Ba-boom! Uh-o, hear that whup-whup-whup? That means my time is up-up-up, and all I can say is it's been swell, Isabelle, swell. Thanks, everyone, and let me leave you with one last thought; never invite a Russian to your tea party. Haha, there's a joke in there somewhere, but I'm gonna let you figger it out... hey, here comes my ride...yee-haa!

KR: Wo, and there he goes, Fynn, he's being hauled back up into the helicopter on the rope ladder. The crowd is going totally bonkers. What an incredible performance. I didn't understand a word of it, of course, but obviously this guy's got it all. By the way, what did he write?

F.F.: O just a bunch of big books full of gobbledygook, nothing to concern yourself about. Hey, I want to thank everyone for such an incredible half-time show. But wait, what about you, Katy? Surely you know a little about what's coming up in the second half?

KR: Not at all, not at all. I think the only person who knows for sure is...

Ernie: Fynn?!

Howard: Fynn?!

KR: Fynn?!

F.F.: O gosh, look at the time, well, folks, that wraps up our half-time show. Hope you enjoyed it. A special thanks to Fyodor Dostoyevsky, and, of course, to Ozzie, and the beautiful, tantalizing, amazing -Ernie and Howard. O, and you too, Katy. Now everyone, sit back, relax, and enjoy what should be a stunner of a second half...

Part II

Ozzie in Oslo

Abu-Harim d'Akbari was late.

Ozzie was worried. This wasn't high school, where tardiness is an indiscretion. This was life and death. Literally.

Not one generally given to panic, Ozzie nonetheless fretted. The café was sparsely populated, a few scattered sippers and chatters. Ozzie stayed alert. Here, a young man was scowling over his laptop. Didn't like what he saw. Ozzie could relate. Over by the window, a mother was desperately trying to corral her two young boys, who would have none of it. They wanted ice cream. They wanted to break the toys. They wanted to be little snots.

Ozzie fretted. Abu-Harim was already 10 minutes late. Ozzie would hang around another 5 minutes –at most. And then...

But just as that thought flashed through his brain, he spied Abu-Harim across the street, sauntering up the sidewalk. By the puffs of blue-gray breath one could see he was laboring. He passed a group of young boys, none of whom looked his way. His long black robe billowing out, his head covered, his eyes glancing suspiciously this way and that. The big dope. He's looking too obvious. Ozzie shook his head in disgust.

Harim pushed through the door and a whoosh of frigid air followed him in. "Hello, cousin." Harim said, pulling up a chair across the table from Ozzie.

"You're late," Ozzie was not pleased.

Abu-Harim shrugged, "And yet, here I am."

"Do you have the information?" quietly, as if asking after his health.

"Of course, can I get something to drink?"

Ozzie flagged down a waiter, "Tea, coffee?"

"Tea," Harim said.

The waiter nodded.

Ozzie looked at Harim, "And so?"

Harim reached into a fold of his robe and pulled out a piece of paper, "What the fuck," Ozzie snapped, under his breath.

"Wah? It's nothing, a reminder…"

"Destroy it immediately we're done here…"

Harim's tea came, and there was an awkward pause as cup, saucer, spoon rattled and clanged onto the table. The piece of paper dangling. Ozzie kept his eye on the waiter to see if his eyes drifted to the paper. Curious. Did not seem to. But, you never know.

"Numbers," Harim said.

"Sunuvabitch. Numbers of what…never write anything down."

Harim was unmoved. "You want to know what activity goes on, so here it is…" he started to pass the paper to Ozzie.

"Keep the goddam thing, pretend it is a shopping list or something." He was anxious.

"Okay…then, here it is, always on either Tuesday or Thursday between noon and two, a car with this license plate," Ozzie glanced at the numbers on the paper, he recognized them, "pulls up to the gate, two guards, not obviously armed, appear, they talk to the driver, but not to the Visitor in the passenger seat, they look in the backseat, walk around the car, and then the gate opens. The Visitor gets out of the car, and with the two guards goes inside the gate. The gate closes behind him. The car remains parked outside, the engine running. His meetings with The One last anywhere from 5 minutes to an hour. If more than 15 minutes, the car pulls away. And circles around the neighborhood, until it's signaled to pick up the Visitor. As soon as he comes out the gate, the car is there waiting for him. He gets in and they drive off."

Ozzie seems pleased, "Is it the same car every time?"

"Yes."

"And driver…?"

Abu-Harim winced, darted eyes back and forth…

"That's okay," Ozzie said, "And you say, Tuesday, Thursday, is this every week?"

"No," Harim looked uncomfortably around, "it is not unusual for weeks to go by with no meeting. The longest period between visits was a month or so."

116

"Do you remember when that was?"

"February."

Ozzie nodded. That gibed with other information he had from different sources. But what to believe...who to believe?

"Do we know how many guards, how many people are even in the compound?"

Abu-Harim, shook his head. "No way to be sure. It could be two, it could be eight. Their backs are always turned, they huddle around anyone they're with. But usually two at a time. There's very little activity, occasionally a few people hurry outside, usually for a taxi or big van, but it is it difficult to follow-up, as we can't be obvious, if we get caught observing..."

"I understand..." Ozzie pauses, takes a lengthy, thoughtful sip of his coffee, "you have done well. Anything else?"

"There are others who visit..."

"Yes?"

"We don't know who, they may be simply locals..."

"No!"

"Well, then, we –I- don't know. There is no regularity, not like the Visitor."

"No idea who they are?"

"No, and they're all different. Some tall some skinny, some fatter than me, but it is thought they are some kind of messengers. The unimportant ones. One was even left outside the gate waiting for an hour. Then was gone."

"Car?"

"Bike. Sometimes on foot."

"There will obviously be others, but if we focus on The One, if we know his routine, if we understand where all these connections lead, that is enough, we don't need to follow every contact out into the world, so long as they always lead back to The One. And everything you have said here confirms what we have suspected for some time."

Abu-Harim was sweating, despite the cold which filtered into the café with each opening of the door. He kept glancing about anxiously.

"Don't worry," Ozzie said, "for you, it is all over. When you return to your apartment you will find a ticket to Frankfurt. Your flight leaves tomorrow morning. When you check your bank account you will find the money we agreed upon has been deposited. Enjoy it. We have tried to be indirect and deliberate, the money comes from various sources with no way to be traced. We hope."

Suddenly Abu-Harim erupted, "Yes, yes, I understand, but what of me? If this is not done swiftly, and if I am discovered, you will find my hands, my feet, and my head in different parts of the globe... if they're found at all."

Ozzie was calm. "Like yourself, we have all lost someone in this struggle, and we know the risks involved. Danger is inherent. But if all the information we have gathered is correct, our job will be done, as soon as possible. No one will be able to trace anything back to you. Besides, you have been remunerated well. Now go. And Abu-Harim?"

"What?"

"Destroy that fucking piece of paper."

As Harim turned, wound out of the café, buckling again the chill, crossed the street, turned right on Norbygata, Ozzie could see him shredding pieces of paper and dumping them into the gutter at three different points along the way.

'Either we are doomed,' Ozzie thought, 'or victory and retribution is within our grasp. And we will probably find Harim's feet in trash barrel in Frankfurt.'

He pays for the coffee and tea and with a glance around, leaves.

Ozzie set off down Motzefeldts Gate to Gronland, then took a weaving, winding variety of gates till he came to and scurried across Stenersgate, then flitted inside OSL-City, went up two stories on the escalator, pretended to window shop at a men's clothing store, down again, around the train station, along Fred Olsens Gate, crossed with the light. weaving in and out of the crowd of shoppers, business-people, until he came to Karl Johans Gate, and hurried along the pedestrian thoroughfare, stopping every now again to glance into a shop, looking for reflections in the window. He rushed past bars and restaurants along the way, until he came to took a left on Kirkegata, and walking swiftly about 20 paces, turned suddenly. No one was following him. He was fairly certain. He took another left along a street mostly apartment buildings, a few businesses at street-level, turn right, another right, and finally into the Ona Bar and Grill.

"Hey, here he is," a beefy male voice called out, "Ozzie, over here." There was a small crowd around the bar, his face lit up into a smile as he approached, Ole, the leader of the team, said gleefully, "Ozzie, you're late."

Ozzie laughed, "And yet, here I am!"

He looked sharp in a Banana Republic black double-breasted, belted wool-blend coat, Ralph Lauren pleated wool serge slacks, GO rabbit fur lined leather gloves, black Gucci lace-up shoes, Thorlos over the calf black socks, and underwear, well, from Costco. But no one needed to know that.

"Why didn't anyone tell me it's freezing here in April?"

Ole laughed, "Pah, this isn't cold? It's downright balmy." This despite his fairly dark-skinned cheek was blazing red with chill. Ole introduced his colleagues, Otto Helve, Vor Thorgesson, and a very pretty, Marte Marsten.

"Good to meet you all in person...at last...but first, I need a drink." He scooted down the bar a bit, towards the bartender. She looked at him, bored, "What you having?"

"Something to warm me up..."

"Not that kind of place."

"I meant drink-wise."

"So did I."

Laughing, "O you're a smart one, aren't you?"

"My job, warm you up."

She was very pretty, long blonde, hair, blue eyes, rather large nose, slightly weak chin, thin lips, but her bright eyes, and smart-aleck calm redeemed any flaws, and Ozzie thought ahead to maybe...just maybe...but duty first.

"Do you have anything red, say, from the Rhone Valley?"

The bartender drummed her fingers against the zinc bar, "A little St. Joseph number. Not bad."

"Okay, I can live with that..."

With glass of wine in hand, Ozzie slid back to his companions, "Well I hope you didn't drag me all the way over here for bad news."

Ole glanced around at his team, and said, "And so, in a word, you're in."

"But of course," Ozzie said, clearly relieved. "Never any doubts, right."

It was a deal Ozzie had been working on for over a year. Representing his family's textile business, the bidding war, the back and forths, negotiations, with faces at the Norwegian company constantly changing, and shifting, along with attitudes and demands, until finally Ole's group took charge, got everything on track, and since then it's been a straight-forward matter of specs, design, measurements, etc., until that moment. Ozzie had always been optimistic. But skeptical. These things have a way of blowing-up in your face at the last minute. The contract was to create over one hundred international flags, to be hoisted up at the 9-11 Memorial Plaza...ground zero. Whatever messiness had preceded, this was the icing on the cake. Done deal.

"A toast," Ozzie said, raising his glass.

Marte Marsten spoke up, "Sorry this took so long, but I think all parties have finally gotten what they wanted. Contracts are on their way to your home office."

"Perhaps we were being over-optimistic, but my cousins have already completed designs, plates, colors, the fabric and machinery, everything is set, all we need do is push a button and go."

"Excellent," Ole said. "Now, we keep our eyes close, and heads down and march forward, because one fuck-up and we're undone."

Ozzie liked the term 'fuck-up.' Not very Norwegian sounding, but effectively blunt.

"From our end there will be no problems, I can promise that..."

"The Americans have a way of interfering with their demands... but, I think we're past that point." Marte Marsten did not seem to enjoy working with her American counterparts. Ozzie let it pass.

"And now," Ole said smiling warmly, "if you set your red wine down for a moment..." On cue the attractive bartender pulled from under the bar an ice bucket, with a bottle of Champagne poked out at a conspicuously jaunty angle, "...a little celebration."

Ozzie checked the label, "Indeed, Tattinger, very nice."

The bartender had chilled glasses ready, poured each a moderate amount.

As they all sipped sighed in respect, awe, and "Let me ask you something my friends," Ozzie said, "our business, an Arab business, manufacturing flags for a 9-11 tribute...ummm, and I know there were scads of others biding on this, but...I guess, in short..."

"Why you?" Ole finished his sentence for him.

"Yes. Exactly. Why us?"

Ole, Marte and the others glanced around at each other, almost daring one or the other to speak. Finally, Marte spoke up, "In our minds it was an opportunity to present a show of unity, not one of divisiveness. Not exactly a 'statement', mind you, a matter of openness…reaching out, perhaps even a sense of…forgiveness."

"Forgiveness?" Ozzie nearly laughed, "odd choice of words. You forgive me for 9-11?"

Awkward moment. "Forgiveness for us all," Vor Thorgesson said, "it is as if the entire world were complicit…and besides, you're in Oslo, my friend, the beating heart of world peace. If I may disagree with Marte, I think that yes, it is a least a bit of a statement…"

Ozzie said, "In any case, we embrace the opportunity."

Commerce. Liability. Love. Revenge. Yes, Ozzie understood.

"And so," Ozzie said, rubbing his chilly hands together, "I'm starving."

They got a table in the dining room. The rest of the evening was suitably warmed by appetizers, a bottle of red, a bottle of white, Ozzie doing his best to melt Marte, who proved to be too stern a package, dropping repeated hints she was married, kids, and quite clearly, not interested. Marte Masten was in fact the first to excuse herself. After a jolly meal (Ozzie had a delicious duck confit), the boys decided they wanted to be naughty and do some bar hopping. Ozzie respectfully begged off. Jet-lag, need to send out emails, etc.

After they left, Ozzie, hoping to go home with the young smart-ass bartender, bellied-up to the bar for another glass of wine. Only to be vastly disappointed as her boyfriend, a cook at a nearby restaurant, just arrived to have a drink and usher her home. She gave him a defiant, seductive, too-bad glance as they left.

Ozzie walked briskly in the biting cold to his hotel, across the bay from the Opera House.

In his room, he reflected upon his strange day. Got a bottle of (lesser) Champagne from the mini-bar. He spent several hours on his lap-top communicating to his brothers in Pakistan, Iran and Lebanon.

On the morrow he'd take a puddle-jumper to Amsterdam, then a non-stop to Haven, New Connecticut, and there resume his faux life as playboy, raconteur, and all-around man of mystery, and then, soon… blood will be spilled, as wine from a broken glass.

Workout

This guy walks into a bar. Wait, it's sweaty guy, or as he's known at ThreeBs, Workout Guy.

He plants himself at the top of the horseshoe wooden bar, flexes his shoulder, takes off his jacket, and leans against the bar.

Katy Riley approaches, "Been working out?"

"Nah, just threw some water over me to make it look like sweat..."

"Smart ass. What're you having? White wine?"

"Sure. Surprise me...so she showed me a naked picture of my wife...haha, old Rodney Dangerfield joke."

Katy Riley, rummaging through the wine cooler, pulls out a bottle, surreptitiously pours, and slides the glass in front of Workout Guy.

He accepts ceremoniously, tastes, pompously, "I approve... what the heck is it?"

"Bobal Blanco, I don't know, Fynn recommended it."

"Very nice."

"Well, get your fill," Katy Riley warns, "It's coming off the list soon as this is gone."

"What?! That's insane."

"It's February, people aren't drinking a whole lot of white wine right now."

"People? Who are these people I keep hearing about? I want a word with them."

"Having anything to eat?"

"What's the soup today?"

"Curried butternut squash, with aioli and fried sage leaf. Or dishwater."

"Hmmm, tough choice, well, I'm gonna bet the bank on the butternut squash. Sounds light, but filling, just the thing after a ferocious workout."

"So what'ja do today?" she says, punching order into the computer.

"Shoulders. Biceps. Treadmill. Weights. Good workout. O and quads."

"So, that really is sweat?"

"Hard earned. How about you, how're you doin' today?"

"Lessee, I had a check bounce...to my Day Care! The car is running funny. The heel on my shoe busted, now my feet are killing me... so, all in all, it's been a real good day." The hostess seats a table of three in the corner of the bar section. "Could've put them a little closer," peeved.

"Lights, camera, action," Workout Guy says as Katy Riley swings around the bar to wait on the newbies.

Workout Guy stands, does not sit, at the bar. He doesn't like the height, or weight, or butt-fit of the stools, too rigid, unforgiving, unyielding. Besides, standing makes you looks so dang cool.

He lets his eyes drift upwards to the TV above the bar. Not much into TV, eye candy, a pretty distraction, made even more enticing with no sound. He watches enough to determine it's some kind of cop show, or, something. Frenetic camera-work, X-rays, scalpels, pincers, what the heck? Marcus Welby meets Columbo? Nothing he'd ever purposely watch, unless stranded at a bar with no one around, and nothing else on. But then he spies a character actor he recognizes. Was he on Seinfeld? Very familiar.

Erin Gobra, the ranging day manager, comes striding out of the back room, making the rounds, chatting up customers, smiling, then back to his ofice to continue his nap. Tough job, but Erin can pull it off. He gets around to Workout Guy, "What're having?" indicating the wine.

"Bobal Blanc. Not bad. Crisp, refreshing."

"We're getting rid of it, Hard to sell anything called Bobo Blank."

Suddenly, Katy Riley is in front of them. Ignores Erin, says to Workout Guy, "So this working out, is it doing you any good?"

"Absolutely. I'll tell you, my thighs are like tree trunks, my buttocks like iron jaws. I can crack walnuts in them."

Erin cries out, "Excuse me, my customers are trying to eat here."

"Hey I just crack 'em, I don't eat 'em."

Katy Riley had burst out laughing, not her charitable, O you're a good customer so I'll laugh at your stupid joke, but a heartfelt, tummy-rumbling guffaw.

She spies dollar signs walking in the door, a foursome, but the hostess does not sit them in the bar area. They want a window booth. Don't look like big tippers anyway. Just then her table of three are all wiggling their fingers in her direction, and she heads over to help them, whilst Erin wanders off shaking his head.

It is the detritus of the lunch crowd. None of the regulars have showed up...but, no one can eat at the same time every day, With the exception of...

"No Buck today?" he asks of Katy Riley as she rings in an order.

"No." Tersely. "Hospital." Eyes on the keys of the register.

"Uh-o, everything ok?"

"Hope so. Just some tests. He has a growth on his neck."

"Growth on his neck? That's his head."

Ignoring him, Katy Riley rushes out to hand back the credit card to a table of four.

Workout Guy tries to concentrate for a moment on the TV. If nothing else some clever freeze shots, flashbacks, hallucinations, quick jolt, then a man and woman looking seriously over a series of X-rays of bones fragments. Grisly.

Katy Riley is back. Obviously bored. Two tables, and him.

"What show is this?" pointing at the TV.

"Bone Hunters," she says.

"Hmm, seems kinda convoluted for a cop show."

"The main guy is an ex-con pediatrician, turned coroner."

"Seems like a natural transition."

"It's actually pretty good." Not very interested. "So, where is all of this leading to."

Workout Guy diverts his eyes and mind from the TV, "What, working out?"

"Yeah. Are you training for the Olympics or something?"

"No, just...I don't know, something to do while waiting to grow old and flabby...besides, what's wrong with looking like a total stud?"

"I figured as much," Katy Riley shook her head. Then groans, the table of three needs her guidance again, "High maintenance," she mutters, and is off.

He glances back up at the TV. Hmmm, it seems like his character actor, who may or may not have been on Seinfeld, is the prime suspect, as he's skulking down dark hallways, opening doors, and turning his head to see if he's being followed. Either that or he's a natural born paranoid. Then the flash to skeletal remains, X-rays, two investigators, looking distraught, as if they were caught in the act of actually trying to act, but they're obviously on to something...ahaha, cut to our Character Actor...what the hell is his name? Uh-oh, he's opening a drawer...a gun? A knife...no, insurance papers. Hmmm, deadly. Suppose you could paper-cut someone to death...new spinoff cop show...'Cuts'. Followed by 'Hang Nails', OK, this is getting weird, now a chase sequence, on foot, we can't see who's being chased, "Hey, Character Actor, stop, or I'll cut you with this post-it note!"

A couple of work gentlemen take a seat two stools away from Workout Guy. They're speckled with white dust and dirt, which scores them ten points. Roofers? Sheet rockers? Pipe fitters? No way to know, unless of course he were to ask them. One is an older fellar, boss, the other young hipster, bossed. The mentor and the menteed.

As they study the menu, Katy Riley sneaks up behind them, "Drinks, guys?"

Wha...who are you, o, bartender. "Yeah, couple Coors Lite."

You can tell a lot about a working man by the beer he drinks. These dudes are high class.'

Katy Riley cranks the lever on the tap, and sets two slippery wet cold ones in front of the boys. The older fellar says, somewhat cantankerously, "You don't have that chicken thing anymore?"

"Nope," Kay Riley says unapologetically.

There is a brief moment, where it seems like he's going to slam the menu on the counter and stomp out, 'No chicken thing?! I'm outta here!' But instead he says, "Shoot, I really liked that."

Katy Riley laughs her charitable customer laugh, and says, "Yeah, it was pretty popular, some people love the fire-roasted Cornish game hen...."

The old fellar, very dubious, says, "Okay, I'll give a try."

The younger mentored one says, "I'll have the buffalo burger with German potatoes and pickle soup."

"Excellent," Kay Riley says, "thank you gentlemen."

There's a guy on the TV show who, clearly is the villain, as he's hufing and pufing, after a good chase. The good guys couldn't catch him? Weasels. And this guy, he's never been on Seinfeld. Now back to our very guilty looking Character Actor. Dang, what is going on?

There's a spell where Katy Riley has nothing to do, leans on the bar in front of Workout Guy, "Slooooooow Day...how's the soup?"

"Good, tasty. I could stand it to be a little hotter, but that's just me..."

"Want me to run back and get you some jalapenos?"

"No, I'm good...hey, do you know who this guy is?" points to TV.

"Hmmm, he's been in a lot of things..."

"Seinfeld?"

"Couldn't say...see him in a lot. He's like everywhere."

The high-maintenance crew is waving again to Katy Riley. Under her breath, "What now." But carves a smile into her cheeks, and rushes over to help them.

Workout Guy finishes his soup. Only a dribble of wine left. Have another? The two sheet-rockers are in quiet confab, muttering every now and again to each other. Seem to be in a good mood.

Katy Riley returns, mutters to Workout Guy "They don't like their hangar steak, it's too chewy. Like that's my fault."

"You're being harangued over a hanger steak? There's a joke in there somewhere."

"They're nice...just...." she's off to deliver.

He glances at the TV. Commercial.

Katy Riley slips back behind the bar, drums her fingers a while, checks everyone's drink level. Then without asking, pours Workout Guy a bit more of the Bobal Blanc. Suddenly the older feller says to her, "Say, would you mind turning it over to sports," he points to the TV. Workout Guy looks stunned.

Katy Riley grabs the remote, flips through channels, "Rugby, boxing, curling, nothing, ohhh, Super Bowl highlights..."

"Yeah, can we watch that…"

Workout Guy looks on in disbelief. He takes a couple disdainful sips of his Bobal.

"Are you going to get them a new steak?" he says to Katy Riley.

"No, they said they'd chew their way through it."

"By god, that's the spirit." He pulls out his credit card, sets it on the bar. Katy Riley takes it, rings him up, hands him an arms-length worth of paper slips.

"Ah, our paperless society." Workout Guy signs what he thinks to be the correct scrap of paper. Takes a last sullen swig on his Bobal, pulls on his jacket.

"You outta here?

"Yeah, I guess, since I'll never find out how that show ends…"

The old fellar looks alarmed, shoots Workout Guy an apologetic glance, "O no, I'm sorry, were you watching that? Didn't mean to…"

Workout Guy laughs, "Just kidding, I was only watching it to keep my eyes off the fetching barkeep…"

"O shut up."

Farewell to Katy Riley, passes behind the sheet-rockers, "Have a groovy lunch, o and by the way, the Cornish game hen is crazy good. Cheers."

He pushes out into the chill of a sunny, but chilly February afternoon. And…it's windy. Thanks. The sweat has dried. He braces himself against the cold, and burrows his way through the wind toward his car. Dead leaves are skipping across the parking lot. As he opens the front door, he stops, looks around, can't help but wonder, 'Yeah, how will it all end?'

Passport to Happiness

Rounding the last corner off the tree-lined backroads of Littlefield, Fynn Fnüdl always got a sense of awe, wonder, and sometimes…shock. From a brace of tightly spaced spruce trees, to a wide-open grass field, a soothing respite before entering the madness of the various gardens, orchards of fig, cider pears, cider apples, cherry, pomegranate and elderberry trees, small vineyard, berry fields, composting and methane shacks, all in the middle of which sat the Geodesic Dome (modified) which they called home. They.

Yes, all of this hit him at first glance around the final bend.

But today as he pedaled his rickshaw up the gravel path, its basket bulging with two ducks, a rabbit, a dozen eggs (bartering with neighbors), and the day's mail, he didn't so much like what he saw. A big, black, gas-guzzling SUV parked by the barn. And walking to it, sauntering really, was a gray-haired, pony-tailed fellow in Birkenstocks. The denturist.

As Fynn drew to a stop, the denturist, gave him a little wave, just as he opened the
door to his beast, "What a great place you guys have here."

"Thanks," Fynn grimaced. What else was he to say.

"What do you do with all this stuff?" Trying to be polite.

"Eat it, drink it, sell it at the market, barter. Maybe some time we can swap for goat milk." There was just enough facetiousness in his voice that the denturist gave him a wan smile. He got behind the wheel, pulled his seat-belt on, backed up, and rolled down the driveway, blowing toxic shit all over the greenery, until he rounded the bend and was sucked into the tree-lined street.

Fynn Fnüdl tipped his rickshaw against the barn, loaded up his goodies in his hemp bag, and went around to the back door.

Ona Maria was in her meditation triangle in the living room. Fynn recognized this position. It was called the I-Have-Nothing-to-Say-to-You pose. She could hold it for hours at a time. He set his armload on the counter, put one duck in the fridge, the other, along with the rabbit, in the freezer. Ona Maria pretended not to notice him. He shut the fridge door with a little more force than necessary. Went to the counter and started flipping through the mail.

"Thinking about dentures?" he said, not looking up.

Ona Maria took a deep breath, came out of her trance, "No." She did not look his way.

Catalog from Barn's Aplenty, questionnaire from the AG Dept. More junk mail. "Anything you need to share with me?"

She shrugged, shook her head.

Okay.

"O, something for you." He frisbeed a manilla envelope her way. She glanced at it.

"Your passport."

She looked at it, sadly.

He checked the saltwater and grass clock, "I gotta go get Sallie Sue."

Grabbed his keys, out the door.

His daughter was in a boisterous, gabby mood. It had been a crazy day at school. She and her friend Gabriella got detention at recess. The monitor heard someone curse, turned to see Sallie Sue and Gabriella laughing, and assumed they were the perpetrators, and made them go sit in the math room for the rest of recess. They laughed about it the whole while. And then later, Scotty threw up in class. Gross. So, all in all, a great day.

Fynn met this with little bursts of laughter, and nods, but Sallie Sue was not easily fooled.

"How was your day?"

"Good."

"Is everything okay?"

"Yeah." He didn't like lying to his daughter. "Just a little pensive. Lot on my mind."

"Looking forward to Paris?"

"O yeah…speaking of which, your mother got her passport today…"

"Really?! Cooooool."

It had been a long arduous process involving lawyers, immigration oficers, an exportation scare, and all for what? A woman who won't leave the house.

"Is she gonna go to Paris with you?"

Fynn snorted, "Your mother? Paris…?"

They both laughed.

"O right."

They pulled around the final bend in the driveway, and the once glorious site seemed to have lost a bit of its luster.

"I've got a couple errands to run, tell your mother we're having duck tonight."

"Okay, pops…." Sallie Sue dragged gym bag, back-pack, and lunch box, and hauled them all around the corner.

Fynn set out for Bistro Bon Bon.

"Fynn!" Katy Riley fairly bellowed, "What're you doing here?"

"Wuh? Can't a guy have a glass of wine this late…or early?"

"Anytime for you, baby. Pinot Noir?"

"No, I think I'll give that German Riesling another whirl. Any left?"

Katy Riley snooped around her stash, "O yeah. One bottle."

"That's all I need."

Fynn snuggled into his seat. He glanced across the bar to Ben, who was pretending to be flipping through some papers, pen at the ready to scratch, erase one number to add another, looked pretty serious. He checks his iPad. Frowns. Numbers don't look good? Nothing adds up. Fynn slapped down his notebook –his pPad.

Slow day. He and Ben were the only ones at the bar. Katy Riley was having a late snack. It was just after 4, her shift ended at 4:30.

All things have weight, significance.

"Hey, aren't you going to France pretty soon?"

"Two weeks from today, speaking of which, did you get your passport yet?"

"No."

"Should get it any day, my wife got hers in the mail today." Fynn had helped Katy Riley fill out of the forms, and both hers and his wife's were shipped off the same time.

"If you get it in the next couple days you can come with me to Paris."

Katy Riley snorted, "Yeah, right, I'm sure your wife would appreciate that."

"I can just see you on the Champs Elysee, sipping a glass of bubbly."

"Fynn, I met your wife, she'd twist me into a pretzel if I went to Paris with you."

"You'd make a pretty little pretzel."

Katy Riley just shook her head.

Ben, having had enough of this conversation which had no bearing on his figures not adding up, stood. Katy Riley gave him a hug. Ben stopped long enough to say to Fynn, "Don't do anything I wouldn't do."

"No prob. Take care."

Ben was off.

Katy Riley was going around wiping down tables for the next big crush of customers. Or just doing busy work.

Suddenly she looked at Fynn and said, "Fastidious."

Fynn repeated, "Fastidious?"

"Yeah, that's the word I was trying to think of. For Ben. He's Fas-tidious."

"The way you say it, it almost sounds dirty."

Katy Riley stopped, thought, "That's not mean is it? Calling Ben fastidious?"

"No, not at all, he is fastidious. And funny fact about fastidious folks, they're proud of being fastidious. It's all part of the fastidious phenomena."

Katy Riley seemed relieved. She didn't want to insult Ben. "Anything to eat? It's Happy Hour."

"No, I'm good."

Katy Riley carried a trayful of dishes into the kitchen, he could hear her joking with the cooks. Fynn doodled in his pPad, sipped his delicious wine. Notes of pineapple, apricot, bit of diesel fuel…oops. Couldn't help slipping into wine writer mode every now again. Just another one of those things that separated he and Ona Maria. He found wine endlessly fascinating, like diving into literature or classical music. The deeper one dives, the more emerges. Ona Maria pretended it didn't exist. Too busy with her Kombucha and Boba tea. Or Paris. Just like wine, Paris is endlessly fascinating, you can explore it the rest of your life and always have something left to pursue. Ona Maria hated Paris.

"You're looking a little down, baby, everything okay?" Katy Riley was all of a sudden leaning on the bar in front of him. Her concerned look.

Fynn let out a reluctant sigh. "She's doing it again."

"O, honey, I'm sorry. Are you sure?"

He nodded. Lips pursed.

Katy Riley wanted the truth. Not pulling any punches. "What're you going to do?"

"I have two choices. My inclination is to just walk away from it all. Go live in France. But…Sallie Sue. She's more important than Ona Maria or me. And then there's everything we've built…the house, the gardens, a comfortable, if somewhat odd lifestyle. And then, there's the financial entanglements. Leaving just isn't a choice. What to do? What I always do. Let it run its course. Bite my lip till it bleeds. Protect home and hearth. Mostly for Sallie Sue's sake. She loves her mother."

"What about you? What do you want? You can't always be doing everything for other people." She paused, "I've noticed that about you…you want people to like you…so sometimes you give up yourself. You're a person, too, y'know."

"Yeah, you're not the first one to accuse me of that. Wanting people to like me. All I can say is, I just want everybody around me to be happy. Better than struggling with a bunch of idiots. If anything, it's self-serving, if not egotistical…just trying to make my life easier. And if," he huffed, "it means ignoring Ona Maria's indiscretions, well, I bought into the system."

"How many times has she done this to you? Three since I've known you."

"Probably six. That I know of."

"Six? Six?! Really. Really?!"

"Really."

"I'd never do that to you, baby."

"I know you wouldn't…"

Katy Riley plucked a hair from around her ear, "Well, I'm sorry, but, I've gotta run and pick up my own kiddo. Doc's here, he's in the kitchen eating everything in sight before he takes over the bar."

He had half hoped Katy Riley would ask him to stick around

for a drink, or maybe even go out somewhere else for a drink…but, like Sallie Sue, little Jordie awaits.

She had her coat on, and ready to roll, when she stopped and gave Fynn a hug, "I'm sorry, baby."

"Comes with the territory."

"Yeah, well…I'll see you before Paris, right?"

"Of course."

And abandoned once again. Doc took his spot behind the bar, said to Fynn, "Gonna have another?"

"Nope, I've resuscitated my soul for the day…"

Fynn took the long way home, highway 29, a two-lane winding through wheat fields, nurseries, remainders of forests, farms, fresh eggs, the tiny community of Felicity…Ah, Felicity…and the final couple miles skirting the River Yvrl.

By time he pulled up into his marvelously scenic gloomy wonderland, he was somewhere between serenity and surrender. He almost hated walking through the front door. What was she going to be like? Confrontational? Rarely. Contrite? Not likely. Defiant? Probably.

He braced himself as he entered, only to see his daughter and wife staring intently at the laptop propped up on the kitchen counter. They both turned to him and Sallie Sue said excitedly, "Papa, Mother wants to go to Scandinavia…can we?"

"Scandinavia?" Okay, was not expecting that. "Ummmm, when?"

"Not till July," Sallie Sue did the talking, "after school's out, and Mother has some stuff in early July, so like, last part of July…"

Fynn thought a moment. Was this an olive branch? Her way of apologizing? Or something far more sinister?

"We got it all planned out, Copenhagen, Stockholm, and of course, Oslo and Bergen." Fynn's great-grandfather, Ole Fnüdlsson was born in Bergen, his great-grandmother, Marte Thorggeson, was from Oslo. They emigrated, separately in 1908 and 1911, to America, and met in a tiny upstart town (incorporated 1906), of Littlefield, New Connecticut in 1912. They married in 1915.

"Can we?" Sallie Sue pleaded.

"Scandinavia, huh?" Fynn thought about it. "Sure. Why not."

The Hawk, the Dove, and the Power of Imagery

A hawk crashed into the bay window.

I was standing in the kitchen, reading the paper, and bang! I looked up just in time to see the hawk flip over backwards onto a lounge chair below. He lay still for a moment, as I ran to the window. What was I to do? I'm no veterinarian, and I'm not about to go out and tangle with a wounded hawk. So I watched. He was a big fella, mostly brown with gray tipped wings. He stirred, like, wo, dude, what just happened? He shook his head, wiggled his wings, yep, all in one piece. He shook out the cobwebs. Dazed. He finally gathered himself, looked a bit embarrassed, and tipsily flew off.

We get a lot of hawks around here, edge of a housing development, beyond the berm is probably 20 or 30 acres of wooded land, a dry creek running throughout. Dry until about January. You see the hawks circling above the preserved wetland, catching a ride on a thermal and just floating along, never having to flap a wing. Sometimes their shadow is the first thing you see, depending on where the sun is, and where the hawk is. Parallax view? Frequently smaller birds pester the hawk, dive-bombing him, circling, chasing, playing, and teasing him. When he's had enough, the hawk launches his powerful wings, and zips off, like the Duchess. Extremely graceful to watch.

134

But to see one crash into your window. That was weird.

If that weren't weird enough, a few moments later, I logged on, went to FratBook, and scrolled down through the dregs, when I saw…holy crap! Are you kidding me?

Checked my watch, it was 11:25.

I threw on my jacket, grabbed my keys, and rushed to Threebies. To see Katy Riley. I like to get there about 10 before noon, just ahead of the lunch rush. Have a couple minutes to chat with her. But as soon I pull into the parking lot, I saw it -the rickshaw. Damn, Fnüdl beat me to it. S'okay. He's a nice guy. As rivals go.

Sure enough, I walk in, and Katy Riley is leaning on the bar, in confab with Fnüdl. He's in his usual seat at the bar. I take my equally usual seat, two stools to his right. On my right, one seat away is Buck. He's grumbling over his soup.

"Brad!" Katy Riley greets me with her usual show of false enthusiasm.

"Hey Brad," Fnüdl says. Tip of my pretend hat to him.

"Brmmmp," Buck growls.

"Whaddaya having today?" Katy says.

"Anything new and exciting?"

Katy Riley points to the cruvinet, "Just got in this Tennat, big monster red."

"Tennat?"

"Yeah, southern France. Usually a blending grape, kinda along the lines of a, ummm, what is it?" She glances over at Fnüdl.

"You were doing so well…."

"O shut up…I'm trying."

"Mourvedre…."

"Yeah, whatever he said."

"Is that what you're having?" to Fnüdl.

"Yeah. It's a huge tannic thing. Strip the tartar right off your teeth."

"I'll give it a shot."

"Wanna taste first?"

"No, let's just go for it." She pours me the full glass. Always a little bigger pour for regulars.

"Having lunch today, baby?"

"No, thanks. Had a huge breakfast."

"Okay…" I'm just about to ask her about the dove, when she races around the bar to a new table, where Darryl, the contractor, is in serious discussion with a gent I don't recognize. Client? Potential client? Boss? Dunno. I do know he has a thing for Katy Riley. But I think he's married. I was at Starbucks with the kids a while back, and he walked in with his wife, and a teen-age girl. I assumed wife/daughter, but who knows, coulda been a date and her daughter. Darryl made a point of not making eye contact with me. Whatever. Katy laughs and chats it up with Darryl, then she's back behind the bar whipping up a coffee drink, pouring ice tea. She rushes the drinks to Darryl and his friend.

Then Ben comes in with his son. Don't often see Ben for lunch. They sit at the bar. "Ben," Katy says. "What's going on? You're early today." Ben always looks a little self-conscious, rigid. His son, whose name I don't recall, looks nothing like him. He's taller than Ben, has a broad forehead, and unruly hair. He also has a goofy smile. All in defiance of his father's visage. What's the joke about the milkman?

Too many suitors today. May never get a chance to ask Katy about the dove.

Katy, who is manic in her customer service, in front of Buck, says, "How's the onion soup?"

"Too cheesy," he grumbles.

"I'm sorry, want me to take it back?"

Buck glanced up at her, spiteful, "I'm almost done."

"I'm sorry…"

"It's fine," Buck says in way of compensation, "but the cheese is gumming up my moustache."

Both Fnüdl and I laugh. Classic Buck.

It's only minutes after noon, but already the bar is filling up. I know I'm doomed when the Cowboy mechanic comes in with an older fellow. They belly up to the bar. The older guy, I smell uncle. Why? First, he speaks to Katy Riley, as if a spokesperson for Cowboy. I didn't catch much of what he says, but I do hear Katy's reply, "I've been seeing someone…not too serious, yet."

"We had some fun when we went out," Cowboy says. "try it again some time." Not a question, the floating of a desperate idea.

Katy merely smiles and rushes off to fetch Ben his stinger, and his son a bottle of Bud.

Katy's seeing someone? Or is that a ruse? Polite way to brush off Cowboy. And why must the older fellow speak for Cowboy? Or is that a dumb question? Then it occurs to me. All the suitors are here, except for one...I say out loud to Katy, Buck, Fnüdl, and anyone within shouting distance, "I haven't seen Ozzie lately. Has he been around?"

"Probably out bombing a train station," Buck growls. He doesn't like Ozzie.

"Hasn't been in for a couple weeks," is all Katy Riley says.

Well, one less suitor.

Suddenly Katy Riley is right in front of me, smiling. "How's the wine?"

Gotta admit, "I'm not terribly fond of it. Might be good with a sizzling hangar steak." Damn, that sounds like something Fnüdl would say. "I mean it's okay," I start back-peddling, but then, I realize I got her attention for at least 2 seconds, "So what is this about the dove?" Katy suddenly lights up.

"Did you see that?"

Katy Riley doesn't often get worked up about details, but when she does, drop everything, fork, spoon, take a long sip of your beverage then sit back, relax, listen and pay attention. Because you ain't going nowhere. Captive audience. And no one gets served till she's done.

"My daughter and I get home last night, putting away groceries, she wants a snack, is running around, then stops and says, 'mommy, look.'

"It was a dove. On our back porch, just sitting there...this dove..."

"How'd you know it was a dove?" Cowboy asks.

"Just wait. Just wait. I'm going like shoosh, shoosh, fly away little birdie, but instead he comes closer to window staring at me. It didn't look hurt, or anything...Jordan said, 'Mommy, I think he wants in...' So I open the door, and this bird flutters into the house! Like he owns the place..."

"No doubt someone's pet..." Ben says.

"Just wait...so I'm trying not to freak out, Jordan's laughing, but kinda nervous. Suddenly he flies up and lands on my shoulder...and I'm going okay, this is weird. Then he kinda nudges me, so I'm thinking maybe he's hungry, but it's not like I keep bird food lying around. Then I remember, my friend Patti, works for PetGo. So I call her, this bird on my shoulder! Fortunately she was working, and she's says, 'yeah, no doubt the bird is domesticated, obviously someone's pet,'" Katy points at Ben, "so she tells me to bring it down to the store, they can keep it there, and see if they can find the owner. So how am I supposed to get a bird in the car? Really?! Patti says, get a stick, or wooden spoon, something sturdy for it to perch on. 'Then you should just be able to walk him out to the car. He's probably been in a car before.' OK. The only thing I could find is a spatula, and I hold the handle out, and he jumps from my shoulder onto the perch, and clings for dear life. I walk around a bit, talking to him, 'How's birdy, how's a little birdy, little birdy hungry?'

"So slowly we head out to the car, and the bird's like, 'nice ride.' Slide carefully into the car, and he flutters around and lands on the head-rest of the passenger side, and settles in, makes himself at home. I thought about putting the seat-belt on him, no, but Jordy has gone from laughing, to being really nervous, 'Mommy, I don't like this...' I'm not too happy myself. What if the bird panics, starts flying around the car, I smell an accident. But no, he behaved the whole way there, only 10 minutes. We get to the store and Patti comes out, she's got a cage, takes one look at the bird and says, 'O god what a beautiful dove.'" Points at Cowboy. "It dives right into the cage, there's food in there, and o yeah, he was hungry. We go into the store, and all the clerks are oohing and ahhing over this gorgeous dove. And Jordy's all happy again, and now she doesn't want to leave the bird. So they're going to put it on their website, and FratBook, post it on their bulletin board, and Patti said the owner's got to be frantic. Such a beautiful bird, and so smart. Probably just got a little too curious, and ended up lost and confused. 'Can't we keep him,' Jordy says. 'No, honey, he belongs to someone else, someone who really misses him right now.'"

Katy whips out her phone and gets to the pictures of the dove, and hands the phone around. Some I'd already seen on FB.

"I'll have to 'share' your post," I say.

"Everyone should, that poor baby...and imagine the owner. Well, hopefully he'll be returned to his home."

"So now you're going to get a dove?" Fnüdl says.

"No," she almost snarls. Everyone laughs. "Lessee, Ben you need another one?"

"Yeah…and him too," he points to his grinning son.

"Amazing…" I say and am about to introduce my own compelling, for opposite reasons, story of the hawk crashing into my window. Sans photos. But before…

Ben says, "He didn't nip you or Jordy, did he?"

"The dove?" Katy Riley says incredulous. "No."

"You never know, even a highly domesticated bird might be carrying some infectious virus…"

"No, no nipping," Katy says, almost offended.

Trying to salvage some respectability, "I ask, because there was a noted ornithologist, he was a longtime caretaker of owls at the Nature Museum. One day he was feeding an owl and it took a little nip out of his thumb. From that little nip he contracted a rare neurological disease…and eventually died from it…so, you never know."

"No, no nipping."

Then Katy wheeled out to wait on all the customers she'd been ignoring, while Ben is saying to his son "…Well, I'm, just saying, you never know…" Odd bird, that Ben.

Katy returns to me, points at my glass, "You don't like it, do you?"

"No."

"Wanna go back to Syrah?"

"Yeah, is that okay?"

"Of course," she took away my Tennat, dumped it out. Poured me my favorite California Syrah. I can see Fnüdl, peripherally, smiling. Enjoying my discontent.

"I don't blame you," he says, noting my noting of him, "it's a tough bugger to cozy up to."

My encounter with the hawk and its relationship to the dove is receding further from possibility, as Bill, the carpenter, bellies up to the bar. Bill's a talker. He's one of those guys, no matter what the subject, he's got an opinion, and usually a story to go with it. The gap is closing –between Fnüdl, Ben, Cowboy, Bill, Darryl, there is no way to slip through the cracks. The hawk will have to bide his time.

Buck in the meantime is wiping the cheese from his mustache, "I'll be tasting that for a week."

Katy Riley is her usual whirlwind of activity, waiting on everyone seemingly at once, chatting, smiling, laughing, in fact, I don't think she could stop. And everyone wants a piece of her. As she's handing Ben his plate of duck salad, he says, "Have you had any resolution with your landlord?" Just a little too much concern in his voice.

"Not yet," she smiles and whizzes away.

"How's that beater of yours running," Cowboy says.

"Great," she lies. It's been sitting in the parking lot for three days because she can't afford a distributor cap. Borrowed her mother's car.

"Should be needin' a tune-up pretty soon. Just lemme know, we can work out a deal."

Katy Riley, ever diplomatic, says, "Okay."

Bill's describing his latest roofing job to Buck, or Katy, or maybe to the rafters. Bill just keeps talking.

I glance at Buck, the grumpiness is rising like steam off a sizzling griddle. He finally gets up, moseys, little shrapnel in the leg, we're never sure if he's joking. He pats me on the shoulder, then sidles up to Fnüdl. "Getting too crowded around here. Too much noise, I'm leaving."

"So, what're you up to today?" Fnüdl asks.

"Well, unless my wife finds me, nothing. She's always got something for me to do…mow the lawn, trim the hedges, clean out the gutters. If I can hold out long enough, her son comes over, let him do it…" Buck chuckles at this. Then says "think I'll just hop on that bike out there, and peddle myself home." Fnüdl's rickshaw. Actually a big bike with a carriage on back.

"Well, you'll have to pick up my daughter, then."

Buck waves his hand, "Forget it," chuckling, then, "Ya'll be good, now, hear?" he limps out the door.

"You pick up your daughter on that thing?" I say.

"No, no, I do actually own a car…but I have to get home in time to go pick her up."

"Is that that Bulgarian thing with a burlap roof?" I ask. He told me once about test-driving it, how it ran on wind and will-power.

"No, it's the Protean 3, electric hybrid."

Then Cowboy, who's been listening with a snarky grin says, "You see my F-150 out there, better for the environment than those hybrids."

Fnüdl's jaw drops, "What're you talking about?"

"Seriously, check it out, everyone says the F-150 is better for the environment."

"I don't know what car mags you've been reading...but that's BS." Fnüdl snaps, and you can sense every sphincter around the bar tighten.

Cowboy sits there, mouth agape, eyes narrowing, "No, look it up, all the studies show it's better for the environment than that Protean..."

Fnüdl laughs derisively, "The Protean is zero emissions, is your F-15? And don't even talk to me about emissions, just gas mileage alone, what you're burning up in that beast is 10 times more toxic."

"I'm saying if you take into consideration everything, y'know, shipping them over from Japan..."

"Sorry, pal, the Protean is made in America."

"...but I bet you the parts are made overseas...if you take into consideration..."

Fnüdl shakes his head, laughing sardonically, "I don't know where you're getting this information..."

Cowboy's uncle, intervened, "No, need...no need to get... y'know, no reason to be so..."

Fnüdl is getting more disgusted by the second, "Well, I sleep well at night knowing I'm not burning holes in the ozone. Can you say that about your F-15?"

"It's actually an F-150."

"I know what it is, it's an F-15 on four wheels."

"Hey look, there's no reason to get personal..."

"You're right," Fnüdl nods, thoughtfully, "you're absolutely right." He returns to his salad. "Enjoy your lunch." He picks up his wine glass and takes a fair engaging sip, then gently sets it back down with a pleasurable, if smug, look on his face. Discussion over.

I've never heard silence before. Not like this silence. It was bruising. Big chunk of nothing drops among us. Everyone's looking down at their plates. I twiddle my glass. Gotta admit, Fnüdl may be my rival for Katy Riley's attention, but he's got *cahones* to spare.

Cowboy and his uncle chew relentlessly on overdone steaks, heads down, chat quietly with each other. Ben looks as if he's scared to move. Might touch off another avalanche. Bill says this roofing job was more complicated than it needed to be. And he can't sub-contract it out, all he'd do is lose money.

And Fnüdl, unperturbed, scratches away in his notebook. Sipping his wine. I don't know that any of us (maybe Katy Riley?) have seen this side of him. What got him so riled up? That Cowboy once dated Katy Riley? Hmmm, could be. It is kinda funny seeing Cowboy put in his place. For her part, Katy Riley is running around waiting on tables, chats it up with customers, 'everything's fine folks, no worries.'

After a very short and quiet while, Cowboy and his uncle ask for the check. Uncle pays. As Katy Riley plops down the change, Cowboy says, "Need some work done on the car, let me know."

Katy Riley whispers something, and Cowboy and Uncle slink out the door.

She waits a respectable nano-second then turns and leans on the bar in front of Fnüdl, "So this is how you treat my customers..."

"Sorry," he says, "you don't say shit like that to me, and think you're gonna get away with it."

Katy Riley shakes her head and walks away.

Bill, god love him, continues to ramble, housing market hasn't hurt his business any...

Everyone else around the bar is a little shell-shocked. Ben is sitting so bolt upright we may have to pry him off the seat. His son, who seems to be an amiable sort, quietly sips his Bud.

Katy Riley who'd been running around trying to assuage customers, and make sure everyone was okay, was back in position in the horseshoe shaped bar, "Everyone having fun?" assuming this was meant as a tension breaker, we all laugh, or at least pretend to.

I'm trying to decide how to diffuse, distract, or otherwise ease the tension, and handed the moment, I blurt out, "I had a hawk crash into my window this morning..."

There was like this beautiful groggy, somnambulant, subconscious, dreamy, cognizance, and everyone looks at me...and though no one specifically said it, the word 'Huh?!' floats up like a thought-balloon in a comic strip.

"I was reading the paper, that story of the Funicular Project, in fact, you were quoted in it, Fynn."

"Probably mis-quoted," he says.

"Reading the paper, coffee, sun shining, when all of sudden...WHAM! This enormous hawk flew into the bay window. I think it was a red-tail hawk, banged into the window, fell into a chair, outside, and was staggering around, shaking his head, and then, he got on his feet, kinda shuttered, and woozily flew off. I'm standing there, and I can't process this, a hawk crashing into my window. I just...I just..."

"Wow," Ben's son says, "an English major's dream come true..."

Huh?

"A hawk. A dove?"

"That's just it," I say excitedly, "soon as I finished reading the paper, I go online, and I see Katy Riley's pictures of the dove on FratBook, and, I'm like, omigod..."

"Beautiful imagery," Fnüdl says, "an artist would kill to have a powerful image like that that drop in his lap."

"I don't know about that," I shrug, "but, afterwards I went out and looked at the chair where he'd fallen, and there was a dead mouse, the hawk was probably carrying it when it flew into the window..."

"Ah-hah!" Fnüdl laughs. "Another distracted driver incident. He wasn't texting, was he?"

"Just checking his email," Ben's son says.

"Y'know," Fnüdl says, "it wouldn't work at all if it were the other way around, a dove crashing into a window, and a hawk on Katy Riley's spatula. Lousy imagery."

"Hey leave my dove alone." Katy Riley says.

"Thought you said you didn't want a dove," I remind her.

"Yeah, but you don't have to make him crash into a window."

Fnüdl laughs, stands, slips a twenty on the bar, "Well, all this real-life imagery is making my head spin, besides, I gotta get home in time to pick up Sallie Sue."

Scooping up the bill, Katy Riley says, "Seeya, o, and hey, thanks for cheering everyone up."

"No problem," he says, smiling broadly, "that's my job."

We all nod or mumble g'bye, as Fynn departs. Once he's out the door I say to Katy Riley, "Are you okay?"

"Yeah, why?"

"Fynn was a little rough on...on...your friend."

"He's a big boy."

I pause, "So what's this I hear, you're seeing someone?"

Katy Riley gets that duplicitous smile, "Maybe. I don't know. We'll see."

I try to read behind the smile, the elusive words, the sparkling eyes, "You're not sure?" I say, as sarcastically as possible.

"We'll see," then she flits off to get Ben & Son their dessert.

So is Katy seeing someone? If so, who? Certainly, not Cowboy. Ben? Bill? Darryl? Fynn? Or, is she putting me off? Or putting me on? Or maybe I'm the 'maybe.' What if she's asking me to ask her out? Shouldn't I oblige?

"So," Katy Riley leaning on the bar, smiling at me, her long bangs dabbling above her eyebrows, sometimes intermingling, with her bright blue/green eyes, "...what about you, are you seeing anyone?"

Taken aback, I say, "Maybe. Could...could...be."

Katy Riley pouted, "Maybe, could be...sounds like some kinda date to me..."

"Katy..."

She points at my glass, "Having another?"

"No, better not." Dammit. Gotta get home to greet the kids. Back to real life. Besides can't ask her out with all these rivals around.

"Well, if you are seeing someone, maybe we could double date..." being a smart ass. I think.

I pay for the Syrah, leave a healthy tip.

Driving north on the freeway. Lost in a muddle of thought.

A diverted hawk crashes into a window. A lost dove perches on a spatula.

I fly home on wings I don't understand.

The Hawk. The Dove.

Buck

Only once did Brad von Easley ask Buck about his limp. It was a miserable rainy day. Buck, who had been complaining bitterly about his leg, struggled off the bar stool, and was on his way out, having gotten 'everything going in the right direction,' when Brad had the temerity to ask after the limp. Buck leaned an elbow on Brad's shoulder, squinted, winced in pain, and said, "Shrapnel, Beirut." Then he let loose one of his patented grim chuckles, patted Brad on the shoulder and straggled out of Bistro Bon Bon.

Buck wasn't much to elaborate on what may have been a rather interesting, if not sinister, or sordid, secretive past. O, he would drop snippets, like confetti fluttering over a parade. Katy Riley was clearly privy to much more of Buck's details, but she herself was as secretive about it as he. That's what you call friendship.

So Brad was left with snippets. He pieced together the wafting confetti into a really bad tapestry, too many threads dangling, in case he ever wanted to write a biography of Buck: Here's what is known; Roswell, late 1950s into early '60s, Vietnam War, at least two tours of duty, something vague about minuteman missiles, DOD, Australia, missions in Beirut, Nicaragua, Philippines, maybe Iraq, Serbia, Syria. With side adventures in parts unknown, unnamed, or unshared.

After Roswell and Vietnam, or maybe there was a transition phase, or overlapping, Buck officially became a 'diplomat', or agent of the DOD. Apparently (and one must always say 'apparently' in discussing Buck's history), the soldier blended into the diplomat, agent to soldier, to the degree there was little distinction between the two. To complicate matters, the DOD was just an umbrella, and the agency he really worked for was the Company. He never referred to it by its true name, it was just the Company.

The regulars around the bar, especially he and Fnüdl, tried all sorts of insinuations, tricks, and wild-ass guessing to get Buck to open up about his life in the Company. But Buck was elusive, at best. Contemptuous, at his most snarky. Fnüdl tried the direct approach once, asking him about his 'work' in Beirut. Buck shot him a withering glance, and said, "If I told you, I'd have to kill you." Followed by the grim chuckle.

The grim chuckle was Buck's singular calling card. It's meaning and intent changed with the ambient chatter. It could mean 'shut up,' or 'just having a little fun with you,' or even 'None of your damn business.' Whatever it was, it signaled the end of that segment. The conversation will resume after we return from this commercial break. For instance, one night the bartender, Doc, was recounting a recent hunting trip where he bagged an elk. He was about to offer some amusing tidbit about the whole affair when Buck interjected, "Funny thing, the sound of a bullet hitting an animal, is the same as a bullet hitting a body…bmp…bmp…bmp…" Grim chuckle. Doc returned to mixing his Moscow Mule.

Another time, the bar was full of lunchtime regulars, Buck, while adding ketchup to his prime rib sandwich, getting it good and gooey, mused almost wistfully about a little incident. He and his buddies were gathering bodies from a roadside explosion. Some bodies were whole, some in bits and pieces. He described effortlessly the scene of splattered blood and grime, wading through the guck, and then right in the middle of their task, they stopped… lunchtime! They wiped off their hands, sat down and ate beef sandwiches. The locals were alarmed and horrified, "Women were crying," Buck said, "their face on the ground. One guy even threw up. What did they expect? It was lunch time!" Grim chuckle.

This presumably was Beirut, but could as easily have been Viet Nam or Serbo-Croatia. No one asked, and no one had ketchup with their lunch.

Then there was the Australian stint. Alice Springs. Middle of the desert. Buck only gave up that information laterally. Fnüdl, was talking about duck, for whatever reason, and Buck snarled, "I hate duck, it's so greasy,"

"Not if you cook it right," Fnüdl said, "you gotta render the fat."

"Only time I had it, it was swimming in grease."

146

"Well, Buck, you're just gonna have to come over and have dinner sometime…and where in the world did you have duck that was swimming in grease?"

"Alice Springs," Buck griped, "us Yanks had our own mess hall, and every day, one of those trays was filled with this awful stuff floating around in grease…duck. I never ate it since."

"I'm surprised," Fnüdl said, "I thought the Aussies if anyone would know how to cook duck…"

"Wo, wo wait a minute," Brad said, "Alice What? Australia?"

"Alice Springs, right in the middle of the desert, nearest city was about 70 kilometers away."

"So you were forced to eat greasy duck?"

"That or starve…"

"And what were you doing in Australia?" There were very few moments when Buck seemed ready to open up, and Brad felt he had to pounce on every opportunity.

"Staring at radar screens all day. If the Rooskies or Chinese sent up a missile we had our eyeballs on it all the way…we recorded it, and reported it. Tedious stuff."

"When was this?"

"Lessee, after Viet Nam and before Beirut…70s." Buck was in a chipper mood that day, and went on, "There was only one bar on base, and I'll tell you, don't ever try outdrink an Aussie…they'll put you under the table. What a wild time, I told you it was only bar on base, hell the only bar within 70 kilometers, and just about everyone was there getting looped just every night. Then about once a month some sweet little gals from the city would come in, and whooop-ee! That was wild. Little young missy comes up to you, 'buy me a drink,' next thing you know you're in the back room humping, then ten minutes later you're back at the bar, while she's off hustling another guy."

Seems as though much of Buck's escapades had more to do with sex, or at least lusciousness, than intel.

Of Polynesia he said, "Walked off the plane, first thing I saw, all these topless gals just walking around going about their business… all ages! and 1 don't mean just bare breasts, I mean, they were… were…" not being able to think of the appropriate superlative, Buck just shook his head.

Polynesia was furlough. He returned several times.

147

There were drive-by mentions of dropping out of planes into the jungle in the middle of the night, probably Viet Nam, maybe Nicaragua.

No fond memories, just tedium, blood, and espionage. He said the most boring time of his life in the Company, was running messages, or whatever it was, flying back and forth between Tokyo and North Dakota so frequently he rarely knew what day it was. He had to wear two watches so he'd know the time of whichever day it was. Mostly he remembered an attaché case, which he was under strict orders not to open, nor let anyone touch. Cargo planes shuttled him back forth, his seat was among, well, the cargo. Sometimes he would share the ride with others on similar unknowable missions, and that's when hooch began to flow. Propped up against crates waiting for the landing gear to go clunk, they'd get nasty drunk. Even then he clung to that attaché case, for whatever was in it was deadly. Or so he assumed. Maybe it was just a change of undies for his supervisor. All he knew for sure is it won him a free-pass through customs. Hold up his special passport, and he was waved through. The supervisor waited in a car for him outside the airport, took the attaché case, and was gone without a word being uttered.

He did admittedly get the heebie-jeebies every now again, if he thought too much about it. Hence, the hooch.

Of active duty, that was pretty much Buck's story, at least from what could be gleaned by the regulars. Fnüdl once suggested he should write his memoirs (perhaps with his help -ghostwriter in the sky?). Buck just shook his head, "Why would anyone want to read that?"

Brad asked when he retired from the DOD. Buck grumbled, "You don't retire from the DOD."

Civilian life was a different matter. Retired, after about thirty years in a private firm buying and selling packaging material. After the service, Buck was just a typical suburban rube. He was more than happy to talk about his wife of twenty-five years. Even though she never accompanied him to Three Bs, some people have actually laid years on her. Katy Riley says she's cute as a button. Giggles a lot, shy but talkative. She's a Master Gardener, which ticks off Buck, "I told her, I ain't pulling no damn weeds." He obviously cherishes her, she's a saint, mostly for putting up with him. She has two sons from a previous marriage. One lives locally, married with kids (whom Buck dismisses as 'critters; and avoids as much as possible. "They know enough to get out of my way when I'm in the room...I ain't nobody's grandpa." Yes, grim chuckle. The other son is a teacher in Vermont. Married, no critters yet. None of these people had names, by the way.

Buck has two siblings. One a sister, Sandra, who occasionally joins him at Three Bs, along with her husband, Dave, one happy gent who, though squarely in Buck's demographic, is lean and fit, and could probably bench-press the whole bar. And the son, Scott, did a lot of yard work that Buck cannot, or refuses, to do.

If Katy, Brad and Fynn were discussing their kids with affection and pride, as they often did, Buck would break in with a counter-punch, "Treat your kids like little wimpy spoiled brats, that's what you'll get. Just lucky they didn't have my parents..." An old story, often repeated, not for enlightenment, but disputation. Buck's father was ramrod strict. Whupping stick, you will obey Marshall law, no talking at the dinner table, and no dinner unless your chores are done. A bloodless tyrant, carved of granite and shale, unyielding, unloving, unfair. Buck was the youngest of the three. They were given a bath once a week, in the same tub of water, and he, being the youngest, went last, splashing around in lukewarm to cold dirty water.

That was Buck's childhood. Apparently. Was he resentful, envious of these new parents and their pampered, wussy kids? O, you betcha!

Buck's favorite father anecdote, "The day I turned 18, I walked out the door," he says, then warming up his grim chuckle, "and my father had my suitcase sitting, packed, on the front porch. 'Come back and visit some time,' The father said.

Buck joined the Navy.

Buck only had two true loves in his life. His wife. And the Duchess. Of his wife he spoke often with teasing affection. But the reverence, awe, afforded the Duchess, lifted him to an eloquence and spiritual plane that was unparalleled. The first he mentioned the Duchess to Brad von Easley was in reference to Roswell, and he literally heaved a sigh, with eyes distant and moist, "She was the most beautiful thing I'd ever seen," he said, "sleek, elegant, perfectly gentle curves, soft as silk, and fast? She topped out at Mach 3." It was only then that Brad realized we weren't discussing a woman. The Duchess was in fact a plane, the SR-71.

While Buck could talk his head off about the Duchess, Brad did a little research, and found the Duchess was a spy plane, of the SR-71 family. One version was built for reconnaissance missions over China and Viet Nam, efficient and reliable. But, oh, the Duchess. Brad could find no reference to the plane ever being called the Duchess, so obviously it was Buck and his buddy-crew that bestowed that name on her. Specifically modified as spy plane, the Duchess had a one-seat cockpit, for the pilot. She was coated with 'Stealth' material, and curved to deflect radar. She was the invisible invader. Silent, efficient. And gorgeous.

"A Russian defector told us," Buck said, "only once did they try firing missiles at the Duchess, but she was gone before the missiles ever got in the air. She's in, out, and boom, gone. Three thousand miles an hour. She was listed at Mach 2. Bullshit, Mach 3, easily. God, she was thing of beauty."

And photos it took? "You could see the pimple on a Rooskie's butt," Buck said. "We learned more from the photos she brought back than all the spies in the US put together."

The only time an SR-71 spy plane was downed, was due to mechanical problems over Russia. Bad luck. Unlike the U2 spy plane shot down by the Russians, no missile could take down the Duchess.

It fell to the buddy-crew, which numbered close to one hundred, on the ground, to prepare the Duchess for flight. Buck must have been one of the more romantic in his maintenance and protection of the Duchess. He only once got to sit in the cockpit, whether he snuck in or was allowed, he never did say. But sitting there, playing pilot, behind the controls, knowing what this baby can do, and had done…it was nothing short of a rapturous experience.

Of Roswell, Buck would always say, "No, I never saw no aliens, unless they were the illegal kind, trying to sneak into Area 51. Couple shots over their head usually encouraged them to scamper off. If that didn't work, we aimed a little lower."

Roswell was the Duchess's landing and resting place. Like the Duchess she was, stretched out on a divan, eating grapes, and fanning herself. It was easy to visualize Buck walking alongside her, running his hand over her subtle curves, dreaming of all her conflicting charms.

The retirement of the SR-71s is still a topic of contentious debate. Politics, big business, government contracts, etc., all forced her to the ground. Buck still gets incensed, insisting she could today outrun, and outperform, any plane they tried to replace her with. She was a species unto herself.

There are a number of the old spy planes in various museums across the country, one about a two-hour drive from Haven.

"You ever been?" Brad asked him once.

Buck sighed, "Nah." Maybe, like an old love, why agitate old memories, best to remember her as he did. Lounging in the hanger, her enticingly gentle curves. No, didn't want to reawaken those memories.

Buck's final unsettling anecdote concerning the Duchess. At some point it was decided to lodge a number of the planes closer to their targets, in the Philippines. Buck and the buddy-crew were called upon to go in advance to "Curtail the indigenous personnel," of the chosen island. 'Curtail the indigenous population?' Brad had to ask. Buck in reply, flicked a flea off his shoulder. 'Okay, I get it.'

Brad could only hope 'curtail' didn't mean…curtains.

The lunchtime crowd at the bar of ThreeBs, mostly guys, there to fawn over and be fawned upon by Katy Riley, occasionally got so crowded, imbibers had to roam free-range around the not-so-spacious bar area. It was one of those days, an elevated decibel level, lots of laughter, a bartender, running around sweating, but with tip-dollars floating in her eyes, when suddenly an invisible, stealth figure, elbowed through the crowd and squeezed in right next to Buck.

Slightly startled, he turned to see this smallish lady, dressed in alarming gaudy shawls, head bands, her wrists draped with cheap jewelry, wearing bright lipstick. Buck looked at her with casual disdain for violating his airspace, and was about to ask her what the hell she wanted, when the lady launched into a tirade, "That's it, I had it with you, buddy," she shrieked, "this isn't the first time, but it's gonna be the last, you may think you've gotten rid of me, but I'm getting rid of you, I'm not taking any more crap from you. I deserve better! Don't ever come near me…ever again! And here, a little gift for you, I hope it ends up in a fire pit along with your rotten soul. And it's the last thing you'll ever get from me, you sonuvatbitch!" She slapped something onto the bar in front of Buck, turned and in a mist of anger, confusion, and displacement, was gone.

Time froze. If an artist were amongst the hangers-out, she could easily have sketched the scene, taking her sweet time, as not a movement was made by anyone. Stunned.

Katy Riley was literally frozen in place while handing a plate of sausage and sauerkraut to Jim and Margie, like a still life, her mouth

151

agape, her eyes a steady stare. But it was she who was the first to break the spell, she finally set the plate down, so that Jim and Margie wouldn't starve, and said what everyone was thinking, "What the hell?"

No one looked more freaked out than Buck. Like he'd been slapped silly by an underworld troll, unblinking eyes, mouth open, his hand holding the fork, still life. But maybe it was Bill who finally found speech and said, directly to Buck, "What was that all about?"

"I...I don't know," Buck gasped. "I've never seen her before in my life."

A snicker sputtered through the bar area, giggles, and back and forth glances started, 'O right! Never saw her before in my life?'

"Does your wife know about her?" Cowboy asked.

"I swear...I swear, I've never seen her before."

Fynn offered an explanation, "Maybe you just got punked."

"That would actually be kinda cool," Workout Guy said, "walk into a crowded bar, randomly pick out someone, and start screaming bizarre nonsense in their face, then poof, gone. Look around, is there a camera capturing all of this..."

Some customers actually scanned the rafters checking for cell phones. "This is gonna look great on YouTube," Jim said.

Katy Riley was the only with the presence of mind to pick up the item that had been so ceremoniously slapped on the bar. It was a tiny notebook, brown, fairly beat up.

"What is it?" Brad von Easley asked.

Katy Riley flipped to a page, read aloud, "Roswell, 1959," turned the page, "Saigon, 1971," next page, "Hanoi, 1975, Beirut, 1982...Granada, 1984...El Salvador, 1987...Lebanon, 1990, Bosnia, 1994...are these all places you were...involved in?"

Buck nodded, "Except Bosnia, that was 1995..."

"Who is she?" Katy Riley asked, now showing some concern herself.

"I don't know...." Buck paused, and looked behind him, in the wake of the whirling dervish, and said gloomily, "But I think I'm a marked man."

And it was not followed by his trademark chuckle.

She's All That

Fynn Fnüdl

Nice bowl-cut, babe. Razor-sharp bangs, a clear and precise crease in a straight line around the back of her head, from ear to ear. Hair fiercely dyed an ebony hue, as shiny as C-Sharp on a Hammond B-3. Light is absorbed and killed in that coif. She seems a bit self-conscious, sipping her white wine. She's waiting for her boyfriend.

On her cellphone. The boyfriend is late. She's chiding him, 'hurry up.'

Now she's texting him, 'bastard, where r u, ther's this guy at the bar staring at me in the mirror, as if I cant tell.'

In defiance of all things irrational, she stares wistfully out the window, onto the fjord-like River Yrvl. A placid day, a rancid barge tramples the sheen of verdant azure stillness.

She texts her boyfriend again, 'Where r u? Bastard keeps staring at me like he's drawing a portrait of me or something. Creeping me out. Hurry up!'

Small mouth, lush lips, little too much red neon lipstick, pale –almost too pale-skin, accentuated by the ebony hair and page-boy bangs and lipstick. Pensive. She holds the wine glass by the stem. Must know something about wine. Novices crib the bowl in their fat sweaty hands. Her hands seem quite delicate, if not petite. And holds her glass with an elegant tilt. She's been in a tasting room or two. Maybe her boyfriend is a wine geek.

She looks around frantically as Erin, the night manager, enters. Sorry babe, he's not yr boyfriend.

'Where is he?' She tries to appear calm.

She's All That

Wait...he's talking to the manager...about me? 'Do you know her, is she single?' O hmm, seems to be a regular here, as everyone, hostess, waitresses and waiters stop by say hello to him. The bartender has been cozying up to him. Leaning over the bar, whispering, smiling at him in such a way...is she his girlfriend? Are they having an affair? The manager talks to him for quite a while. Someone important? He's got the contagion, for sure. Hmm. Another waitress passes by, "Hey, Fynn..." his name is Fynn.

The manager excuses himself. Fynn checks me out in the mirror, fleetingly, barely catch him at it...the tiny, young hostess sneaks behind him, taps him on the shoulder. Sits next to him, they chat softly. What, is he having an affair with everyone in the restaurant? She leaves. Fynn does not glance up at the mirror.

More than likely some loser barfly with nowhere else to go. But here, by golly, he is Lord of the Drinks! A toast to pathetic loneliness. At least he's drinking wine. Hmm, swirls, sniffs, sips. Is he just being pretentious?

The bartender is talking to him again. Whatever is going on, they are intimate.

Are they talking about me? Whatsamatter with me? Maybe it's this haircut. Doggonit, I told Stephanie it was too extreme for me. But o no, 'you can handle this look.' That's why he's staring at me. Stupid coif. Going back to Stephanie, 'chop it all off and start over.' Why do I listen to people? My skin's too pale for jet black hair.

Finally here...

FF

O wait, not a boyfriend at all, a lady friend. She finely shows up. She's the 'contrast' girlfriend. 'I'm attractive, hip, sharp dresser, Xtreme haircut, and so I pair with a friend who is overweight, sloppy dresser, unkempt hair, glasses sliding down her nose. Backdrop, foreground.

154

"Omigod, yr hair, I love it!" Contrast fairly shouts.

She's All That looks pained, "I don't know…"

"You don't like? I love it…it's so you. I mean, you –we all, need a change."

Katy Riley takes her time before going over to take the Contrast's order. But first Contrast asks She's All That, "What're you having?"

"Pinot Grigio," she says, "It's good." She glances my way. I'm having red wine.

"Naw, I think I better just have ice tea." Contrast settles in, plops her big fat billowy purse on the stool beside her, fluffs her hair, wiggles her butt, looks my way…smiles. I smile back. 21st century greeting.

I think She's All That is regretting sitting so close to another patron at the bar. Her voice is somewhere between a whisper and that of a chastising boss. I have the funny feeling she's used to being looked at…and why not?

Contrast blurts out, "Well I told you…"

"What?"

"He's back."

"O lord."

"I know, it was the ole 'I can't live without you' BS, but he seems to mean it…"

"So far."

"I know…what am I to do? He comes crawling back on his belly, apologizes for everything, treats me like Queen for a Day…and he took me to the hockey game last night!"

She's All That is having none of this, she can scarcely conceal her contempt. So she tries the dodge…

"How's work?"

"Ah jeez, I told you about my review…?"

"Yeah."

"So now I'm walking on thin ice, I can't afford to lose my job, much as I hate it, this ice tea is weird, are you gonna eat?"

"No…"

"So I'm wearing myself out smiling all the time and trying to make everyone happy, and then today a client comes in demands to talk to Mr. Big, and I say he's in a meeting and the guy's head is about to explode. Sorry, I was told, 'I'm in a meeting, no interruptions,' and so here I am trying to diffuse a bomb, as really, this client is ready to go ballistic on me, he's some big-shot contractor around here, housing developments, and he thinks he owns the county, but I was told, Mr. Big cannot be disturbed, and so here I am ready to lose my job, and this client is furious with me, and I'm saying like look, 'It's not my deal, Mr. Big specifically said...' and he's ready to go off on me, when thank god, Mr. Big comes out of his ofice, and rushes over to make lovey dovey with Mr. Self-Important, and Mr. Big gives me a glance, and I'm ready to pack my desk and go...but very cool, after it was all over, boss-man comes over and apologizes for the idiot's behavior and said I did the right thing, and I'm like 'Yes!' I live to fight another day. So I don't know, I feel like I'm doing my job, yeah, I'm not gung-ho, and it's obvious I ain't going anywhere in this job, but it pays okay, and seriously, I CANNOT afford to lose it, jeez being unemployed right now, can you even imagine. You gonna have another?"

"Sure."

Katy Riley overhears this, but waits a few moments. Steps over to them, "Another Pinot Grigio?"

"Please."

To Contrast, "More ice tea?"

"Uh, yeah."

SAT

O Yeah, he's having an affair with the bartender. She's all over him. While pouring Connie's ice tea he watches her like he's reminiscing about being inside her. Then his eyes drift up to me. Then Connie. What does he think, He's All That?

Connie's had a tough day. Work. Ex-boyfriend creeping back into the picture. But I'm all sympathetic. Yeah, he's a clod, but he does like you, a lot. And so, he's a dope, all guys are dopes.

She got off early and wanted to stop for a drink and chat. With Connie that's usually a bad sign. But, what're friends for, other than to play doormat. She relates her woes with hi-hilarity, like, 'ain't this all a

156

grand joke? And aren't I the best punch line?' Well, I won't say it, but it's one of those, 'sister, you made your bed, now…'

The line of conversation –or is it a circle, Mobius Strip, fractal algorithm?- wends its way through various health issues, mother-daughter dysfunction, car problems, TV shows -she gets a little too intense about reality shows, as if she's competing for a million dollars -and like a snake gnawing on its tail, back to her ex. And then, as if a joke, she says, "So what's up with you?"

Me? There's a me here? Wow. Seriously?

I'm exhausted just listening to her. I have no energy to complain or explain, so I huff a sigh, and say, "Life's grand."

She laughs and we clink glasses.

I do give her a few details, love-life sucks, job's fine, mostly good, don't want to overdo it, sound like I'm bragging. I'm half way through my glass of wine, when she suddenly grabs her purse, "Well, Leo and I are going to see that new Adam Sandler movie, so I gotta run home and get all dolled up…"

She's reaching in her purse, and I say, "I got it." It's only ice tea.

After Connie disappears, I consider a face lift, and tummy-tuck, and maybe one more glass of wine.

"You okay here?" Bartender.

"I think I'll have another."

She gets my glass pronto. "I haven't seen you in a while…" she looks at me, kind of caustically.

"You remember me? Even with this awful haircut."

"What? I like it. I think it really suits you." She has a wry smile like even she disagrees with herself.

"It's not me…at all!"

"We'll, it's cute…whadda you think, Fynn?"

The barfly glances up from his notebook, which he's been slicing up with his pen, contemplating. "Cute, stylish…I can see it with a little ombré."

"O gawd, you know what ombré is?" I kinda screech.

"He's totally hip," Bartender Girlfriend says.

She goes to wait on another customer. Fynn bends his head over his notebook, and begins pen-scratching,

Feeling a wee bit self-conscious, and could always use a good pee, I slide from barstool and casually stroll into the restroom, which turns out to be the kitchen. A cook points me to the other corner. "O, you mean where it says Restroom?"

Gussy myself up in front of the mirror, yeah, baby, not so bad, put a couple pleats in the bangs, fluff it up a bit. Who knows, maybe an ombré would sassy things up. Come back here some day and see if he notices, assuming he's like always here, ("Hey, ombré, you took my advice.") Now, now girlfriend, let's not go dreaming off the deep-end.

I clamber up on the bar stool, struggling like a little kid (why are they so high?), just as the bartender and this Fynn guy are in intimate confab...

"...so you've been two-timing me," he says archly.

Bartender leans on the counter, closer to him, nods her head. "Well, I had to...he fixed my car...for free."

"Nothing is free, toots."

"Yeah, well, I felt obligated...it went okay. He's a nice guy... just...just...I felt kinda dirty. You know what I mean? I don't want to lead him on..."

"Yeah, well, now at least your car runs..."

"Sheesh, yeah. Anyway, what's up with you? You seem in a cheery mood."

"Why not, I'm going to Paris."

"That's right. When do you leave?"

"Wednesday."

"Wow. That's coming right up. And you'll be gone...?"

"Two weeks. At least."

"Is your wife going with you?"

"Ha ha."

"What am I gonna do without you?"

"Come with me."

"Right. I still haven't gotten my passport."

"Put you in the carry-on bin."

Katy laughs, shakes her head then spins out of her horseshoe confinement, and waits on a foursome that just sat down at a table by the wood pillar.

158

"Paris?" I say, not eavesdropping, just caught bits of conversation.

"Yeah."

"Business or pleasure?"

"Yes."

Haha. Funny guy.

"You been?" he says.

"Paris? Once. Same as you, business s, then pleasure." "What's the business?"

"I work for Rancoeur, the French printer."

"Printers. The bane of my existence," and then as if talking to himself, "I oughta make a list of all my banes."

"Well, they've been good to me, brought all us Americans over for a huge conference two years ago. Lavish, food, wine. Huge convention hall, somewhere on the outskirts of Paris. Then at night -parteeee."

"What kind of places did you go to?"

"I have no idea. Couple French gals took us around town, bar after bar...dancing, music. It was insane."

"Then back to work?"

"Exactly. So, what business takes you to Paris?"

"Basically, shit." He pauses. "Sort of by accident I've become the guru of waste. There's a big international conference in Paris, who knows, maybe it's the same convention hall, a big love-in for earth-huggers, like myself. Scientists, philosophers, politicians, journalists from around the globe, converge and discuss the death of our planet. Me, I'm in charge of shit."

"How does one become involved in, ummm...poop?"

"I have a small farm up in Littlefield, and I became alarmed at the amount of waste we generate. I started getting involved in using animal waste, rotting plants, and being in dairy country, cow poop, for good. Do you know you can power an entire home with enough methane given off by...cow shit?"

"Ummm, no. Okay, I'm sorry, as an engineer, I'm curious... how do you convert poop to power?"

"The technology's been around a long time, but the machinery is very rudimentary, clunky, and difficult to operate. So

159

I've partnered with a number of dairy farms in Littlefield, one big time operation in particular, and we're trying to find ways to streamline the technology, make it more user friendly, and cheaper, and more efficient...it can be done. You should be able to go to your local dairy, pick up a couple hundred pounds of shit, and power your house for, I don't know, a week. We just need the people with the technical and engineering know-how to get us where we want to be," he pauses, chuckles to himself. "We were going to call our enterprise Meth Power, and then thought better of it." He looks at me with...okay, I'm gonna say it, a sh-t-eating grin.

"I'll stick with printer boards." I say.

Bartender/Girlfriend pops up all of a sudden, "Is he demonstrating his green toilet for you?" she smiles wickedly.

"I'm way beyond that now, onto browner pastures," he says.

"Wherever he goes, talk turns to shit."

"I'm not even gonna ask, green toilet?" I say.

"You need to see it to believe it," Katy Riley says...is she being protective of her beau? Am I interrupting something here?

Now she's looking at me quizzically, "O god, I just realized," she blurts out, "her hair...even the face, a lot like your wife's."

Fynn studies me, and not just my hair, "Yeah, a little, maybe..."

"By the way, that is a compliment," Katy Riley says to me over her shoulder.

I'm starting to feel like an object. Studied, examined, considered, discussed, which could all lead to ...judgement.

She bolts out of the bar loop to some dog-whistle that lets her know customers' orders are waiting. Fynn goes back to head-down over his notebook. Scribbling. Better not be about me.

When she returns, I say to Katy Riley, because I'm not sure I'll ever get her attention again, "I'm ready for the tab."

Katy Riley nods towards Fynn, says, "He took care of it."

I tip my glass to the generous gent, "You didn't have to do that."

"Who knows, I may need an engineer to bounce ideas off some day. It's all about making connections."

"Well, it's been nice chatting with you," I stand, a bit woozy, "thank god I took the afternoon off," I say. We all laugh.

160

"Farewell."

"*A bientot*," Fynn says. French?

I walk as steadily and careful to the door as possible, and out into the brilliant sunshine.

FF

She's All Gone.

"Do you have to flirt with everyone?" Katy Riley was leaning over the bar, violating my private space.

"Just trying to make you jealous."

"It ain't working."

"Nothing seems to."

"Do you know her?"

"Of course, she's every woman, she's Ona Maria, she's you, she's my Mom, my sister, she's the moon and the stars...She's All That."

The Baron von Easley
Or; I Shoulda Turned
Left at Albuquerque

"So what's new with you, Brad?"

"Well, I just found out...I'm a baron."

Katy Riley barely flinched. She looked deeply at Brad von Easley and said, dryly, "Really? I didn't know guys could be barren."

Brad laughed, "No, no, I'm a baron. Not barren...except maybe in imagination."

"A baron?" even more quizzically.

"Yeah. A real baron."

"Hmmp..." Katy Riley raised a finger, "hang on." Spun outside the bar, and greeted a husband wife team taking a table. "Hi you guys, long time no see." She laughed, they laughed. She took their drink orders, then got busy.

The Baron von Easley sat brooding. Smiling, but in a brooding way.

Yes, he was a baron. The last of the Barons von Easley.

His great-grandfather, the true, one, only Baron von Easley emigrated from (some say 'fled') the Old Country in 1910 –or thereabouts. No sure biography of the Baron has ever come down, or to light, in part because he was a fairly shady character, and sly enough to fudge, fabricate, and finesse the facts. Especially about himself. Which cast enticing shadows on his motives, aspirations, failures, travels, and his simple whereabouts. He left no paper-trail, that's for sure. One can easily imagine the crafty immigrant, wending his way across the country, getting involved in all sorts of disreputable and vaguely illegal activities. Why, one could write a novel about what is not known.

All that is certain is that he did finally settle in Santa Fe toward the beginning of Prohibition. More than likely tried his hand at cattle ranching, trading, and various vaguely con-man schemes, but finally found his niche as the owner of a cantina in 1920, a singularly odd choice, for someone with his virtues and proclivities. Although one farfetched rumor had it that he won the cantina in card game.

The Baron, being the character he was, and the times as they were, had two wives, kept separate by some ten miles, and much subterfuge, silence, and the complicity of both families. He sired 22 children (at least that survived, and were accepted by one or the other family). The wives' names were Esmeralda and Emma. Nothing else is known of them.

If the Baron's success as restaurant/tavern owner seemed coincidence, the year of the founding of the Cantina de Tepuddl was not. Prohibition had been voted in and bootlegging became big business.

Santa Fe was still a rough and tumble town, the capital of a fledgling state, and growing haven for artists and outlaws, con men and visionaries, and all it really took for the Baron was to grease the palms of local authorities to keep his business lucrative. Just his status as Baron already bestowed upon him privilege.

It will never be known if the Baron took much lively interest in the running of cantina. The first few years it limped along as a source for booze, women, and something resembling food. It would be his children, all 22 of them, who would eventually take over the cantina, changing its name to Cantina de Tilapia, and turning it into a thriving, family-oriented dining and entertainment venue. A fish motif enlivened the façade and walls of red stone masonry. An outdoor *plaza* draped with bougainvillea and epazote, a fountain with fish flicking about, and tables turned from local tree stumps, with red, green and yellow pepper-decorated umbrellas, was a favorite gathering spot. A peculiar twist gave the cantina a notoriety that spread all the way from Taos to Albuquerque. For, in a divine clustering of genetic material, all or most of the von Easley children were possessed of marvelous singing voices. Even at an early age, they would stroll among the guests, charming them with little ditties, and nursery rhyme tunes. Sometimes solo,

163

sometime in pairs, and eventually as a whole chorus. At first it was merely a novelty ('hey, look what my kid can do!') until the children grew older, developing routines, performing skits, with vaudevillian panache and giddiness. By the end of Prohibition, the cantina seemed more a theater than a place of drinks and food, and its popularity was second to none in Santa Fe.

As the Baron aged, he retired from whatever it was he had been doing, and took to being the crotchety old doorman and greeter, usually cupping a glass of local hooch. Boisterous and cantankerous, he would sit weaving stories and whoppers, adorned with lies and gossip, as customers filed in and out, often stopping to listen to the grand old geezer spew forth. He himself became a piece of entertainment. He was visited by local dignitaries, politicians, and journalists, in particular, who slobbered over his spurious reveries and recorded them in the local and not-so local papers. He was dubbed The Gatekeeper of Spit and Wisdom. Some even said the Baron was the inspiration behind Yosemite Sam. The Baron, no surprise to himself, eventually turned into the legend he had always pretended to be.

In the meantime, the children began showing as much business acumen as creating heavenly and complex harmonies. Using seed money from the Cantina, they bought up all the surrounding property, and piece by piece built a mercantile center, renting out spaces to artists, craftsmen, clothiers, butchers, and bakers. An entire block was now the hub of Santa Fe's creative and business scene, what locals called The von Easley Square, though it was never given an official name.

Georgia O'Keefe was known to take her tonic at the cantina whenever down from Taos (she would try to sing along with the kids, but it is rumored she couldn't carry a tune in a bucket), and cartoonist Chuck Jones loved the local version of schnapps, giving his Hollywood friends a bit of the down and dirty dusty world of the desert.

By time the Baron passed in 1941 or '42, the children had amassed enormous wealth, prestige, along with a diversity of interests and pleasures. A Santa Fe Cantina can't hold 22 siblings for long, and soon they began one by one branching out into other ventures. The Great von Easley diaspora was on.

Some went to squander their fortune in New York, Hollywood, London or Paris, in often well intentioned and widely imagined

164

business ventures. Others more mundanely used their wealth to maintain a lowkey lifestyle, marrying, raising their own children. A small contingency of siblings, mostly the elder of the children stayed behind to keep the Cantina and surroundings vital and profitable, and still the hub of activity.

It wasn't until the revival of all things Tepuddlian that a renewal of interest in the Baron and his legacy began. Books were written, and the von Easleys, spread across the globe, were the only source of information about the wily, mystical ex-pat, the Baron. Most of the children and their scion could care less. They were unaware or listless about their heritage, until they needed to borrow money. A few survivors did take enough interest to poke around and find out that the eldest son of the Baron, the Baron von Easley II, (AKA Scooter), was, as fate would have it, Brad von Easley's grandfather.

Grandpa had not squandered his Easley gained wealth, but instead joined the army in 1940 to fight the Nazis. For the entirety of the war he was stationed at Fort Brigadoon, roughly 5,000 miles from the nearest Nazi soldier. He became a career military man, because, after losing his chops as a singer, he really hadn't much ambition to do anything else. He married, had two children. One, Brad von Easley's father, Phil, was the oldest of the two and had dibs on the old man's money.

He used it to seek his fame and fortune in the Great Mid-North-West, first in timber, then mining, but not terribly adept at either, found he had more talent in banking. After settling down in Haven, he made a modest success of himself. He married, had the required two children (a von Easley trait after the Baron). Upon his retirement he took on two partners and started a winery, spending the last nickel of the old man's money. The winery endured for five years, then it was sold at a break-even loss to a conglomerate California wine distributor.

Brad knew little of his uncles, aunts, cousins, grandparents, great and not so great, spread around the world. The most recent contact he had had from anyone in the family tree was on the occasion of his grandmother's 88th birthday fete, which was some ten years ago, and held at the Cantina de Tilapia. Brad received an uninspired invitation to the party, and to this day regrets he did not attend.

To say the least, therefore, Brad was astonished to find not only was he the last male in the von Easley clan, but that he had inherited a Baronship.

Brad was slapped from this brooding reverie, by a flat-hand to his right shoulder.

"Brad! How are you?"

It was Ozzie. One of the many rivals for the considerations of Katy Riley. Who herself had finally returned from running around waiting on the dozens of people clamoring for her attention. She was now standing in front of the Baron von Easley and Ozzie, smiling her heartless smile, "He's a baron...don't you know." She said whimsically.

Ozzie stepped back in deference, "Indeed? A baron? I am among royalty?"

"I've never met a baron before," Katy Riley said, "do we bow?"

Brad von Easley was beginning to rethink his approach to announcing his new title.

"How did you just suddenly become a baron...did you win a contest?" Katy Riley, finding much amusement in the situation, said.

He tried to explain the Tepuddlian connection, the old baron, the revival of historical archives in the lost country of Tepuddle (now defunct, with its fragmented remains subsumed by surrounding countries) and the tracking down of the baron's family, trying first to decide which of the two Santa Fe families was the most legitimate, none of which he knew squat about, until two days ago, when he received a packet of papers (FedUp) declaring he was the Baron von Easley.

"Did they ask you to send money?" Katy said, still grinning.

"No, I thought that too, it's a scam, but later I got a call from the attorney representing the von Easley empire, and it was legit. I am officially the Baron von Easley."

"Baron, hey...honey, did you need anything to eat?" to Ozzie.

"What's the sandwich of the day?"

"The Weenie Panini, a spicy sausage on a bun with pesto."

"I'll take it, with the side of beet goat cheese salad."

"With Funny Fnüdl's arugula?"

"If I must."

Katy Riley looked down at her phone and smiled.

166

"Fnüdl on his way?" the Baron von Easley said, caustically. That was his usual way of announcing his imminent arrival, by texting Katy Riley.

"No…no, he's in Paris, actually."

Ozzie cried out, "Ahh, my favorite city…what is that wastrel doing there?"

"International Climate Change Convention," Katy Riley said without a hint of facetiousness, "he's chairing a symposium on…on… wait…" she grabbed her phone, flipped through it, "it's called 'What's That Smell? Urban Leachate Management.'" She smiled.

"Fascinating," von Easley said.

"He thinks so, and…he is in Paris," she said with stark snarkiness. But always adding a smile.

"And we're not," Ozzie said sadly.

"He's having dinner right now, posting on FratBook…"

Ozzie looked at his watch, "Kinda early for dinner in Paris, it's only 9 o'clock there. Does he say where he is?"

Katy Riley glared at her phone, squinted, scratched her chin, "Our Peg, Our Peggy…" Ozzie looked baffled. She spelled It out, "A. R. P. E. G…"

"Arpege? One of the finest restaurants…in the world!" Ozzie cried.

"He posted a picture of the first course…" she held out the phone for them to see.

"Ah yes," Ozzie said, "the famous soft-boiled egg with foie gras…"

"You've eaten there?" Brad von Easley said, rather contemptuously. He was being marginalized, and didn't like it. Come on, guys, I'm a Baron!

"Yes, yes, it's the chef's signature starter…I am so jealous," Ozzie said.

Yeah, me too, Brad thought.

Suddenly one of Katy Riley's more brazen customers signaled for her attention, and she hustled over to the table.

"And so, Brad, this Baron thing, it is real?"

Brad nodded, "'Fraid so. I was even invited to a ceremonial celebration of all things Teppudlian next January…in Belgium."

"You're going, of course?" Ozzie said.

"Thinking about it…"

"You have a passport, don't you?"

"Yes, I think it's still good."

"Hey, I finally got my passport in the mail yesterday!" Katy Riley, having returned from calming another customer, said excitedly.

"Katy! Now at long last I can take you to Singapore, to Rio de Janeiro…the Riviera!"

"Yeah, right…o look here's another course…" she showed her phone around.

Ozzie looked at it, squinted. "What is it…o there, it's beets in a coconut milk black forest ham sauce…hmm. The chef is vegetarian, but black forest ham?"

"Beets?" Katy Riley, shook her head, "Yuckkk."

Brad laughed, "Katy, you work in a fine dining establishment, what do you do for lunch?"

"Go across the street to Burger Hop."

Then she laughed, still looking at her phone. "I asked if he was alone and he says, 'no, there's about a hundred people here.'"

Even thousands of miles away, he's a smart ass, Brad thought.

"Hey wait a minute…wait just a minute." Ozzie stepped back, gave each of his compadres a quick glance, then said, "A Baron. With, say, his fiancé, attending a royal wedding…you both have passports. It would be perfect."

"What are you going on about," Katy said.

"My brother, a life-long bachelor, finally found the woman of his dreams, and they're getting married next week. It's gonna be a huge bash, with diplomats and members of our extended families, close to 200 people, all on my brother's sprawling palatial home, with gardens, fountains, totally extravagant. And the food! I can't even begin to describe…"

Katy was unimpressed. The Baron didn't believe a word of it.

"So, where is this wedding?" Katy Riley said.

"Pakistan, city outside Islamabad, Abbottabad," Ozzie said.

All Brad could think about was, 'Fiancé?'

"I can get your tickets right now…" he flipped on his iPad, spent several minutes staring, and banging on the keyboard.

Meanwhile a very circumspect Katy Riley said, "I have no idea where any of that is."

Ozzie, intent on his screen, muttered, "Well that's too bad..."

"What? No go?" Brad, hopefully.

"No, nothing left in business class. We'll have to travel coach, is that okay?"

Katy Riley and the Baron von Easley glanced at one another.

"Coach is fine with me..." Brad said, sensing he was being swept into a crushing river, headed for a waterfall with a thousand-foot drop.

Ozzie, looking at the ticket info, "We'll need your passport numbers, birthdates, address, blah blah blah, you can fill that out, or I can do it, probably be easier that way...contacts, blah, blah,blah..."

"I can't afford..."

Ozzie waved it off, can't be bothered by something so petty as money, "No it's okay, I got it. It will be an honor for me..."

"Wait a minute," Katy Riley, beginning to realize maybe this wasn't just some insane schoolyard made-up game, this was for real. "We can't just drop everything, kids, work, and run to to...what? Pakistan? That's crazy!"

"Of course, it is! I do it all the time. A passport, yes, money, and the simple desire to do something on the spur of the moment, drop everything and go! Didn't you ever want to just go nuts and run off somewhere...everyone does. Here it is, your chance!"

"I'm not a spur of the moment kinda guy," Brad said, "although. Pakistan. Sounds exotic."

"It is."

"Sounds scary." Katy Riley said.

"No, you're in the big city, it's like Haven...and you're with Ozzie. No problem."

"Don't know...I have this weird feeling, you got something up your sleeve..."

Ozzie laughed. "Me?! Come now."

"Yeah, you. What're you up to?"

Ozzie was on his second glass of Cotes du Rhone. He leaned conspiratorially closer to the two, "Okay, I'll fess up," he looked behind him, to both sides, and seeing no one other than his two co-conspirators, leaned ever closer and said, "my friends, we are going to kill Osama bin Laden."

Ozzie on a Plane

Ozzie was alert to everything and everyone around him.

From the tilt of the air vents, who was watching what on their monitors, the movement of each steward and stewardess, and the intonation of every voice around him.

He was no doubt being followed, spied upon. But by whom? And for which reason? The Taliban, DHS, FBI? Each had different motives. What did they want? Just to observe...what's he up to now? Or interfere. He was fairly certain he was nearly always under surveillance. Some, the benign kind, some not so much. It was always a guessing game. Which is the way he preferred, if not arranged, it.

The sheepish looking guy standing by the bathroom, reading a newspaper. Little too obvious. But...

The Russian woman who pretended to understand nothing, and groused about everything.

The black fellow, Nigerian, probably, well dressed, focused, intently on his laptop.

The mother walking her baby up and down, up and down, the aisle.

All of them innocuous, blend in, don't jump out at you. The perfect cover. The good spy is the one who keeps you guessing.

It could as easily be the mouthy teen-ager behind him, talking incessantly about himself, foul-mouthed, loud, and extraordinarily rude to the sad looking but efficient stewardess...jerk. But...who knows.

And that's why it was good to have Katy Riley and Brad von Easley seated to his left. They offered diversion. They took up the middle seats, a bit crimped, but secure. It was the final leg from Frankfurt to Islamabad.

Ozzie kept up a steady stream of conversation with Brad and Katy, playing up the glories of the wedding they were soon to attend. A tad different than what they might be used to. The ceremony was simple, pretty much out of sight, then the party began. Non-stop music, hundreds of people, tons of food, fireworks, and to ease their minds, most people speak English.

Ozzie was still miffed at himself. His horrible and embarrassing blunder, blurting out the intent of this trip. But he tried to use it to his advantage. Just a joke. Wouldn't that be funny? Who'd believe they were on the way to an assassination? No, honeymoon there. Katy and Brad von Easley had other worries occupying their minds. Getting the time off work was simple. Brad had accumulated way too much vacation time and they were begging him to take a week off. Katy traded shifts with Doc, mostly because he needed more hours. And kids? Isn't that what grandmothers are for? Visas? Do we need visas? No. Ozzie had a solution to every obstruction they threw up. Finally, wearily, they said, "Okay...let's go to Pakistan."

The 'brother' whose wedding they were attending, was actually a very distant cousin, notoriously gay, wealthy, who had lost a brother in a suicide bombing, and by some cosmic coincidence ended up living in a wealthy neighborhood in Abbottabad. He was needless to say, sympathetic to the cause. But for Ozzie, in this business, no one is above suspicion, no one would be trusted with your life in his or her hand. Not a cousin, not a friend...maybe Katy Riley.

The cousin, Abrim Saluud, had months ago gotten into contact with Ozzie through a number of surreptitious interlopers, and when Ozzie realized the magnitude of this coincidence, that Osama bin Laden might actually be living withing shouting distance of this cousin, was too much to believe. Once substantiated, the gears were set in motion, and once they determined that it was almost certainly their quarry, they had to act. And quickly.

Who knew how long bin Laden had been living there, and how much longer he'd stay? Best to get this done as quickly as possible.

There were those among his country-men a slew of ex-soldiers eager to lend a hand in this...thing. Ozzie chose five of the most formidable and trustworthy, and all with an ax to grind. Cousins, with guns.

The kid behind him was rifing on his sexual escapade in Berlin. He was talking to someone next to him who was not entirely interested but kept listening, and asking just enough questions to keep the kid running off at the mouth. He had paid 100 euros for a lap dance from some little tart in a cabaret last night, and didn't even get off. He was totally pissed, but who do you complain to in a foreign sex joint? His seat mate was more or less sympathetic. As much to get him off the subject than to agree with him.

The mother with the baby would pause for a half hour, then begin walking the baby up and down the aisle again. A common practice, keep the baby active, hopefully it would go to sleep. But Ozzie was timing her. Was she coming within range just enough to catch everything said?

The Russian woman turned out to have a sister (or mother) who was sitting in another part of the plane, but kept coming over and leaning over the seats to complain about her situation.

The sheepish looking guy was done reading his newspaper and had taken his seat. Ozzie couldn't tell where.

He had last been in contact with Saluud two days ago. Everything was looking very promising. His wife to be, a concubine, was prepped for an arranged marriage, that once done, given that she going under a false name, would be nonexistent. She'd get plenty of money for her trouble. Go buy herself a hotel room for three nights. A common enough occurrence.

The 'team' had arrived, all of whom had some experience with weaponry, intrigue and disappearing into the night when a job was done. Ozzie just hoped they were able to keep their mouths shut.

But this was…big. If Ozzie counted correctly, there were maybe ten people intimately familiar with this operation. But it's always a gamble. Listening devices, cameras, all too sophisticated and virtually invisible, that even without a human hand or mind could sniff out trouble. If there were a crack in the system, and someone found them out, or even got a hint that something was going on, the whole operation would crash. And if discovered, it would depend on, by whom. The wrong side, and they were all dead.

"I need to go pee," Brad von Easley said.

"May as well go too," Katy said.

"While you're back there could you see if we can get a refill on our wine?"

The mother got up and marched her baby up and down the aisle.

The kid behind him (Ozzie refused to turn to see what he looked like), was raving about his sexual conquests in Amsterdam.

The Nigerian almost never took his eyes off the laptop. That's a bit too intense.

The Russian women were jabbering back and forth (the one language Ozzie did not know!)

Ozzie got his refill of wine. His friends wiggled their butts into place.

He was getting worried. Still another 4 hours before touch down.

The wedding itself seemed to be coming along quite nicely. Most of these affairs are thrown together with huge fanfare, on almost a moment's notice, and being in an affluent part of town, spacious grounds, it shouldn't attract any more attention than from a few envious neighbors. Still, their target would be alert, is this wedding legit? Who are all the guests? How many? There was no way anybody could trace the guest list. Who knows, maybe the body guards would come and enjoy the fun. O yeah, right.

As far as could be determined, there were at least six guards, total. Were they all on duty all the time? If his boys, working silently, swiftly, efficiently, caught them by surprise, at least two should get through, if not all. That was Ozzie's hope. He never spoke of this as a suicide mission. Who knows, if the guards are lulled to sleep by yet another boisterous wedding, with the noise, music, fireworks, all it would take is split second to break through…

He closed his eyes. The kid behind him was silent. The mother was way late on her walk with the baby. Asleep? Maybe, just maybe, this was all going to work out.

The in-flight meal was a choice between pasta and chicken. Daring selections.

Katy Riley was not looking well. She hadn't slept much the night before. Anxiety. She overpacked, and Brad and Ozzie were forced to carry two of her bags and to pay extra for the effort. That's okay, Ozzie thought, typical tourists. An assassin would never drag along so much luggage.

"Water," Katy Riley said when the stewardess asked what she'd like to drink.

"Chicken or pasta?"

"Nothing, thanks."

Ozzie got more wine and ordered the chicken. Brad had the pasta. Both dishes were slathered over in Chef Boyardee sauce.

The stewardess had to ask the Russian sister to return to her seat, which angered both Russians.

Two rows in front of him, to the right, across the aisle, an eye flashed, turned away, a reflection in the monitor. Glancing at Ozzie.

If he were the spy, what a rank amateur.

Ozzie first realized something was wrong when without announcement the plane began to descend. A full two hours before their presumed destination. The descent was slow, barely noticeable. Unless you were paying attention.

Beside him both Brad and Katy Riley were either asleep or pretending to be.

Ozzie braced himself. More than likely they'd make their move soon. They certainly wouldn't wait until the plane landed. He had a choice. Unbuckle, stand, and force their hand. Or stay buckled up and enjoy the ride. He asked a passing steward for another glass of wine. May as well go down with a bit of a buzz. More than likely the stewards and stewardesses were on alert that something was about to go down. But it was just as likely they wouldn't know what until the action started.

All around him was quiet. Shades were down on every window leaving only the lights of the monitors casting a gloomy glow about the cabin. Dark. He got his wine. The Nigerian pretended to sleep over his laptop. Even the Russian woman was silent. He sighed. He wouldn't resist. What would be the point? Where would he run to?

Maybe they'd wait until the landing gear clunked down. No, more likely before that. Make sure everyone was safe before it became obvious that a landing was imminent.

He got about halfway through his glass of wine when it started. Two stewards positioned themselves in the forward aisle blocking any passage. That means, whatever was coming down would be from behind him. The teen-ager? Or his seat-mate?

Suddenly a hand was on his shoulder. It was the sad stewardess. "Sir, could I ask you to stand…"

Ozzie took one long slug of the wine, set his cup on the Katy's tray, unbuckled, and no sooner did he get upright, then a flurry of hands had him around the throat, pulled his arms pinned behind, and the click of the cuffs, kicked his legs out from under him, and he slid to his knees. There were a few gasps from passengers nearby. But it happened so fast. Only Ozzie could appreciate the efficiency.

They let go the choke hold, since they realized he wasn't struggling. He turned to see his captors. Yeah, the 'teen-ager'. Although, now he could see that he was no teen-ager at all, mid-twenties, maybe thirty, "Back of the plane," he said. He was good. He still had his teenager voice. The fellow he'd been talking to, nudged him and pushed him into the aisle and spun him around. Suddenly Brad said, "What...?" he started to get up, maybe come to his aid.

"It's okay, Brad, just stretching my legs."

He was pushed down the aisle could see a few stunned faces. Glances that said, 'Haha, another Muslim.'

"Brother, are you okay," a bearded, turbined man said.

"Fine."

They got to the steward cabin at the rear of the plane. There were two goons, one in each aisle, standing guard.

"FBI?" he said to the teen ager.

"Something like that," he said. "Just be a good boy, and we'll have a nice, soft landing."

It was only then that the pilot came on to announce a sudden departure in plans, they'd be landing soon. Slight emergency. Everything is okay, everything is fine. Please relax, and remain seated.

He was seated, back against the wall. His captors stood over him. Every now and again addressing questions from the guards, and stewardesses wondering what they should do. Or not do. Nothing. Stay away.

"Don't suppose I could get another glass of wine?"

Nope. They'd have to take off the cuffs.

He sat quietly. Wondering who else was caught up in this mess. The five-man team? Abrim? The concubine?

The landing gear went clunk beneath his feet.

Well, at least it was the Americans that got him.

Damn, he sighed, everything had been going so well.

Paris

Fynn Fnüdl awoke to the sound of water running. Felicity was taking a shower. He rolled over to take a peek outside. It was a cloudy morning in Paris. What he could see of it. The apartment building across the courtyard with its sheen of green and gray tile and metal roof blocked most of his view.

He glanced at his watch. Little after 9 am. His flight wasn't until 1. Plenty of time. Maybe Felicity was up for one more bout... maybe he could sneak in the shower and take advantage.

The previous night's adventure had been an artful, sensuous exercise, part gymnastic, part sensory explosion, and all this after a wonderful multi-course meal at Che Louis...nothing *too* fancy. After dinner, they popped into a wine bar for a nightcap, when she began flirting unmercifully. Hands on his cheeks, caressing his shoulders, playing with his hair. Their rendez-vous the day before she had seemed a little...hesitant. Reluctant. She was just off the train from Brussels where she'd had a meeting with European counterparts. Industrial Insurance. The first night she fell asleep next to him with nary a touch.

But then last night, by time they got back to the hotel, they were practically undressing in the elevator. Just the recollection aroused him. Now...should he slip into the shower with her?

The point became moot when there was knock on the door. Had she ordered room service? "*Un moment.*" He called out. Got up, put on pants, tee-shirt, opened the door, and...

He was thrown against the wall by two UZI toting, black-booted, bullet-proof vested, soldiers in black uniform, helmets and visors. Generally a pacifist, Fynn struggled for a moment, until one of

176

them had his arms pinned behind him. He relented. Relaxed, His first thought was Felicity. Second thought…what the hell is going on?

"Easy, big boy," the first soldier said, American, obviously, "and we won't have any broken bones."

Now he had to say it out loud, "What the hell is going on?"

"Just doin' our job."

Their job was apparently to inflict as much pain and aggravation on a very vulnerable, unsuspecting and generally accommodating guy. Struggling was useless. No point.

"Just tell me what the fuck is going on…"

Instead they jerked him across the room, pushed him into a chair and clamped his arms behind his back, the click and sting of hand cuffs.

"You got a choice, big boy, sit and shut up, or make everyone's life a whole lot more difficult."

Fynn said nothing. The shower continued to run. Had Felicity heard nothing? Impossible. Certainly she felt the rumble…

"Fine."

There was a tap at the door. Soldier number one opened the door carefully, in walked…Felicity. Dressed in black, armed, black boots. Fynn's jaw both figuratively and literally dropped. Like a brick.

"Ummmm, Felicity?"

"Everything okay here?" She said. Not to him. To her comrades in arms.

"So far, so good."

Felicity walked into the bathroom, and turned off the shower.

"Good." She looked at her watch.

"By the way," Fynn said to her, "I'm fine."

She glanced at him, heartlessly. Then turned to her comrades. "Now we wait," she said.

Fynn scrounged around his inner resources, understanding, comprehension, infinite void of nullification of all things reasonable. Then a fire cracker went off behind his eyeballs. "This wouldn't have anything to do with Ozzie…Islamabad…a wedding…would it?"

"Just sit back and relax," Solider number one cautioned.

It did. It was Ozzie. Something sounded fishy about the wedding. The abruptness. The need to gather other people. Like peering through the wrong end of a telescope, the picture was vaguely coming into focus.

"Can I at least get some coffee," he said. "*Café?*"

The three soldiers exchanged weary glances.

"I'm sure if my hands were free I could take out all three of you. And still finish my *café* and croissant."

Soldier two said, "I'll get it."

"Servant of the people," Fynn said.

"Shutting up would be a real good thing right now," Soldier number one snarled.

Soldier two left. It was nearly 15 minutes before he returned. "They're bringin' it up."

"Is that a proper thing…" Felicity.

"Ames has it."

"Ah."

Ames? How many of these thug soldiers are there?

"I almost hate to say this, but I've got to pee really bad. I think I could even do it with an UZI upside my head."

"AK-17," Soldier number two said.

"Go ahead," Soldier number one said.

The snap of hand cuffs, his arms free, Fynn stood up. Guns were all aimed at him. "Just gotta pee, kids. Really."

AK-17 waved him into the bathroom. Door almost shut, ajar, Soldier number two stood directly behind him. He didn't have to look to see where his gun was pointed.

He unzipped, "Y'know what, dude, this thing was inside your lady friend last night…a lot. From every angle. You know she likes it from behind? Offers up her juicy ass, wet pussy just starving for some action…and when she comes, omigod…" there was thud upside his head.

"Just piss and shut up."

"…and when she sucked on this thing for god, I don't know, ten minutes, jesus."

Another rifle nudge.

When done, Ames had arrived with the coffee. He was a sniveling looking sort. Cream colored suit, fashionable shoes, balding pate. Maybe under different circumstances, Fynn wouldn't have taken such an immediate disliking to the sap. Maybe.

178

Now, hotel rooms in Paris are rather small and with three bulked soldiers, waving AK-17s, along with two civvies, "I'll take my *café* standing up," Fynn said.

Ames and Felicity went into the hall, door shut behind them, short confab.

There was only one thing for Fynn to do. He pulled up the chair to the little table welded into the wall, crossed his legs, sighed excessively, then took a sip of coffee. Ames must be a slow walker, as the coffee was only slightly above lukewarm. Still, a pleasurable sigh.

The incongruity of the scene was not lost on Fynn. Two burly soldiers, each loaded down with military gear, cradling an assault rifle, pointed at a civilian, causally sipping coffee and gnawing on a *pain au chocolat*. Fynn quite nearly broke into laughter. Surprisingly, the two soldiers were not so amused.

"So, I suppose my flight to Islamabad is out of the question."

Silence.

"Which means either the wedding is off, or was a hoax, or knowing Osmond Hussain as I do, that something for more insidious than a wedding was plotted, and I and my friends were somehow sucked in, coerced, and knowing Ozzie, bamboozled into taking part in whatever shenanigans he had up his sleeve. And gathering by the finely tooled weaponry pointed my way, I would assume that our Ozzie did have something far and away different from a wedding in mind. I only hope my friends, who were, or are, with him, are not in any way held responsible. I also wonder how long the lovely Felicity has been in this. And why me? She can fuck anyone she wants, but why me? These are things I ask myself, my friends." He took a thoughtful bite of the croissant. The two soldiers seemed bored by his soliloquy.

Until he'd said it out loud, he hadn't had time to consider his history with Felicity. She was just an habitue of the farmers market, who constantly chatted him up. They had lunch several times. With wine. But a clarity, if not a solution was forming. Rather like deconstructing a jigsaw puzzle with the same precision and uncertainty with which it was put together. Felicity pursued him. Or, in retrospect, trolled him. Was it because of his tenuous connection with Ozzie? What else could it be? At worst he was an environmental activist. No need for AK-17s, as toxic weed killer was enough to disarm him. So she kept tabs on him. He was a mole to her, but he didn't know it. And then when Ozzie acted, they (what was it, Homeland Security, FBI, the Company? Or all in collusion?) had to be the perfect accessories prior to the fact.

Good strong French coffee, even of the hotel type, stimulated his brain, looping a thread through all the disparities and seemingly unrelated events and connections. Felicity had always kept her distance from him, while at the same time reeling him in. He could only imagine how many others around Haven, New Connecticut she had similar ties to it. It's funny she didn't sink her fangs into Brad von Easley. Or had she?

The more senseless, the more sense it made. Felicity, probably not her real name, the Industrial Insurance broker (is there really such a thing?), flitting about the area keeping tabs on anyone who had some connection with Ozzie. And that's it. It all comes back to Ozzie. Is he Taliban? Al- Quaida? Or their opposite? Pakistan or Afghan government operative?

On the one hand, Fynn felt vindicated. All this to stop him from diving into whatever pot Ozzie was stirring. On the other hand, it's really not a whole lot of fun having a gun pointed at your head while you're trying to relax over a cup of coffee in Paris.

Felicity returned to the room. It was a like a beautiful painting had spun around and become an ugly crusty gargoyle. She was just a lying piece of shit, who had deceived him to the max. Fynn thought a moment, then said, abruptly, "Arugula pesto." There was a quick flick, Felicity's fierce eyes darted to him, then as quickly, back. Gotcha. "Would be great on a croissant," he said, seemingly apropos of nothing.

She turned immediately to her comrades, "We should know in a couple minutes."

"Good, this one's been brooding and talking to himself, and I don't like it."

"Not the thinking type?" Fynn said.

"Fuck you." Soldier one.

"Already been done."

There was tension creeping around the eyes of Soldier number one. Should he push him harder? He was himself an

American citizen. What could they do to him? He was only in this spot because of Ozzie.

"And it was a good fuck my friend," he said, thoughtfully, "but not as good as the one I got from my own country. Rights? Not from you lying pieces of shit with guns pointed at my head."

"There, there, everybody relax, let's just take it easy," Soldier number two.

Fynn was right, they couldn't possibly do him any harm.

Felicity remained unmoved. Truth be known, she wasn't so good of a fuck at all. She didn't come. She did everything she could to make him come, get it over with, so she could be done with it. He was actively beginning to hate her.

"So, when these couple minutes are up, what happens, we all go back to being best friends?"

"Shut the fuck up."

"Shut me up, asshole. Go on, try it."

"Hey!" Soldier number two, took a step in between. "Why don't you get out of here," he glared at Soldier number one, "just go, we got this. Get out. We don't need this shit."

"I'll get Ames," Felicity said, and along with a soldier much in need of anger management, marched back out into the hall.

"Good ole America," Fynn said.

"And you, I suggest you do shut up, relax, finish your goddam coffee."

"Yes, sir. Yessirree, Bob."

"You know what's really hilarious. My name is Bob."

Soldier Bob made sure Fynn and 'Felicity' were not alone in the room at the same time.

Solider number one was in the next room, banging around, which means that probably all of the soldiers had been one thin wall away from Fynn and Felicity. Were they amused by the prolonged fucking last night? Or were they out having a beer? 'Felicity's got this.'

Agent Felicity stood by the door. "It's all over now, we're just waiting for the official word."

"Good. Just wish I'd been there. You know who did it?"

181

"SEALs."

"Makes sense."

"I know you're purposely keeping me on the edge of my seat," Fynn said, "but if anyone can enlighten me as to what's going on."

Felicity rubbed her nose. Dang itch.

Soldier Bob filled him in, "You'll know soon enough."

Tapping at the door. Felicity opened it. It was Ames. "All done. President's going to announce any second."

"Excellent," soldier Bob said. "our work done here?"

"Yup. Gather your gear. Truck's waiting downstairs."

Without a glance back, Felicity slipped out the door. Gone. Solider Bob gave Fynn a way-too-close for comfort sympathetic glance. "Seeya, Chuckles."

He too was gone. Just Fynn and Ames. He looked at Fynn the specimen, "So Mr. Fynn Fnüdl..."

"You pronounced it right."

Ames had soft hands, white flesh, and wore a white jacket, somewhere between a sports and lab coat. Was he the evil scientist here to experiment on Fynn? He looked the part. The only thing missing was the monocle, bald head, foreign accent, and a hook for a hand. Yes, gotta have a hook. But Fynn could superimpose those features on him. Just to make the game more interesting.

"If you think you're going to get information out of me, I got nothing."

"No, no, we know all we need to know." He sat on the edge of the bed, rubbed a hand over his head, "We have quite a predicament here. You see, you are not able to leave, and yet if you stay, your life could be in danger."

Ames looked out the window. Fourth floor. "It's a long drop."

"Am I about to have an accident?"

"Osmond Hussain, Katy Riley, Brad von Easley?" Ames said, as if quoting from Shakespeare.

"Never heard of them."

"I don't want to know what you know about them, I want to know what you don't know."

"Ummm, that could take a while..."

"What don't you know about this Ozzie?"

"I got nothing."

"I surmise you can't have known him for long, a year or so? Yet, somehow he chose you to be part of this umm, adventure. Any thoughts on why?"

"Why don't you go ask this Ozzie guy yourself?"

"If he's still alive."

It was only then, right at the moment, that it hit Fynn like a ton of bricks -this was some serious shit. Time to re-organize the brain. This, whatever this was, was far more dangerous, and serious, than anything he'd ever gotten himself into.

"Are his friends okay?"

Ames glanced at his watch. "We'll know more in about an hour. Right."

"Are they in that deep of trouble?"

Ames smiled at him, "I got nothing."

Fynn pondered. "I sure could use a glass of wine."

Ames stood. "Mr. Fnüdl, you are in a heap of trouble. We'll all know more in a while, how much trouble. If there is good news, it's that you are of absolutely no consequence, so you may skate away unscathed. But in the meantime…relax. O, and by the way, life, as long as it persists, might be a lot easier for you if you never mention this little show of American hospitality. I can't follow you around forever, but just know, a word here, a word there, your life wouldn't be worth a plugged nickel. And no one will be there to bale you. But, let's not think about that. The less you say, the less you know, the better off you are. And now, on my way out I will have someone bring up some wine. Red or white?"

"It's French, who cares."

"Anything else?" almost facetiously.

"Steak and eggs?"

Ames opened the door, and paused a moment, "I'm sorry Mr. Fnüdl, but you are going to have to miss the wedding. I hope you weren't the best man."

"Far from it."

As two different soldiers, less weighted down with gear, and far more congenial looking, entered, Ames departed. As good as his word, Fynn got a half-bottle of wine, red, a small baguette, and some butter. The two soldiers, whispered among themselves, only every now and again making their weapons, handguns, apparent.

It was around 8 pm, that a third soldier, unarmed joined them, and packed Fynn's bags. "This yours?" he said holding up a tee-shirt. Who the hell else's would it be? But, he seemed pleasant enough.

He was allowed to get dressed, and at nearly 9 pm, handcuffed, feet cuffed, the two soldiers escorted Fynn to the elevator, downstairs, where oddly enough not a soul was about. He could see the swirling red, white lights, spinning outside lighting up the surrounding windows on the street. In between cars and armed soldiers, he could see across the street in front of the creperie, a bunch of baffled onlookers. He got rushed through the door, stuffed him into the back seat of an unmarked car. They peeled off down rue Delambre.

He was treated like royalty at the airport, chaperoned onto a plane, and the next thing he knew he was in Frankfurt, alone. No guards, no supervision. No guns. Nothing. But a ticket to Haven, New Connecticut in his hand.

It was only then he saw a headline… 'No, no,' he sputtered. 'Not possible…even Ozzie…even he wouldn't…omigod, it is…possible.'

Drained of all reason, sensibilities, he found a bar. More than two hours to kill, had a glass of Champagne. When he lifted the flute, he noticed for the first time his hand was shaking uncontrollably. He nearly spilled his Tattinger. Sat back, sipped. Deep breath. Calm. Had some crackers. Brain spinning inside his head like a roomful of gyroscopes. He sipped. He sat, resisted further speculation. Contemplated life.

Or whatever was left of it.

184

Katy Riley in Pakistan

She awoke to that awful buzz of silence. Like flies, miles in the distance. Cars honking, thousands of miles away. Cloud sneaking from ear to ear. A rush of white noise, accentuated by the sheer accommodation of silence surrounding her.

She was alone in a bare, Spartan room. On what appeared to be a mere cot. Had she simply gone to sleep, or had she been drugged? Sure felt like drugs.

The flip-flop inside her stomach, the ringing in her rears, the bare room which for some reason she could not bring into focus. A load of bricks inside her head. She kept her head on the pillow (if that's what you wanted to call the hard, scratchy lump under her skull), and tried to gather everything into something coherent.

Everything over the past however many hours (she had no idea) was a blur. Her and Brad, whisked off the plane, not exactly handcuffed, by dark skinned, plain-clothes cops or FBI, or whatever the Pakistan equivalent might be.

Rushed through the airport, surrounded, hemmed in, by these cops, and what she could see was a dizzying array of color, crowds, and the noisy babble of foreign tongues, the smells, musty and pungent, frightened her nose. Brad looked confused, alert, but resolved, and held her by the arm as they pushed through crowds, noise and aromas, outside, ten steps into a van, and the swarm of whatever they were maintained by, body to body contact, a scrum. pinning her and Brad in the middle, doors slamming, and radio jabbering, and the van sped off, horns honking, the wail of sirens, they were indeed inside some sort of police car.

Fatigued, bewildered, her and Brad exchanged glances, he tried to smile, "Always wanted to be in a James Bond movie," he joked.

185

Then as the van became subsumed into hellish traffic, over a period of time, a calm ensued. The cops seemed less taut, flexed, even joked among themselves. Not to Brad or her. But it somehow reassured her. And somewhere along the route, she fell asleep.

Very scant recollection of being hustled out of the van. Her and Brad separated, and she led by two uniformed women, through glass doors, a labyrinthine hallway, people glaring at her in derision.

Then into this room. She was allowed to use the potty. It took her a while to figure out how to flush the toilet. Only one of the armed ladies stayed with her, a cot was rolled in. That's about the last cogent thing she remembered.

And now she was alone. Tattered, her thought mechanism in shreds, she finally focused enough to scan the room. The yellowish walls, with white outlines here and there hinted at some kind of furniture or shelving, now absent. A stand, wooden, on shaky legs against the wall next to the door to the bathroom was empty, but carried some import. A plastic chair in the corner on curled metal legs. A vent, grilled. More spots here and there where once a phone been, a clock, maybe photos. This room had been something once, an office maybe.

She sat up on the cot. She had to go pee. She must've been asleep a long time. There was a mirror in the bathroom, a sink. Paper towels. The water from the faucet was more a dribble, but at least it looked clean. She dashed water on her face, and only then dared look at herself in the mirror.

Well, Katy Riley, what have you gotten yourself into? Considering all she'd been through, she looked decent. She never used much make-up anyway.

Suddenly there was a commotion in the hall. Her door rattled. a woman entered, uniformed, armed, one of the ones who had led her here. "Ahh, look who's awake." Perfect English. Thick but workable accent.

She had two bottled waters in her hands. Set them on the rickety stand. And then from under arm, she took and handed to Katy Riley her purse. "You may need this," she smiled. And left.

This brief exchange only served to further confuse Katy Riley.

Then there was more commotion outside the door, rustling, the door opened, and in walked...Brad von Easley! If matters were different she'd run over and hug him, but he looked only slightly less nonplussed than she, so that they merely smiled at each other, then slowly sidled up to one another.

"Yeah, you two get acquainted," the woman said, "my name is Camla, I'll check in on you later."

She slipped out the door, there was a loud click. Locked.

Finally, her and Brad hugged. After a moment, she all but pushed him away and cried out, "Goddam Ozzie, I knew this was trouble." She ranted for a few seconds, then collapsed back on the cot. Brad sat on the rickety chair.

"What now?" Katy Riley said, exasperated.

"I don't know...I don't think we're in trouble...I don't think... no one's mistreated us...at least not me..."

"I wouldn't know, I slept the whole time. So, just how long have we been here?"

Brad consulted his watch, "About twelve hours."

Too many questions, too much confusion. "What the fuck was Ozzie doing?"

"I don't know. Whatever it was, it was illegal, criminal, but we are not complicit."

"You don't think he really wanted us to kill bin Laden?"

Brad snorted, somewhere between contempt and dismissal. "Who knows with Ozzie. But I doubt that even he would have the audacity...it was certainly something criminal. Probably smuggling. Two innocents, engaged, slipping through customs. Who would think we have a sack full of heroin, or whatever, in our bags. But I don't know, somehow he seems more imaginative, simple smuggling is cheap and dirty. Then again, Ozzie's fifty percent bullshit, forty-nine percent brag, and the rest? I think he likes it that way."

"I just had a scary thought...."

"What?"

"Fynn."

Brad's face turned sour. "If he's here, I haven't seen him."

"God, I hope he didn't leave Paris." Katy Riley was starting to feel like a human being again.

"So if we're not in trouble, why are we..." she waved her hand around the Spartan room, "here?"

Brad thought a moment. "Protection?"

Suddenly Katy Riley stood, stiff, awkward, and started pacing the tiny room, "Goddam it, I could kill Ozzie. How the hell did he talk us into this? Goddam it, I got a kid at home, a job, a life, and here I am in this freakin' hole in the wall, no idea what's going on, no idea where I am, what I'm doing here, goddam it, I'd rather them torture me…but, they are! Ozzie! Did I tell you I'm furious? Jerk. Let's go to Pakistan! Yaya, what an adventure. What fun. A royal wedding. A baron for a fiancé! And I even have a passport! Yay. What kind of idiot am I? Look, I'm not the sharpest tack in the pack, but goddam, don't I have any common sense? I knew something was rotten, terribly wrong, I don't even listen to myself! What kind of dope drops everything and runs off to freakin' Pakistan…Pakistan! A pretend royal wedding? Royal wedding? Really? Really?! There was no wedding, the whole thing was a ruse, he was getting into boiling water and needed company. Us! We were accomplices…in what? Driving the getaway car? Who knows, maybe he had something even worse up his sleeve. Revolution. Military coup? Maybe it was all just a big joke to him. Royal wedding! Goddam you, Ozzie! What a dope I am."

"Umm, I'm here, too."

"Folly a due."

"What?'

"French phrase, two stupid people falling for the same stupid fantasy."

"Huh?…"

"It's French. Fynn says it a lot."

"O."

"He better be okay. Goddam it."

"My guess, he didn't get very far."

"He better be okay…"

Katy Riley sat back down. Steam fizzing off the top of her head. Fzzz! "What a nightmare…and don't say we're gonna look back on this someday and laugh. I won't, if I look back it'll be to kill Ozzie." She huffed. She felt a lot better. In her head. "I just realized something…I'm starving to death. Even though my stomach is killing me. I'm starving."

"I had some kind of doughy thing, sweet, it was pretty good."

"Maybe we could ring room service...O Camla," they laughed, a small unwarranted but much needed giggle.

She rifled through her purse. She had stuffed some snacks from the flight in it. But they were gone. Then she remembered. She ate them. O well. "I'd kill for a sweet doughy thing right now."

"I wonder..." Brad stood up, went to the door, and rapped on it, not a frantic pounding, just a polite, 'Hey, little help here.' Nothing. He tried it several times, then returned to the rickety chair. "Worth a try," he muttered.

"Fine, I'll just starve to death."

"I'll try it again in a couple minutes..."

"What time is it back home?"

Brad checked his watch, did some mental gyrations, screwed up his eyes, moved his lips as if counting backwards, "About 6 pm."

"Dinner time. I haven't eaten in..."

Suddenly there was commotion outside the door, coming down the hallway. Voices, lots of heavy footsteps, one of the voices sounded American. Muffled, at least in English. A female voice, another male, not loud, but loud enough, not an argument, but concerned conversation. The English-speaking voice was clearly American, and sounded menacingly familiar.

Somewhat in alarm both Katy Riley and the Baron von Easley stood, and with nervous expectation stared at the door. What now? The portal to their future? The rabbit hole to hell? The voices halted right outside the door. No, definitely not an argument, almost a command, an order, the American English voice seemed in charge, then the door opened, and in walked...

"Buck!" Katy Riley and Brad screamed in unison.

"Who'd you expect, Bugs Bunny?"

Katy Riley started blubbering and ran to hug him. So tight he nearly fell backwards out the door again.

"Easy, I've got two hip replacements..."

Katy Riley was laughing and crying at the same time, and hugging Buck tightly.

Buck let it go on for a few seconds, then pried himself loose and stepped further into the room. "Got everything you need in here?"

Between paroxysms of sobbing Katy Riley blurted out, "I'm starving."

Buck turned to Camla, "I got it," she said.

There was an emotional pause when everyone looked at each other in wonderment, disbelief, awe, embarrassment, contriteness....

"So," Buck said baldly, "could you two have screwed things up any worse?"

Now they both looked sheepishly at each other.

"Do you have any idea...any idea at all, what you were getting yourself into, and how much you could have totally fucked up things?"

"It was Ozzie..." Katy Riley blurted out, though understanding her own culpability.

"Ozzie, hell. You just blundered into one big mess, and just about screwed everything up..."

"Buck, we didn't know...hell, we still don't know what's going on...we were told it was a wedding, Ozzie's brother..." To Brad it all sounded pretty stupid when he said it out loud. Katy's right. What a couple of morons.

Buck looked so disgusted at the comment that he nearly burst a seam.

"But...what're you doing here?" Brad said.

"I told you, you don't retire from the Company...."

Just then a uniformed fellow walked in with a....TV? He excused himself marched between everyone and plugged the TV into the one plug in the wall, and set the TV on the little table. The Baron noted it was a fairly nice flat screen TV.

Buck demanded, "Can you get the right channel?" The solider/agent nodded. He fiddled with knobs and wires, until a scratchy noise erupted, and wiggly picture floated up into the screen.

"That should be right..."

"What's it, a couple minutes?"

"Yes,"

Buck dismissed him,

"We're gonna watch TV?" Katy Riley said.

"New reality show," Buck said.

Just then Camla returned with a tray of rice, the doughy things, some bowls of vegetables, none of which would normally have looked appetizing to Katy Riley, but in her current state, she'd gobble up anything not moving.

The TV squawked with voices in Pakistani, or whatever language they speak here.

"Here it comes," Buck said.

The picture on the screen clarified a bit, the voice-over stopped, Katy Riley and Brad von Easley picked out on the screen a long hallway, festooned in white and red and a figure approaching a podium. It was the president of the United States. Brad nibbled on one of the doughy things, and Katy Riley watched while scarfing up rice and veggies.

Barack Obama with a very serious look on his face stood regally behind the podium. Hands on the lectern, he intoned into the camera, "Ladies and gentlemen, tonight, we took down Osama bin Laden…"

Brad nearly spit his doughy thing out on the floor. Katy Riley's face went white, and though famished, stopped chewing, and listened intently as the president went on to elaborate, maintaining a calm resolute look. His speech lasted nine minutes.

Buck turned off the TV, and looked scathingly at the two, "See what you and your friend almost fucked up?"

Katy Riley, said, "O. My. God."

"He really was going to try to kill bin Laden?" Brad said.

"He would have failed," Buck said, "and in the meantime screwed up the most important mission in American history."

No exaggeration.

"Jesus," is all Brad could say.

"Congratulations," Buck said.

"I think I'm gonna puke," Katy Riley said. But she didn't move. And in fact, resumed eating.

"So, as the world's most efficient and intelligent secret agents, tell me, what did Mr. Ozzie tell you about this mission, how much did you guess, and what the hell did you think you were doing?"

Brad and Katy stumbled over each other trying to explain, exculpate, and otherwise extract themselves from guilt, all the while, fully aware that stupidity is no excuse. They spread the blame from Ozzie to themselves. Ozzie creates excitement, Ozzie made everything sound so like little kids going on a space ride in a kiddie wagon. They described Ozzie's arrest on the plane, the rather awkward descent and landing of the plane, with three agents crushing against them, then rushing them off the plane, everyone staring at them, 'criminals!'. "And here we are, in Pakistan," Brad summed up.

"Well," Buck nodded and grimaced, "you're not in Pakistan, the flight was diverted to New Delhi. You're in India. Folks are a little more friendly here."

Buck went on to elaborate, in generalizations, Ozzie's plan. He had pretty much had the same info everyone had. Various tips led everyone (in the biz) to believe bin Laden was in Abbottabad, where, coincidentally one of Ozzie's distant relatives owned a nearby house. They cooked up the wedding idea as a smoke shield, crowds, music, fireworks, partying, late into the night, while Ozzie's cronies slip into bin Laden's compound…not Ozzie himself, he would never bloody his own precious hands, too dirty. "Besides he might've gotten killed. And frankly, he would've."

"Fynn? What happened to Fynn?" Katy said.

"Fnüdl? He had a, umm, chance encounter in Paris, that kept him…detained, and as far as I know, he's still there. Safely."

Phew.

Buck, the diplomat, government agent, said harshly, "Now that you know what kind of shit you got yourself into, you also know this is the biggest kind of hush-hush stuff. First and foremost, if the wrong elements knew as much about Ozzie's goings on as we did, you wouldn't still be on this side of the sod." Both Katy and Brad got a petrified look on their faces. "Our best guess is, no one outside of us knew what Ozzie was up to…and even we didn't really know exactly what he was up to, at least that much can be said about the con man, he's very, very careful. So, for you two, the fewer people know about this little escapade, the better. I wouldn't even tell my dying grandmother if I was you. Can I be any more clear on this? Keep your big fat mouths shut. And maybe you'll live a long, rich life."

"I really don't think either of us want to remember any of this," Brad said, still a bit shaken.

"So what becomes of us?" Katy Riley said.

"We're going to detain your sorry asses here for the rest of your life," grim chuckle. "No. You're going home."

The New Delhi Airport seemed far more friendly, happy even, with all the outrageous smells, spices, the jangling music, the foreign chatter, it all felt pleasantly warm, and welcoming. There was even a slight hint of remorse from both Brad and Katy that they didn't get to spend some 'down' time in India, just to get a feel for the lifestyle. Maybe even take in a wedding or two.

Buck was not with them. He had a military jet -not the Duchess!- whisk him home.

Followed by invisible agents, they made it to Frankfurt, where in the layover, had a couple flutes of Champagne. And 12 hours later, Katy Riley picked up her daughter, and soon enough, she was asleep. In her own bed.

She dreamed that it was all a dream.

Back in the good ole US of A. Talk about the readjustment blues…Gone three days (though she and Brad had cooked up a pretense that they had been gone the full four days, as originally planned, and just took off an extra day of work, hiding), and Bistro Bon Bon was wallowing in stagnation, the bar, a tepid zone of indifference. Customers, co-workers, everyone and everything looked familiar, but still. Quiet.

Katy Riley was focusing on squelching the memory of the last couple days.

"How'd the vacation go?" Doc asked her.

"Pretty crazy. Lots of people. Noise. I pretty much never got over jet lag, so don't remember much. I guess it was fun."

"How was the wedding?"

"Didn't happen. Groom got cold feet at the last second."

Her and Brad had rehearsed all of this on the flight from Frankfurt.

"The whole thing did sound a little fishy," Doc said.

Then she saw it. His rickshaw pulling up, watched as he untangled his long legs, not on a stretcher, or crutches, he appeared to be in one piece. Fynn Fnüdl came through the door like always.

Doc returned to the kitchen.

She rushed up to him, "Hey, baby," put her hands on his shoulders, "my god, you're okay…!"

"Of course," Smile. A bit painfully.

"Jesus!" she almost started to cry, "we were scared to death… we didn't know…we didn't know anything!"

"Wait, wait," he said, "what about you guys…talk about worried sick…"

"Long story," she said, glancing around, "tell you about it… all, sometime…I'm just glad you're safe."

"Yeah," took his place at the bar, "they made it sound like you guys were all gonna die…"

Trying not to cry. She brought him a glass of Riesling without asking. "Are you okay?"

"Just barely," he said.

"Was it bad?"

"Well, if you call being handcuffed in a tiny hotel room, by jack-booted, military cops, each pointing an assault rifle at your head, bad, then yeah, it was pretty lousy. But what about you guys, with Ozzie?"

Katy Riley tried to explain everything that happened quickly, quietly, but emphatically.

Fynn kept a grim look of concentration on his face, then said, "Holy fucking crap…" took a breath, "Ozzie…what the hell was he thinking? And you, Brad, me…now, just specks of dust in in the eyeball of history. Katy," he looked at her in wonderment, "we could've been killed."

"Tell me about it!"

"And Buck was in on it…" amazed.

"Shhh, don't say anything…I don't think he wants you to know."

"Buck. Brad…Ozzie," shaking his head in frustration.

"Ozzie," she said bitterly, "if I ever see him again, I might kill him."

"He bamboozled us all," Fynn spoke into his glass. "I'll tell you one thing, after all this, I don't think I'll ever trust another person for the rest of my life."

"Even me?"

"Okay, one exception."

"Goddam Ozzie, why did…" Katy looked up, her eyes popped wide, "Uh-o…Buck."

194

He rumbled into his seat, "Howdy ya'll."

"Hey old soldier, how you doing?"

"I'm doin…"

"Your usual?" Katy Riley, very uncomfortable.

"You need to ask?"

"Who knows, you might surprise me someday."

Buck rattled his newspaper, ducked his nose behind it, sipped his ice tea.

"How's Fynn?" Buck mumbled.

Dramatic, accusatory pause, "Good. Real good."

Buck just kept pretending to read. "Glad to hear it."

It was getting on noon, and the lunch rush would begin.

It wasn't long before Brad von Easley took his usual bar seat between Fynn and Buck, leaned against the counter, watching Buck eating soup. Glancing at the newspaper. Pretending not to be there. Turned to his other side, "Fynn Fnüdl," he said gleefully, "how are you?"

"Groovy."

"And Buck?"

"Whatever he said."

"Good. Good, good, good…Katy!"

"Brad!"

"Good to see you again. How you been?"

"Good, you?"

"Fabulous."

"So…." Katy said, and Buck tensed up a bit, "what's new?"

"What's new?" Brad said, "not much. You?"

"Just back working."

"Fynn, what's up with you?"

"Same old, same ole."

"Nothing ever changes around here," Brad smiled. A smile that held the universe in its groove. "Does it?"

Buck glanced over the edge of his newspaper, "Let's keep it that way."

App Pro Poe

I just downloaded my Free Association App, and I am so excited, unrelentingly, justifiably, inconsolably, weeping like a child at the gate of the Cemetery of Gnomes, ruins to runes, the run of the mill, a gust of wind, the grain is ground...wo, hey, this thing really works!

And it's only $9.95 (plus tax) a month, though you have to be a member of the Underpublished Writers of America. Your UWA membership ($100 annual fee), allows you access to the hundreds (maybe thousands!) of apps available, ranging through every literary category imaginable. I started with the 'training wheel' apps, freebies, many of them traditional, like the Henry James App, which offers unlimited words per sentence. I also have the Dickens App, aka the Inflation App –too many words chasing too few ideas. I rely on these when I need to fill up space between the margins.

For the short story writer, The App Pro Poe is interesting, though a bit weird. The swish of the ax is always in your head. I thought about getting the O. Henry App, but how many rabbit-out-of-the hat gimmick endings can the universe endure?

Journalist related apps are mostly free, like the Wine Writers App, and the Jazz Columnist App, both of which I have, and both of which are totally useless.

The more popular ones can be expensive. The priciest app, and -not uncoincidentally- the #1 bestseller is (duh!) the Harry Potter App, at $29.95 a month. Number two on (this week's) Bestselling App List is (double duh) The Chill Vampire App. The Stephen King App has been on the list ever since there's been a list. There are some head-scratchers, like the Danielle Steele App (but who am I to judge?). Way down on the list is the New Yorker App (now you can write like scores of other little under-A-Cheevers and Updikes!)

You can also get a lot of self-help apps, like the Strunk and White App, which teaches good gramma. There's the Spell Chequers App, but it's preddy unrelyable. And the Comma Sense App for all things punctual. I always keep handy a few thesauri apps, as well.

All sorts of apps aim at specific genres –mystery, sci-fi, fantasy, romance, humor (which ironically, does not come with punchlines). Some are fancifully if not enticingly named, like the Mr. Ed App (writing for TV), and the Eszter-Ass App, for writing horribly wretched screenplays. Speaking of which, I often use the Smart Ass App for polishing my sarcasm.

Steer clear of the Shakespeare App, I hear it's addictive. And if you think you're underpublished now, just wait till you get your first rejection slip for a play studded with 'methinks', 'alas' and 'begobs' (although that last may be Joyce, I can't recall).

Also, be careful of the Hemingway App, it suckers you in with its ease and simplicity, and suddenly you're writing with such sparsity and terseness, an entire novel clocks in at under five pages.

While all of these have their finer points, I prefer the more elusive apps, appetizers, calamari, egg rolls, rice patties, hamburger, hot dogs, Frankfurt, strolling the Bremerstrasse, taking the U line to the park, glass of wine on the Romerplatz...

Woops, there it goes again! This App can be dangerous.

I had a tough time deciding between the Free Association App and the Stream of Consciousness App (free samples are available), and while the two are similar, I just felt that sticking my toes in the Joycean stream encouraged my writing to be a tad too -how shall I say this –overwrought...rot wood wrought of knots and what not, slip knot, brass chamber pot...oops, sorry.

If nothing else, these apps are great for writers trying to get out of a rut. But they're especially useful if you suffer from writers bloc, comrades staring at a blank screen, the cursor blinking, the mouse still, a faint hint of patchouli oil in the background, soft jazz playing, outside the window the fog lazily lifting, dreaming of summer days long ago, o youth, where hast thou gone?...wo, I didn't know this thing had a poetry setting.

Once I get this under control, I'll probably check out the S. J. Perlman App -although, now I think on it, Woody Allen has pretty much beaten that horse to death (App-aloosa!).

In fact, it's kinda hilarious, you can often spot a writer leaning on an app. I don't want to hurt anybody's feelings, but will you please put away the Dan Brown App. You know who you are!

In the final assessment, these apps should be used wisely, discreetly. Unless, that is, you want to be an overly-published author. Then you'd be kicked out of the UWA.

And now if you'll excuse me, I'm gonna get this baby out on the open road, turn her loose and she what she'll do...do...doo-wop a diddy...sh-boom, boom, yessir, she's my baby, moonlit low-rider, scratches contours in the sand, dune, buggy, flees, hits the wall of thought, dispersed, unimaginable, yet brittle, like candy caught between yr teeth, brushing aside all fears while aiding and abutting the grazing sun, her eyes on, quiet, insistently, with no consideration for another's outrage, and then a shot rings out, and all ends in dearth...

A Joke
(Edited for Clarity
and Brevity)

Thank you for your submission of the short story 'A Joke'. I thought the idea very refreshing, unique and pointed. Though the idea at its core is satisfying, it requires fleshing out, and I cannot see publishing this story in our magazine without substantial rewrites. As we would like to see further work from you, allow me to give you suggestions as to what we look for in a polished, electrifying, publishable piece. I will use the current submission as an example of what we look for:

A Joke

Three editors are walking down the street.

(Where? Under what circumstances? We need context. Detail. A sense of time and place. Let's say these editors are just getting off work. They are rivals from three powerhouse publishing companies. Obviously set in New York. Why New York? Because it is the cultural center, the artistic soul, the intellectual beating heart of America. Even people who hate New York, regard it with awe. Its history and culture are second to none in the country. So, we have our time and place. A good catchy opening line is an absolute must, and while I'm just tossing this out, you can use it in the future or alter it slightly to suit your needs: 'It is a warm autumn evening in New York...' See? Time, place. And they are not just walking down a street, they are walking down 6th Avenue. They

199

meet at a curbside near 53rd each waiting to hail a taxi. Since it is rush hour, they know they will have a long wait, and because they all have different destinations, they cannot share a ride. Conversation ensues.)

They spot what looks like a pile of shit on the sidewalk. The first editor says, "Is that shit?" The second one says, "I think so." The third one is not so sure.

(Shit? That's no good, not in New York. That's an insult. Let's say instead, they each have recently received a submission, a novel, and all three are aghast at having to read such a lousy piece of writing. Little do they know an unscrupulous author has submitted a manuscript simultaneously to three publishers –a huge no-no. No writer in their right mind would ever do such a thing, not if they ever want to get published in this town. But the Editors don't know that. Yet.)

The first editor bends down and scoops up some of the substance on his fingertip, "Boy, sure feels like shit," he says.

(Come on, we need more dialogue here. The first editor, let's give him a name, Ty. Ty is the newbie on the block, Publishers Row, he's the cock-sure millennial. He describes his reaction to the novel he has just been assigned: "There wasn't one moment I didn't want to throw it out the window. The writing is atrocious. Overwrought. He has Henry James Syndrome, the more words to say the least, the better. These are the kind of manuscripts that make me wish I'd gone into the aluminum siding business." This gets a big laugh. A touch of humor is always a plus.)

The second editor sniffs it, "Sure smells like shit."

(The second editor, Brie –we need a female character here, to create a little sexual tension- goes on to top Ty's story, "You think you had a terrible manuscript, the dreck I read today made me want to scream. The plot, such as it was, was lifted from every TV cop show of the

'70s, the characters were cardboard cut-outs, the tin-ear dialogue was unbearable, and the only good thing about the ending was, it was finally over. I had to share some of the clumsy tidbits with my cubicle cohorts, and they were laughing their butts off. How anyone could submit such drivel…and in New York!")

The third editor tastes it, "Boy, sure tastes like shit."

(Ralph is a senior editor at his publishing house, an old, revered house, that has withstood the mergers and disintegration of the rest of the industry, and done so by maintaining high standards of excellence and quality. Nearing retirement, Ralph has been through thousands of these kinds of manuscripts, and the last thing he wants is his legacy to be associated with trash. "I've tossed hundreds, maybe thousands, of manuscripts that were superior to this one, so you know where this one will end up. But there's always a little mental post-it note I keep in the back of my mind. Many, many years ago, I was forced to read what was the most awful novel I'd ever read. It was long by ten times, bloated, stuffed with fluff, it made absolutely no sense, like it was written with crayons. The plot was absurd -characters, dialogue- nothing rang true. I was horrified that I had wasted any part of my life reading this heaping mess. I wrote a nasty note to the chief-editor, dismissing the author as worthless, and rejecting the manuscript outright. Wash your hands of this catastrophe, I cautioned. Well, a year later that book got published by another house, and you know what it was? Stephen King's "The Stand.'"

Ty and Brie gasp.

"That's outrageous," Ty says. "Some editor must've been forced at gunpoint to brush it up."

"Must've taken months," Brie says.

Ralph says, "And then, maybe I was wrong. What do I know?"

"More than most of us," Ty says. "But, y'know, I wonder, you don't think we all got the same submission today. Is that possible?"

"Highly unlikely," Brie says, "but stranger things have happened. It takes a lot of chutzpah to write this badly, so the author obviously has no scruples."

"It is doubtful," says Ralph. "But who knows, what if it ends up being the next Stephen King rip-off blockbuster? It could happen,"

Ralph says sadly. "All the same, this manuscript really did stink up the place." They all laugh.)

The editors continue on their way, saying, "Boy, sure glad we didn't step in it."

(That's it? That's all you got? There are two kinds of endings in fiction. 1: Everything is sewn up neat and tidy. No dangling threads. 2: The ball is left up in the air, leaving a sense of the unresolved, hope, and spiritual connection with the ultimate unknowable universe. Your ending however just leaves us wondering, 'Huh?' Here's how we could do better. 'Almost by miracle, for New York, three cabs all pull up to the curb, one behind another, at the same time (this *is* fiction, after all). Ty, Brie, and Ralph wave to each other congenially, wishing each other better luck on their next submission. Ralph says while stepping into his cab. "Maybe we did all read the same manuscript today, if so, all I can say is, 'Boy, sure glad we didn't publish it.'" And they are off to their various destinations.)

Good luck sticking this piece somewhere.

The Editor

Molly Begolly

I went to the book signing with reservations. Reservations I found I did not need.

The book in need of signing was 'Alas, Poor Yorick,' by Artold Antoid, the 15th in a series of mystery novels based on Shakespeare quotes.

The author, Antoid, is an old friend, actually an ex-old-friend (we had a falling out over -what else- a woman), and while we went our separate ways, in both writerly and worldly matters, I kept abreast of his authorial triumphs, however trite and inconsequential. When I saw he was in town for a book-signing, I tucked my ego underarm, doffed my beret, and headed downtown.

I read his debut novel, 'To Be, or Not.' It was awful. Laughably so. Antoid knows less about Shakespeare than any two-year-old does about the universe of sub-atomic particles.

What surprised me most, other than the unequalled shoddy prose, was the utter lack of humor. For you see, Antoid is one of the funniest guys I've ever met. In any group, any setting, Artoid was the cut-up, his sarcasm, wit, bizarre observations, were often insightful, far-out, or straight-up Rodney Dangerfield. He was a hoot. In person. And like most comedians, he had a most boisterous infectious laugh.

Weird then that his writing was so wooden. You could whittle a toothpick out of it.

Now, I suppose it's not fair to assume his books should be funny (they are, but not in any way he intended), but doesn't it seem odd someone so funny in person, is so drab, odorless, and dour, and downright boring on the page? I thought so.

I wasn't sure the little beggar would recognize me. After all, it had been 5 years since he ran off with the woman of my dreams, Molly Begolly.

About the same time he pilfered my gal, Antoid started cranking out the Shakespeare tomes, to the tune of three or four a year. Which alone could drain the most energized of creatives talents. And that's not exactly what we're discussing here. One online reviewer suggested the author demand a refund from the Creative Sperm Bank.

'To Be, or Not,' was dedicated 'To my muse, my spark, my Molly Begolly.' The second travesty in the series, 'Out Damned Spot,' was dedicated 'Again to my muse...' etc. I hadn't paid attention to his subsequent attacks on world literature.

Of the first two, I must say, 'To Be, or Not', was the better written and plotted, but the characters were paper thin, cut from the TV cop-show cloth, and the dialogue was unbearably tin-eared. 'Out Damned Spot,' seemed to be written on the back of a cocktail napkin at closing time, with a plot thinner than beer foam on a stein (a gay murderer comes 'out' -get it?), but at least the characters were a little more quirky, with a passing resemblance to real human beings, and the dialogue had some zip to it (did an editor get ahold of it?). It was set on a college campus, which made me think Antoid wanted readers to assume he'd attended an institution of higher learning. He may have visited one, but only to take a selfie, and scamper off.

I flipped through the third book, 'A Horse, a Horse, My Kingdom...', apparently set in the shady world of horse racing, gambling, etc., a world that Antoid was intimately unfamiliar with, though at least from his search engine he could get a glimpse of it from Dick Francis.

The much-heralded Antoid book signing was held in the storage bowels of Ploughman Books. I purchased a copy of his latest, 'Alas...', my ticket into the signing.

I was directed down 2 flights of stairs, where I took a sideways elevator underground across the street, rode a donkey along a creek bed for a couple hundred years, shimmied down a manhole, stumbled through a sewer tunnel, then climbed a ladder to a stone ledge, inched along for a several yards, then and finally reached a door with this ominous sign, 'Book Signing.' Must be the place. I rapped on the door. Through a speakeasy peep-hole a pair of beady eyes appeared, a mouth below the eyes spoke, "Who are you. What do you want?" I told him the truth.

I was allowed entrance. I had expected a crowded room of fawners, fan-boys, and groupies, queued up, sipping pomegranate, caramel, extra soy Frappuccino, all the while discussing the international literary significance and influences of Antoid. I was wrong. Some 20-feet away, barely illumed by a single bulb dangling from a pair of tenuous wires swinging above his head, was a solo Antoid, stretched out, yawning, at a wobbly card table, his fingers tapping on his pPhone. As I approached, he looked up, and hardly changing his droll expression, "Ho, ho, look what the cat dragged in. How are you, my friend?"

My friend? That stung. He did not offer his hand for the shaking, nor did I mine.

I allowed I was fine, and in response to my query, he too was in fine fettle. I glanced around quizzically, not exactly saying 'where is everybody' but sort of insinuating it with my caustic gaze.

"You just missed the first big wave," he said, I think, sarcastically. "So how long has it been? Couple years, decades, eons?"

"Five years. Three months. Two days..." She left me on my birthday, so it's rather etched on my brain's Page-A -Day calendar.

"O right. You're not still upset about that...are you?"

"Totally over it. Totally...so how is Molly?"

"Molly? Good lord, man, I haven't seen her in...I don't know how long. You should know how it is. Poof, she's gone."

Hmmm, hadn't heard. But then, why would I?

"She seems to have a preference for writers, she left a sci-fi author for me, than me for you..." I mused.

"She didn't leave you for me. She left you for...her."

"And she left you for?"

"Herself of course."

"Maybe she's going through every genre of literature to find herself," I said.

"Fits her MO," Artold said. "Loser Sci-fi writers. An avant-garde writer, complete with beret, basement-brewed artisanal beer..."

"Wo, that's harsh."

"No, no, you must admit, that's your style. You cultivate it. Obscure, all but unreadable. Although I did come upon something of yours recently, a very funny piece, you even stooped so low as to use complete sentences and punctuation…where was it?"

"Had a couple stories published in online magazines, 'Shirk and Smirk', and 'Spindle'…"

"That's it, 'Spindle'. So how's that working out for you?"

"Made a couple pennies."

"Good. Good, good." He absently tapped his stylus on the stacks of hard cover books on the table. "In any case, she's covered sci-fi, wanabe James Joyce, mystery…what's next? Architectural Digest?"

"Comics? Graphic novels?"

"Graphic novels! By Jove, that's it. She is a Graphic Novel. God, if I could draw a decent stick-figure I'd draw it, Molly Begolly, the Graphic Novel."

"Alien. Femme fatale, Punk Wonder Woman."

"I like it, I'll let you have this one…get on it, lad."

I was starting to get that old-time feeling, the sparring, the fractal unraveling and intertwining of ideas, intellectual one-upmanship, bro style.

"Get a crazy comic book artist, you know you see them staggering around the coffee houses and bars, like Charles Bukowski…I'll give you the name of my agent…maybe."

And then…silence. Click. Pause. We're done with that track.

"I have to ask, but, I don't remember you ever being exactly a Shakespeare scholar, ummm, how did you come up with this idea of a series based on his quotes?"

"Funny you should ask, because it all comes back to Molly Begolly. First time she left me- yes, the first time- I was distraught. I was contemplating suicide…no, I wasn't contemplating it, I'm too much of a coward, but rather I was, in perfect writerly fashion, contemplating someone else contemplating suicide, distance it with a character, head in hands, crying, 'To be, or not to be.' And then, as everything goes into my mental meat-grinder, it comes out as a mystery novel, and so I offed him. It wasn't suicide at all, it was murder! My agent loved it…I mean the idea. I hadn't written a word yet, barely had an outline. Before I had a first draft done, Goronsky sold it for a pretty hefty sum, but there was a catch. The Publisher wanted a sequel, maybe even a series…and that's when the idea came to me. There're mystery series with days of the week, the alphabet, the periodic table of elements, so I said, let's go for something infinite, and it was right there in my first title, a Shakespeare quote. The great thing is I don't have to read the dusty old turd, crack open my Bartlett, and go. Boom! A series is invented…"

I sighed. It's so easy, isn't it? O well, no point in being a Bitter Bobber.

Fortunately, as conversation seemed to fizzle out, like a dander from a dandelion, the doorman ushered in a small crowd, young hipsters, arms sagging with copies of the master's misquotes, laughing and stomping mud from their gladiator sandals and Ugg boots. Seeing he had work to do, and a smile to put on his face, with the flick of a wrist, I bid Antoid a fond adieu.

The doorman, seeing I was about to exit, said, "O you can go out this way." He pointed to a door behind Antoid. "Little quicker," he smiled.

"Huh? You mean I crawled through hell to get here, and there was a door right here all the while?"

Antoid laughed, "You had to prove worthy." Maybe the funniest thing he ever said.

I left him basking in the glow of adoration, pushed out the door onto 10th Ave., right next to Ploughman's Café. I was in mighty need of a cup of Joe, so took an outside table, opened my book, only to realize the bastard never signed it. Joke's on me. I thought about going back (the short way), then reconsidered, 'Nah, I've done my duty.'

I flipped through the pages idly, pretty thin, with large print, coming apace to the dedication page, and sat up straight, startled when I read, in italics, font size 12, 'Once again to my muse, my spark, my wife, Molly Begolly.'

Hmmm.

How I Became a
Bestselling Novelist

My wife was chastising me a few months ago for being a lazy asshole (Hey, yr the one who married me, not me!), when suddenly I jumped off the couch, pointed a finger right between her beady little eyes, and said, "O yea, well guess what, I'm gonna be rich, cuz I got a plan…"

"O really," she said scornfully, "and what might that be, Mr. Unemployable?"

"I'm gonna become a bestselling novelist."

O, you shoulda heard the laughter. The rafters shook, the curtains billowed, the dog hid under the sofa. Har har har.

"Mark my words…" I said defiantly.

"Well, sadly, Koko's the only one who's likely to mark your words," she said, pulling the dog out from under the couch by the collar. "Novelist?!" She shook her over-permed head and stormed out the door, off to her Book Club. Which is sort of what actually gave me the idea. That, and an ad in the paper about a top-notch literary agent, Mr. Goronsky –from New York, no less- hosting a seminar that very evening. Subject: How to Become a Bestselling Novelist.

My first thought was, boy, do I have stories to tell. Take my wife…please. See, that's just one.

So anyway, I pony up the one hundred smackers, get a front row seat, and up to the podium comes this little runt of a guy, shabbily dressed, fat, balding with a really bad comb-over, and I said to myself, this guy's the real deal. First words outta his mouth, "So who wants to be a bestselling novelist?" My hand shot up like a spike out of a nail gun...so did about forty other hands. "Well, listen careful," he said, very authentic New Yawk accent, "because a year from now you will be. If...you follow my advice. Here's the first thing you do. Pick up a copy of the latest number one bestseller, hardcover, not paperback –that's yesterday's news. Don't bother reading it, just flip through it, pick up a couple ideas -plot, main characters, setting. Next, sit down and write out your version of that novel in synopsis form. No point in writing a whole novel. Right now, you just wanna sell it. Now, what do I mean by 'your version'? Let's say this bestseller is about a retired cop. Make your guy a retired FBI agent. Let's say his ex-girlfriend owns a restaurant. In yours, she owns a florist shop. See? And for you ladies in the audience, lemme tell you, if the lead character is a guy, just turn him into a gal. With an ex-boyfriend who owns a butcher shop. Or, for guys, vice versa. But don't do gay –no bestseller there. All I'm sayin' is, change things around. Check out subplots. If there's a back story about a forest fire, make yours a train wreck. If a bunch of people take a trip to Barcelona, ship your group off to Madagascar. You don't have go there. Yahoogle it. Now, take special note of dialogue. Most bestsellers today, the dialogue is more about explaining what's being said rather than actually saying it. You can pick that up in an instant. Just don't make dialogue sound like the way real people talk. Boring. Never listen to the way people speak, it's all wrong. No one talks like that in bestsellers."

Then he went on with a lot of detail about query letters, how to format purloined material, arguing with editors, etc. This lasts about an hour, I'm taking notes like crazy. At the end, Mr. Goronsky handed everyone a card, saying, "I expect to hear from you...soon."

On the way home I stopped and picked up the number one bestseller, 'Kill Die', (by the author of 'Die Kill'). Got home, started flipping through it. Got a pretty good idea what it was about. The main character, Guy Stickert, was a fiercely competitive lawyer. And his ex-girlfriend, Ella Twitchert, was a hotshot working in the District Attorney's ofice. They don't get along, always snapping at each other. Then he takes a high-level murder case, and, what a coincidence, Ella is the prosecuting attorney. This mash-up goes on for the first third or so of the book, until they discover the real murderer is still out there, and this guy Stickert is defending has been framed. Then they start working together to find the real murderer, all the while, the trial is still going on. If I'd had time to read it, it might've been pretty good. Lots of side characters. Ella's boss, the District Attorney, is a real sleazeball. One of the top guys in Stickert's law firm has a heart attack midway through the book…so that's a pretty good little subplot. Then there's a bunch of legal mumbo jumbo that's probably all made up, and a stubborn judge who's on the take, and a dozen dopey jurors, and in the end despite both legal teams up in arms over the two lawyers who are supposed to be going after each other (well, they are, but in bed). Finally they solve the crime and figure out who the real killer is…guess what…the sleazeball District Attorney. Nice twist.

Took me an hour, tops, to get all that. And yeah, I checked out the dialogue, Goronsky's right. Example:

"You're not leaving here without me," she said, looking at him with her steely eyes. He realized right off that she was going to get her way no matter what, and so he may as well allow her to tag along, even though they were going into the seediest part of town, where violence was always one wrong word, one awkward glance away. But he knew in the long run he would need her expertise in speed reading and Tuvan Throat Singing. Besides she was looking more beautiful than ever. Maybe it was the lighting, or the parquet flooring.

"Okay," he said. And she knew the only reason he was giving in was because deep in his heart he still loved her, and this was his way of allowing her to believe in herself, even though she didn't believe he really did believe that she believed in herself.

My wife came home about then, "O, look, his book's already published…and omigosh, it's the number one bestseller, o my hero!"

"Yeah, well, clown around all you want, but one year from now, this is gonna be me…"and I held up the book.

"You're gonna be John Grisham?"

"No, no, no…I'm gonna be the number one bestselling author."

"Of fantasy?"

"Mark it down, Twyla…one year from now."

"Okay. Well, good luck with that. As for now, sorry, but I got the next flight off fantasy island and am going to the real kitchen and fixing myself a real sandwich, because obviously bestselling novelists can't make dinner around here."

The next day I set to work. My main character was Bent Starkly, a baritone saxophone player for the best jazz group ever, holding down the number one gig in New York City, at the Stump Tower Bar and Grill. As they were playing one night, in walked Bent's ex-girlfriend, Wanda Spiggot, a drummer for a punk-Emo band. Suddenly the band leader announces she's the new drummer for the group.

This ticks off Bent to no end, and he and Wanda argue and snap at each other throughout the gig. When Bent goes home that night, he finds his wife brutally murdered (gotta admit that was kinda fun). The cops arrive and immediately name Bent a person of interest. He calls Wanda because she was once a private eye in someone else's novel. As the cops and DA gather evidence to arrest and convict Bent, he and Wanda have 72 hours to discover who the true killer is or they can't go to the Gimmy Awards.

That was the main plot, around which I created a smorgasbord of side characters and subplots, which is actually kinda fun. You take someone you know, give them a different name, a different job, and then just make up a bunch of crap. I made New York come alive, with people jumping in and outta taxis, playing touch football in Central Park, getting mugged, etc., and using words like 'yous' and 'fogettaboutit'. In the middle of all this, the band leader strained a hip flexor while soloing on 'Caravan', causing much consternation.

The big ending comes when the duo discovers the murderer to be the head of Stump Towers, 'Stump' Powers, who had been having an affair with Bent's wife, and when he broke off the relationship, she began bilking and blackmailing Powers, until he had her killed. There's a big shoot-out and chase scene up and down the 112-story Stump Towers, which I thought had movie rights written all over it.

I crammed all that into 10 pages, licked a manila envelope and posted it off to Mr. Goronsky. I added a little note reminding him I attended his seminar, and that I'd done everything he suggested, and I couldn't wait to hear from him.

Eight weeks later I got a post card saying, 'Thanks for giving us an opportunity to look at "Sax and the City", but Mr. Goronsky is not currently accepting unsolicited manuscripts. We hope you find someplace to stick this.'

There you have it; my first $100 rejection slip.

I made the mistake of leaving the card lying around and my wife picked it up and started in on me, "Congratulations! I knew you could do it. Better get to work on the sequel, buddy-o..."

So I started sporting a beret, dangling a lanyard from my belt, riding my bike to the unemployment ofice, and hanging out at coffee shops, indie art galleries and movie houses.

One day as I was sitting at a sidewalk cafe sipping a tall-no-whip-extra-hot-soy-malt mocha, I spotted a familiar looking young lady sitting nearby. It took a while to figure out where I'd seen her before, then it dawned on me, she was at Goronsky's seminar. The sting of trauma still weighing on me, I wondered if she fared any better. I introduced myself. She didn't recognize me but admitted she was at the seminar. I asked if she came away with any good pointers. She just snorted, "What a façade, that Goronsky is such a jerk. It's no wonder every bestseller reads like every other one, they just feed on one another. There's nothing novel about novels nowadays. At least not on the bestseller list."

Wo, that kinda shocked me. So I told her my pitiful story.

She was sympathetic, but not surprised. "You know what would make a great novel?" she said in response. "A couple of nobodies attend a money-grubbing seminar. One of them follows to a 'T' everything he's told, and gets nothing for it. The other one scoffs at the whole affair, chalks it up to a waste of time and money and forgets about it. When the two meet again several months later, they commiserate, but realize nothing's been gained, nothing learned. And that's it. Fini. Story's over."

"Who'd want to read something like that?"

She grimaced, squinted against the sun, picked up her shopping bags, stood, and said, "Probably no one." And walked away.

The Ultimate Pen

Ben sat glowering, fixated, with a look of deep conviction and admiration...at his plate. So long was he staring that Fynn couldn't help but observe, "That hamburger isn't going to eat itself, Ben."

Ben laughed, "You just keep to your side of the bar..." He lifted the top bun, made sure all the condiments were well adjusted and accounted for, one, two, three onion slices, then dove in with a humongous bite.

"Hi, baby," Katy Riley popped up in front of him, "what's going on? You razzing Ben again?"

"Of course, so what's up with you? Pretty quiet around here."

"You're early, it's not even noon. It'll all kick into gear, soon..." She squinted and peered out the window, "Speak of the devil, here comes Buck."

Buck straggled over, struggled onto his bar stool, just as Brad von Easley strolled through the door. Followed almost on his heels by chatty Bill with a co-worker, who took the stools to Fynn's left.

Then Cowboy, the car mechanic sauntered in, and leaned against the bar. Fynn tipped his glass towards him, "Hey brother, how's that mojo machine of yours running?"

A bit startled, Cowboy said, "Like a dream. Just started doing some detailing on it..."

"Make it look like it runs?"

"You betcha...hey gorgeous," everything stops for Katy Riley. "I hear it's Burger Tuesday..."

She was looking leerily at Fynn, 'Why you being so chummy?' To Cowboy?

Then back to Cowboy, "Any burger on the menu, five ninety-nine..."

The two Credit Union ladies, names not known, but who take their spots once a week or so at the bar and shop-talk non-stop to each other. One of them is quite brassy. And engaging. Then lovely Elle plopped her purse on her seat, while wrestling out of her coat, and taking her stool next to Buck. She always sits next to Buck, and her cheeriness, good-natured optimism, is a sparkling contrast to the grumbling dark cloud that is Buck. She always orders the Asian salad, with the same caveat, "Not too spicy."

"How's that granddaughter of yours?" Fynn said.

"Omigod, I can't get enough," Elle, beaming, said. "I'm playing the typical grandmother, if I could, I'd have her with me all the time." She was dancing on her seat like a schoolgirl.

"How old is she?"

"Just turned six months, last week."

"That's a great age…well, they all are."

"I think my daughter's sick of me always hanging around. I don't care…I'm a grandma!" Laughing.

Then Old Pete took a stool beside Fynn. Pete, over the last year had started looking more and more frail and shaggy. At 74, you're allowed to do that. But his mind was sharp. And frugal. He confided in Fynn that he didn't come here as often as he used to because the Chinese restaurant down the road, The Silver Serpent, served merlot at half the price as ThreeBs.

"Can't be any good," Fynn teased.

"It's still merlot."

"Just barely," Fynn said.

"Well, a buzz is a buzz," Old Pete chuckled, raising his overpriced glass for a toast. Can't argue that logic.

Then came in Workout Guy, good and sweaty. "I lost so much weight today I think I can squeeze in at the bar." And everyone was happy to make room, and plenty of it, for him.

Jim and Margie sauntered in, smiling, took their usual table closest to the bar, so they could keep tabs on and gab with the barflies, without having to be associated with them. Jim was a retired postal worker. And once upon a time, a writer. He published a number of short stories in detective magazines, all involving mail fraud. They sure had the ring of truth. And his sense of humor was evident on every page.

Yes, it was a jolly crew. Katy was working up a sweat herself, all the while dollar signs rolling in her eyes (tips, tips, tips!), as she

214

raced from table to bar, to next table, back to the bar...suddenly she cried out, "Holy..." She was staring at the door.

Everyone turned to see enter...Ozzie.

Katy stopped right in the middle of scraping foam off a beer, raced around the bar and gave Ozzie a big hug, "Omigod, you're safe..."

"But of course."

"You creep, you don't text, email..."

"It's only when I do text or email, you know I'm in trouble... and look..." he approached the bar, an arm around Katy, waving with his free hand, "all of my friends have come to welcome me, I'm back. Yay, all is well now, Ozzie is here!" As he passed Buck, he slapped him on the shoulder, "Hey, old buddy, so glad you're here...Brad, Fynn, Omigod, everyone DID turn out, just for me?"

"Hardly," Buck sneered.

There was a slight hum of white noise as Ozzie restlessly went to each of the patrons, joked, roared with laughter, until he came to Fynn and Brad. He draped his arm around them both. "And you two, my friends, almost as much as Katy, I have missed you, and I am so glad to see you here. Now, which one of you is going to buy me a drink?"

Now, if the sight of Ozzie, after months of absence wasn't enough to rattle his already gobsmacked brain, Fynn looked over to see...She's All That enter. She stood by the hostess, wondering whether the bar was too crowded...when she noticed Fynn. He waved her over. They'd bumped into each other several times over the last couple months, exchanged a few sardonic words. Her hair had grown out, the black sheen had settled to a less dramatic glare, and it was pulled back to a small bun, leaving her bangs hanging carefree on her forehead. Fynn got off his stool, "Been saving it for you."

She's All That laughed, "You did not..."

"I'm sorry, I don't remember your name."

"Brenda. And you're Fynn?"

"Right. I like your hair."

"Are you being facetious?" A warning glance. She wore a tan summer dress, sinched at the waist, and a sheer, yellow jacket.

She nestled into the bar stool, just as Katy Riley, who shot Fynn a threatening glance, arrived. He winked at her.

"What are you having?" Fynn said to Brenda.

"Pinot Grigio?" Katy Riley interrupted.

"Yeah, you remember…"

Katy Riley poured a glass, slid it gently in front of her. Then as quickly was off to wait on another table.

"Wow, you're a regular here?" Fynn said.

"O, right." Feeling the weight and volume of the crowded bar, Brenda said, "So how was Paris?"

He paused, took a sip of wine, deep breath, "Well…a tale of two cities. The first was all work, then the pleasure part got interrupted… with extreme prejudice."

Buck let his newspaper droop a bit, glanced Brenda's way, "The Froggies kicked him out cuz he wasn't froo-froo enough."

"Something like that," Fynn said. "Let's just say my stay was cut short. Emphatically."

"Sorry. Anything…bad?"

"No…no. Not really. Just…well, I'll probably go back, someday, to make amends…or reparations."

Buck rattled his newspaper.

"How's with you? Rancouer treating you okay?"

"Just got a raise, not much, but better than nothing."

"Cool. Well, I just tossed my printer out the window, maybe I'll try Rancoeur. Although, I'm a little leery of French technology. After all, they gave us the washing machine that's also a dryer."

"What?" her look of surprise, slight smile, tantalizing eyes.

"Yeah, have you seen this? It's a washing machine that doubles as a dryer. And you know what? It doesn't work. It can't work, there's no way the same vessel that washes clothes, can also get them dry."

"Funny you mention that," she said, looking at him with no irony, "on our new printers, the scanner is also an ironing board."

Fynn laughed, "I seriously would not doubt it. French technology!"

"Well, give it a try…if you don't like it, I don't want to hear about it…"

"Are you eating?"

"Of course. You?"

Fynn held up his glass of white Burgundy, "Yep. Got all the major food groups right here…hey, do you mind guarding my spot for a moment, I need to talk to some friends I haven't seen for a while, and, ummm, don't go nosing through my notebook…"

"Uh-o, have you been writing about me?"

"O yeah, a novel, your life story."

"That'd be pretty boring."

"I don't know, it's pretty steamy."

She smiled, "So it is fiction."

Fiction. Friction? He saw it. "I'll be right back."

She saw him off with a curious smile. Something's going on here, he thought.

He took the liberty of grabbing a seat at Jim and Margie's table, "Hey, how's it going," Jim crowed, "I haven't seen any new stories from you online for a long time, what's going on?"

"Well...I got an agent."

"O that's great!" Margie said.

"Yeah, and he's very optimistic he can stick it someplace, hopefully with a publisher."

They laughed. "What is it...a collection?"

"Yeah, a lot of the stories I've published online, rounded off with a bunch of new stuff."

"That is so exciting," Margie said.

"One thing you got going for you," Jim said, "you're very distinctive, you're way out there."

"Well, it's roomier out there. It's not so crowded. No riff-raff."

Jim laughed, "Well, that is so great. Keep us informed..."

"I shall. But, what about you? When are we going to see more stories from you?"

"No, I'm done...just don't have it anymore."

"Come on, it's like riding a bicycle."

"Nope, all done."

"Okay, anyway, just wanted to say howdy." Fynn stood.

"Good luck," Margie said.

Fynn looked back at his place at the bar where Brenda was chatting with Workout Guy, laughing it up. Good.

He decided to go out for a breath of fresh air, saying to himself, 'It's roomier out there. No riff-raff.'

Sunny, but not hot day. He walked toward the parking lot, past a sign requiring smokers to remain 25-feet from the door. He came upon the Credit Union ladies, gabbing and having a smoke. As he passed, said, "I just counted, and you're only 24-feet from the door."

The (fake) blonde one laughed, "O yeah," taking a step closer to the door, "now I'm 23-feet away,"

"Here comes the ciggie patrol."

Fynn passed through the screen of smoke, and walked to his rag top 'car'. He spotted Cowboy's rig, went over to have a look. On the driver side, against the bright shiny black, was the start of a flame, looked like it might end up going the entire length of the truck. He must polish this baby every week, if not every day. You could eat off it. Like Buck and his Duchess. Cowboy's one and only. It was so shiny he could see himself in the door frame. The artist reflects.

He turned back, took a couple deep breaths, then headed back inside. On his way, he passed Old Pete, leaving, "Going to The Silver Serpent?" Fynn said.

"No," laughing, "that's my one glass for the day."

"Seeya next time."

Brenda was happily occupied, laughing as Workout Guy amused her. He went up to Cowboy, "Took a look at your rig, that's gonna be amazing when you're done."

Cowboy, all excited, "I wanted to do like the flame coming out of a dragon's mouth or something, but my friend doing the detail said, 'that's a bit much.'"

"Yeah, but man, it's you."

"Yeah, well, anyway, thanks."

"Very cool." He could see Katy Riley following him with her eyes. 'What is going on with you?'

He brushed his hand on Brenda's shoulder, "Is this guy harassing you?"

"He won't tell me his name…"

"It's Workout Guy, I keep telling her. That's what everyone calls me."

Fynn laughed, "It is. And we don't want to know his name. You know, in certain cultures if you tell someone your name, they have power over you forever."

Workout Guy, stage-whisper to Brenda, "It's Eddie."

All three of them laughed. Katy Riley set Brenda's plate down, once again glancing up at Fynn, with just a barely noticeable little shake of her head. "Ketchup?"

"Sure," Brenda said. To Fynn, "Want some of my fries, no way I can eat all this."

"I might have a bite or two…"

218

"So what're you doing out in the parking lot....?" She took a sensuous bite of a French fry. Smiling.

"Car theft." He dipped a fry in the ketchup. "Pick up a couple extra bucks."

"So you can buy all the ladies drinks?"

"No…just the special ones."

"Hmmp." With fork and knife in hand, looked at her plate, "This is ridiculous, you're getting half this burger…" She sliced it into two almost perfectly equal pieces. "Please." She scooted the plate over for him to share.

"Only if I can buy your wine…."

She shook her head, impatiently. "So…is that your, umm, car out there?" she looked at him, mix of humor and mockery.

"My rag top? Yeah…how could you tell?"

"It just shouts you."

"It shouts something," Brad von Easley, sitting on the other side of Fynn, interjected.

"What does it run on?" She said.

"Mostly luck…" and he broke into a laugh, as did Brad. "Umm, it's a combination solar, wind, leg power, with a bit of biodiesel…and, really, mostly good luck."

"I don't think I've ever seen one of them on a car lot…."

"It's the only one in the country…maybe the universe…I got it to review…and the Belarusian company that produced it went out of business before I even got to drive it."

"They just gave it to you?"

"Sort of. They wanted some good American press from a hopefully friendly source, and I write for a few conservation magazines. Enough to get me some notice."

"Like the toilet?"

"Yeah! Did I tell you about the Green Toilet?"

She nodded. Chewing. "I'm beginning to wonder if I should believe a word you say."

"Just beginning?" Katy Riley said, suddenly standing before them. "How's the burger?"

"Good, but…too much."

"Fynn can feed it to his rag top," Brad von Easley said.

"Probably get me all the way home."

Katy Riley was staring at Fynn, critically. She glanced at Brenda. Then wandered off.

"So, what about you, what's going on in your world?" he said to Brenda

"Work. Mostly. Feels like something earth-shattering may be coming up. Printer market is stagnant, and has been for years...so, we just keep making them faster, more efficient, lighter, and cheaper... only so much fine tuning you can do. So...we shall see."

"You always been a techie?"

"O, not really until college...and even then, you know, they just kept throwing things my way, and I kept gobbling it up..."

"Do you specialize in any one area...like hardware...or..."

"No, most of my hands-on experience has been with microchips...that's kind of led me into a few good positions..."

"Cool, well, you must have something people see in you...o, Ozzie."

Ozzie, who had been working the crowd, finally made his way back to the Regulars. He stood wedged between Fynn and Brad. "You, my friends...my friends..." almost tearing up, "rare is it that I have so stupidly put my friends through such...an experience..."

Buck was rattling his newspaper.

"Hey, an adventure is an adventure," Brad von Easley said, hoping to stop Ozzie right there.

"I never meant to put my friends in danger...I hope you can find it in your heart to forgive me..."

"Nothing to forgive," Fynn said. "We're just glad to see you back."

"No harm, no foul." Brad von Easley said.

Buck was getting more and more restless and anxious, and so was his newspaper.

"I'm missing something, here," Brenda half-whispered to Fynn.

He looked at her calmly, nodded a bit.

"Okay." Suspiciously.

Buck finally spoke, "Hey Finnie, the French just called, they want their beret back."

"They can't have it, it's all I have left of Paris."

"Well, anyway, my friends," Ozzie said, "we're all good?"

"Fabulous," Brad said.

"Good," Ozzie group-hugged Brad and Fynn, "so now I must go, duty calls." One quick side glace to Brenda. Just checking.

Ozzie gave Buck a friendly pat on the back as he headed towards the door. Katy Riley dropped everything she was doing to run after him.

"I feel like I've walked into the middle of a movie..." Brenda said, a little (faux?) agitation in her voice.

Brad and Fynn looked at each other, then at Brenda. "Actually, it's the end of the movie," Brad said.

"Roll the credits," Fynn said.

"Okay, so don't tell me."

"You going to have another glass of wine?"

"You don't have to keep buying my wine..."

"May I?"

She narrowed her eyes, cautious smile.

"Pinot Grigio?" Katy Riley just happened to be returning to her post.

"Yep," Fynn said, "and I'll take another of that fabulous white Burgundy."

Katy Riley just glared at him as she pulled out and poured the wines. "Everything else okay here?" she said, tersely. Fynn could see by the tension in her cheekbones that she was pissed off, but wouldn't say anything yet, too busy. She'd corner him later.

Workout Guy, who had been trying to drive a wedge into Bill's monologue, next to him, without success, pushed his plate away, "That makes sense," he said, "put in a good hour workout, then gobble a huge burger with fries."

"Isn't that why you work out?" Fynn said.

"So I can eat like a pig? Well, all I know is, now I'm ready to crash." Workout Guy stretched, flexed, slapped a twenty on the counter. "I'm outta here."

Brenda said, "Remember, Eddie, I have the power over you."

Workout Guy looked around, "It's not my real name."

He said goodbye to anyone who would listen and was out the door.

Katy Riley came over to bus his plate, eyed the twenty-dollar bill, o la-la. Nice tip. "Nice guy," she said.

Brenda pushed her plate aside...still nearly half the burger left. "I'll know better next time..." she said.

Fynn looked at her, "You're not talking about me, are you?"

She laughed. Trying to think of some witty reply, but instead dipped her head, gave him a pursed lip smile, a glint to her blue/green eyes, a toss of bangs across her forehead. His eyes fixed, his mind froze. Her smile tore him to pieces. There are those, people from miles around, who swore that at that moment they heard the snap of a heartstring.

The spell was splintered and broken when Bill waved his credit card at Katy Riley, who juggled dishes, cards, money and rushed off.

Jim and Margie, came up to Fynn, "Well, I wish you the best of luck, my friend," Jim said. "It's really exciting."

"Yeah, I'm trying not to get too hopeful…but, he did say he was almost sure he could sell it."

"Sounds promising, doesn't it?" Margie, always a bright smile on her face.

"Very."

"Just stay in touch," Jim said, and with a behind-the-back wave, he and Margie were off.

Brenda was looking at Fynn as if for the first time. What is this aggregate of a human being? He smiled at her.

"Can I get to know you better?" she said, brazenly.

"Funny, I was thinking the same thing about you."

Her eyes, searching, demanding. "Can I trust you with my phone number?"

"Of course."

She started reaching in her purse, then, self-conscious, noticed Katy Riley glancing their way. She looked up at Fynn, suspiciously. "Am I interrupting something?"

"Not at all, it's just a little game we play."

She handed him her card. He scrawled on an edge of notebook paper, tore it off, gave it to her. It felt a little weird to both of them, each making sure Katy Riley wasn't looking during the exchange.

"I'll look forward to it, maybe you can tell me more about this Paris movie," Brenda said.

"Not much to tell."

"Well, I won't pry…yet."

"And then you won't let it go…"

"How do you know me so well?" she smiled.

"It's all right here…" patting his notebook.

"You," mock anger, "you're trouble. I know it." She smiled, shook her pretty head. "But as for now, I'd better get back to work… before this wine knocks me out…I will hear from you?"

"Soon. Y'know, there's a funky wine bar up in Littlefield, a friend of mine owns it, we could meet there."

222

"Sounds nice."

"I'm almost always there Thursday evenings."

"O, ummm, let me…"

"Too soon?"

They both laughed. "Yes," she said, "how about if I give *you* a call?"

"Okay. I got your wine."

Shaking her head, she fiddled around in her purse, pulled out a ten, and set it by her plate.

She slipped from the stool, straightened herself, her and Fynn shared a tentative but warm hug.

"See you?" she said.

"Promise."

And She's All That walked gracefully out the door.

"Sweet move, my man," Brad said.

"Nice gal."

"What shenanigans you got going on over there?" Buck snarled.

"None of your business."

"If you're hitting on the ladies, I wanna know about it…I forgot what it's like." Grim chuckle.

"Well, it was good to see Ozzie," Brad said. "Alive."

Buck looked around, carefully, "He's just lucky we saved his ass."

Fynn suddenly noticed, maybe his attention had been otherwise occupied, but, hey, where'd everybody go? They were the only three left at the bar. He was sipping the rest of Brenda's Pinot Gris. Katy Riley was racing around cleaning, stacking dishes in the hopper, washing down the counters and tables, but then made the mistake of coming inside their circle, "I'll take another…" Brad said, holding up his empty glass, "when you have a chance," he added quickly.

"Okay, I need a breather anyway." She poured him a glass, leaned against the counter in front of the three. "So, Fynn, you seem to be getting along quite well with…"

"Brenda."

"Brenda? O so it's Brenda," she nodded as if this were a useful piece of gossip to have in her back pocket, "and you got her phone number?"

"Yeah. Right here somewhere."

"Don't lose it, I know she's interested in you."

"What?"

223

"She came in here while you were gone, asked about you. I had to tell her the dirty truth, of course."

"Thanks."

"Anything for a friend." She turned to Brad, "You've been here a long time. Get fired?"

"No, I had to watch this guy's moves. I've been taking notes."

"Why, who are you trying to woo."

"Woo who?" Buck said, amusing himself.

"You," Brad said to Katy Riley, then quickly, "actually, I had planned to take the rest of the day off anyway, and now that we have the whole assassination crew together…"

Buck gave him a cross look.

"Well, despite everything, I was happy to see Ozzie," Fynn said.

"You were just a happy little guy today, schmoozing it up with everyone, even my mechanic. Trying to impress your gal friend?"

"No, just…life's good."

"Well, good luck, Linda seems like a nice gal."

"It's Brenda."

"O Yeah, right. Kind of common name, isn't it?"

Fynn laughed, shook his head. "Well, she's battle-tested."

"How so."

"Walking into this den of hungry males, hormones popping like jumping beans…"

"God, it was crazy in here today," Katy said, then maybe reminded of a similar scene, said. "Buck?"

"Huh? I didn't do anything."

"Whatever happened with that nutcase lady? The one that wanted to murder you. Did you ever find out what that was all about?"

Buck chuckled, "Well…remember that little notebook she threw at me? Went through it a few times, and I realized it was all in code, and once I figured it out…it was my mission."

"So, she was…?"

Buck glanced around to make sure no lingering waitress, bus boy, nosy manager, were within earshot, "An agent, giving me my assignment. Pakistan."

"They already knew back then?"

"It's the Company, baby." He rattled his newspaper for emphasis, "Now, y'all keep your mouths shushed, y'hear."

224

Grampa Udresson Recollects

Grandpa leans forward, nearly tumbling from his rocking chair, pointing at my hand, This is NOT for publication. Put that tape recordy thing down. Cuz I'm gonna tell you about a time, a dark time, a time of hate and pain, of poverty, shame, of meanness and pettiness, distrust and deceit, when the sun was too embarrassed to shine 6 months out of the year, when the moon was a muddy brown, and the whole earth sank beneath a cloud of fear, hopelessness, and cowardice.

I'm talking about the Great Recession, two thousand something. Nine, ten, eleven…It was bad. Hellish bad. Brains rolled out the door. No one could agree on anything…relied on hate-talk, screaming, yelling over each other…wrong, wrong, wrong! Everyone else was stupid and gullible…O, except for me! Conversation? Pah! Shouting, snorting, accusations, lies, distortions, filth, disregard for civility or anything close to it. Everyone returned to their caves, throwing rocks, and cowering in skanky trenches. You could cut the divisiveness with a knife and hand out the pieces like poison brownies. Petty, mean, stupid, hurtful…

And the air? Unbreathable. It was so toxic, a whiff, and your face puffed up like a balloon. And the smell? Foul stench. Even if you could breathe, the smell would burst your veins, pop your sinews, it was disgusting. For months everyone ran around holding their breath until they could get into a hollow log, for a few seconds of scuzzy oxygen.

And then, the nighttime screams kept everyone in startled consciousness, there was no sleeping…

Uh, Grandpa, there is a 'but' coming up here somewhere, isn't there?

What? A butt?

A but. 'But then the good times came…'

No! No buts. I tell you, this was dark. Cruel. Ugly. Wanna know how ugly? In my school the handsomest lad was hideous, unbearable to look at, and mean?! He was so mean and ugly, the prettiest of girls fell in love with animals and trees, they'd rather kiss dirt, and hold hands with broken glass. Ugly in mind. Hateful in speech. And cruel to everyone he met. He wasn't just in our school, he was everywhere, he was the Everyman of his day, hated, reviled, but so cravenly clever that he blinded everyone and became the most popular kid on the block. Filthy, and smelled like sewage.

His adversaries slithered into the dark, putrid gray shadow figures, howls and yelping came from their crooked maws, as they roamed the darkness, trying to find a ray of light somewhere. But… there was none.

Food was inedible. Masses of gray chunks clamped together like clay. Instead of food, we subsisted on lies, prayers, and submissiveness. We belittled ourselves so much we fell apart into tiny crumbs, and when the wind kicked-up, we were gone.

Anyone with an ounce of sense in their head…gave up. What else to do? Protest, rattle the cage, carry signs, sing songs? We tried, o, how we tried, but hands were strapped behind our backs, then someone pulled the plug, and the lights went out. We lost energy. We sank lower than the horizon.

So, grandpa, after that, what happened?

Things got worse. He clasps his hands above his head, and rocks back in his chair, much, much worse.

Then resumes, I don't know. I was dead. I'd ripped my eyes out, tore my feet off, crushed every bone in my body, and buried myself in rocks, where I lay clawing at the filth and scum, trying to find light, air, until…he stops, we have come to the end.

He sits for a long moment, savoring the horror. But then a sudden shift, he perks up, he leans forward, That, my boy, was the Great Recession. Now, you wanna turn the recorder thing back on, and I'll tell you all about what it was really like in the 'good ole days…'

That's All, Folks!

So I get a phone call from this Mr. Goronski. Heard of him. Didn't like what I heard, and this didn't figure to be the beginning of a lovely relationship. "Goronski, here, this Katy Riley?"

I guess.

"I got your name from a mutual friend..."

O, I know who that shady character might be.

"You probably heard he ran off to Paris, took his advance, and boom, gone."

He does that a lot, loves Paris, needs to decompress, recharge the batteries, chow down on inspiration and foie gras. And...drink wine, and look at pretty women.

"All well and good, I don't know an author who hasn't grabbed his advance and gotten the hell out of here, but in this case, the bum left me holding more than my...in my hand, anyway, it was supposed to be the final story in his collection, and as he's running to the airport, he throws a handful of notes and scribblings on my desk, no order, no outline, nothing, just a folder full of scrawls and barely legible notes. I took the liberty of mailing them to you. You know him. Personally, so I figgered you'd have some insight into that snarled brain of his, and maybe you can make some sense of it all, at least put them in an order that makes sense..."

I peered over my margarita. There indeed was a manilla envelope in the pile of bills and advertisements. I had just grabbed the mail, but figured me and the couch had to share some quality time first, along with my BF, margarita.

"You want me to edit a bunch of notes? O yeah, I've seen him scribbling away at the bar, sometimes giggling over what he's written, sometimes pensive and glum. In other words, I don't think I want to get tangled up in this."

"Give it a look. There's a place in the Acknowledgments for you."

In other words, no moola.

"No, you'd just run off to Paris."

I laugh. "Okay, I'll take a look…"

Goronski was right. What a mess. Sticky notes, scraps of paper, a notepad from the Shelburne Hotel, scribblings on receipts, and, O look, one receipt from Bistro Bon Bon, guess who was his wait person…me! Two glasses of Riesling. Side salad. Let's see what he wrote on it….

Into a battle of wits, he rode unarmed.

At least wasn't about me. I flipped through the pieces of paper…

The Addict in the Attic

"I'm going to New York to write a novel."
"You can't write a novel here?"

Liters/leaders
Parrish/perish

Beware these common myths

Crastinate, concrastinate
The pros and cons of crastination

What the hell?

Take Advantage of Your Mind

In freakin' credible
Discussed/Disgust

Some were kinda funny:

Undershorts are not to be worn inside out after 5 days of wearing inside right.

228

Defrocked Christmas Trees

Rank and Rancor

She's giving me a Hard Attack (naughty, naughty*)*

Egrets? I've had a few.

I've been a bit combobulated lately.

Couth
Kempt
Long shrift
Wieldy
I'm having these non-negative feelings.
Finally/Finely. He sharpened the knife finally.

I bet his spell-checker hates his guts.

His suit looked like an uninterrupted television pattern.

Criticisms, and witticisms (o no, I'm starting to catch his verbal virus).
Some are frustratingly obscure:

One senses a divergence of assiduousness

The iridescence of redundancy

Tranche

Pay Purview

To succumb? Or overcome.

Bad hyphenations: rear-ranging. Are-action.

Someone 'who studies social awkwardness...' Really? Sign me up.

"Yr way out there."

"Well, it's roomier out there. It's not so crowded. No riff-raff."

Nothing says job security like not having a job.

The primordial snooze

A well thawed-out thought

(O here's one for me): *Received plaudits...in lieu of cash.*

Revellion. To revel in rebelling. (Abbie Hoffman led the revellion.)
Bon bons and Bona fides.
Conviction oven.

Political oxymorons:
Italy's Ministry for Simplification
U.S. Government Office of Accountability. ("Sorry there is no one
here to take your call...")

ALL CAPS PERSON. It's shouting in print.

I think I overheard this one:
Buck: I never could get all my verbs and proverbs straight.
Well, if it works for nouns and pronouns.

    Lois Bidder
    She was involved with the Robuttocks technology (Hmm, his
new girlfriend?)

    Sallie Sue,
    Life is a string of unrelated contiguous events. Enjoy.
    Love,
    Pops

    We'd be happy to receipt you.

    A polarized bear.

230

I was at the Verb and Vowel, when the barkeep said, "Eh, mate, mind yr Ps and Qs." I didn't think that was consonant with the evening's frivolity.

I'm not a bedding man. Or, If I were a bedding man…

Ninja Yoga

Far Tartufo

I'm not Thomas the doubter. I'm Thomas the what-the-fuck-are-you-talking-about? (language, language.)

Are you content with the content?

What a jumbled mess. And I'm supposed to make something of it? Well, here I am still waiting on him.

There was one sticky note, pink, with blue ink, stood out, in a baffling way. I had to go over it several times, he had spilled something on it, wine no doubt. Only one word…but it seemed to have some significance. The one word:

Groovitas!

Just out there all by itself, Groovitas! Sounds like a title of some kind, a story, novel…wait…title? new story? Or title of a book? I flipped through the wild meanderings…suddenly pieces started falling into place, kaleidoscopic, but once they settled into a pattern…Order. I got on the horn to Goronski. "Sharpen your pen to acknowledge me…I think I got it."

"Got what?"

Did he even remember me?

"Of course, you got it all figgered out?"

"I think. All these scrawls, musings, asides, dangling descriptors, they're all leading to one thing…"

"Okay…what?"

"Titles, ideas, phrases, stream-of-consciousness BS…it can only be leading up to one thing…SEQUEL!"

FINI!